Kissing My Old Life Au Revoir

Eliza Watson

KISSING MY OLD LIFE AU REVOIR

ISBN-10: 0989521907
ISBN-13: 978-0-9895219-0-1

Printed in the United States of America

Also by Eliza Watson

writing as Eliza Daly

Contemporary Romance

Under Her Spell

Romantic Suspense

Identity Crisis

Dedication

To my sister, Sandra Watson, for reading the book's first draft and having a crush on Luc. Thank you for having faith in the story and for always believing in me.

Acknowledgments

I would like to thank my husband, Mark, and all my friends and family, for believing in me and supporting my writing in so many ways. I wouldn't have made it this far without your support. Thank you to everyone who critiqued, *Kissing My Old Life Au Revoir,* and helped make it a stronger book, including Laura Iding, Jill Wood Lawrence, Samantha March, Sara Palacios, Robyn Neeley, and Cait O'Sullivan. To my mom, Judy, for reading the book numerous times, in its many versions. To Sandra Watson and Lori Lynch Muchmore, for being first readers and having faith in the story. To Elle J Rossi, for a brilliant cover. To Amy Knupp and Julie Sturgeon for your editorial skills. To Amy Atwell for a perfect-looking interior design. And to Glorianne Pajkich, my Sorbonne buddy back in college. Our summer in Paris was a blast!

This book was written over several years and I apologize if I failed to acknowledge anyone's contribution.

Merci beaucoup to everyone!

Chapter One

No elevator. No air-conditioning. No way was I staying at this dump, even if it was just for one night. The tiny lobby was stifling and reeked like sweat. My sweat, no doubt. I'd been standing there several minutes glaring up the narrow, open staircase to the ceiling above, trying to find the energy to schlep my luggage to the top floor. My younger sister, Libby, lived in apartment 610. The penthouse suite.

Located in Paris's Latin Quarter, the building was smooshed between a flower shop and a bustling café. Thanks to the broken intercom at the building's entrance, the door was unlocked, allowing any vagrant off the street to wander in. With the five hundred bucks a month I'd been sending Libby over the past year, she had to be able to afford something better than this. Although Libby insisted my money was a loan, I'd see retirement checks before I'd see Libby's checks. No big deal. I just wished she would put the money to better use. The place was probably her idea of quaint.

Cranky from exhaustion, I inhaled a calming breath and gave myself a little pep talk. Dump or not, I was staying here because spending time with Libby was what really mattered. I proceeded to lug my two bags up the narrow staircase to the sixth floor. Having sweated off my makeup, I was blotting my cheeks with my fingertips when a guy in his late twenties strode out of the apartment at the top of the stairs.

He had on jeans, a white cotton shirt with a black open vest, and a black fedora. The hat's band secured a dozen cigarettes, lined up at attention along the front. A Celtic cross hung around his neck, and a pair of blue-tinted sunglasses peeked out of the breast pocket of his vest. Our gazes locked, and he spoke French, the smooth, flowing sound of his words making all my aching muscles forget they'd been confined to a tiny airline seat for nine hours. There was nothing sexier than the sound of the French language.

Two years of college French, yet I didn't have a clue what he'd said. I gave him a blank stare.

He smiled. "Your baggage, can I help you?"

"Ah...*merci*," I muttered.

With his dreamy brown eyes, he was undoubtedly used to women panting in his presence. It was my trek up the stairs that had me on the verge of hyperventilating. He wasn't my type with his quirky style, shoulder-length, brown hair, and five o'clock shadow—three days old.

"You are Samantha, *non*?" He hitched a worn backpack up on his shoulder then lifted my bulging garment bag and large suitcase with ease.

I raised a curious brow. "Yes, I am."

"I'm Luc. Libby told me you would be arriving today."

As we headed down the hallway toward Libby's apartment, my pulse quickened while my pace slowed. What if Libby was still ticked at me? She'd wanted me to stay with her the entire time, and I'd compromised, agreeing to one night, since my meeting attendees didn't arrive until tomorrow. I would hardly see her the rest of the week, being on call twenty-four/seven. Libby had been inviting me to Paris for the past three years, but this was my first visit. I traveled over a hundred days a year for work. The last thing I wanted to do was travel for fun. People who didn't travel a lot for work didn't get it. And work had never been a priority for Libby.

Luc rapped on the wooden door. My heart thumped against my chest. He called out something in French, his voice calming my nerves like I'd popped a Percocet.

The door flew open, and Libby appeared. "Sammy!" she squealed. "You're here!"

Her long, blonde hair was tossed up in a clip. The sash of her red kimono robe was tied beneath her breasts, but the robe was hard-pressed to contain her big, round belly.

Libby was pregnant?

I stared in disbelief at her stomach. Besides being shocked, I appeared to be the only one uncomfortable with Libby being virtually naked. Unfazed, Luc carried my luggage inside. Libby placed a fleeting kiss to each of my cheeks then hugged me as best she could with her belly between us. I returned her hug. She ushered me inside, where Luc waited patiently, twirling an unlit cigarette between his fingers while she rambled on about how she loved my new hair color—a chestnut brown—and how great it was to see me.

When Libby finally took a breather, Luc turned to me. *"Enchanté."* He kissed my cheeks, his lips warm against my skin, his breath smelling like cinnamon. The stubble on his face brushed my cheek, causing tingles on the back of my neck.

He kissed Libby's cheeks. *"À bientôt."* The corners of Luc's mouth curled into a warm smile as he disappeared out the door.

Libby wrapped an arm around my shoulder and gave it a squeeze. "I'm so glad you're staying with me tonight. It'll be way better than some hoity-toity hotel."

I was still staring at her belly. "You're pregnant?"

Libby placed a hand lovingly on her belly. "If I'd told you, I knew you'd just worry about me. I'd planned on surprising you and Mom at Christmas."

I hated surprises. They wreaked havoc on my professional life, and I didn't like them threatening the stability I worked hard to maintain in my personal life. Besides, this was major. Not like Libby was surprising me with her new puppy. I couldn't believe she hadn't called to tell me she was pregnant. Since when had Libby been able to keep a secret about anything?

"Thought it would be nice to tell you about the baby in person." Libby nibbled on her lower lip, as if apprehensive to tell me about the baby even *now.*

And in other words, if I'd visited in the spring like she'd asked, I'd have known she was pregnant.

I glanced away with guilt. "When are you due?" I slipped off my black suit jacket before I wilted like the daisies in the vase on the table.

"Six weeks."

"Is Luc the father?"

Libby shook her head. "We're just friends."

Relief washed over me. Luc looked like he probably earned his living standing on a street corner pandering to tourists, playing "La Vie en Rose" on a harmonica or exhaling cigarette smoke in the shape of poodles.

"The father isn't parent or marriage material. I'll be fine. Don't worry."

"Is he at least going to provide child support?"

Libby's smile faded, and her look told me to drop it.

"You should move home, so I can help out."

I couldn't bear the thought of Libby living alone in Paris with a baby. She didn't realize the responsibility of raising a child. I did. I'd raised Libby.

"I could never leave Paris." Libby smiled brightly, gesturing at the surroundings. "Isn't this place awesome?"

Four threadbare rugs covering the scarred wood floor delineated the bedroom, living room, dining room, and art studio from each other. A rice-paper screen partitioned off the kitchen nook, and an orange-beaded curtain with lime green daisies served as a bathroom door. Furnishings were an eclectic mix of garage sale items. There wasn't a single baby item in sight. She was completely unprepared.

I clamped down on my lower lip. "Quaint, just not a lot of space for the money."

Libby looked at me like I'd been sniffing her paints. "This place is a steal. And I help Madame Gerrard with the upkeep, painting apartments, so she knocks money off my rent."

The discount, waitressing, teaching art classes, and my "loan" didn't keep Libby in the lap of luxury. However, living three years in Paris was the longest Libby had ever stuck with anything. When she'd visited Paris with an art history tour and spontaneously taken an au pair job for an art professor, I'd figured it was a passing phase. And that Libby wouldn't leave me alone to deal with Mom off her meds again. But just like when I was ten and Dad had left, it'd been up to me to keep the family from falling apart. Not an easy task when Mom was convinced Libby had also abandoned us. She'd refused to talk to Libby for six months after she'd moved.

"This is the best." Libby grabbed my hand and ushered me over to a set of French doors. She flung open the doors and swept a hand in front of her. "*Voilà*. My terrace."

The tiny cement slab overlooking the narrow street below, housing a slew of potted flowers, must have been the magnificent garden Libby referred to in her e-mails.

"Don't they smell incredible?"

"Mmm hmm," I muttered, inhaling the fumes drifting up from a delivery truck idling below. So much for my vision of the entire city of Paris basking in the aroma of freshly baked croissants and baguettes.

Libby waved at a small elderly man standing on an apartment balcony across the street, surrounded by a colorful explosion of potted flowers. He waved back. She waddled over and plopped down on the orange-cushioned futon. She collapsed back, rubbing her bare belly. I sat next to her and tried to get comfy. She took my hand and massaged it over her tummy. The celestial tattoo around her bellybutton was stretched beyond recognition.

"How about taking in some sights?" she said.

I nodded, stifling a yawn. "I need to stay active so my body adjusts to the new time zone. I just have to make a quick run by the hotel first and check things out."

As a meeting planner for Brecker, a beer company, I usually arrived at a destination a few days before the attendees to get organized, but I was swamped, having just received the program two weeks ago when my boss, Lori, quit. The group was boycotting its annual Oktoberfest program in Munich after getting kicked off the grounds last year. Lori and the president's snooty wife had the brilliant idea of bringing these good ole boys to Paris, the city of fine wine and haute cuisine. So at least if the trip was a total bust, I couldn't be used as the scapegoat.

"We'll take a boat trip down the Seine tonight," Libby said. "It's totally gorgeous at night."

I winced. "I'm meeting Evan for dinner at Jules Verne at seven. Sorry. He wanted to meet before the program begins. It should only take a few hours. Let's do the boat afterward."

She smiled. "We can do it another night."

"I'd invite you, but we'll be talking shop, so it wouldn't be too exciting. I'm...getting a promotion tonight," I said hesitantly, unsure if Libby would be happy or feel sorry for me.

Evan was my boyfriend, but being vice president of North American sales, he'd also been my interim boss since Lori had quit. I'd be reporting to Roger Darwin, global president, once I was promoted from the department's manager to director.

"That's awesome. Congrats." Libby squeezed my hand still resting on her belly. "You certainly deserve it." She sounded genuinely happy for me rather than asking if this position would entail more travel and longer hours, which was undoubtedly what she was wondering. "You're here for two weeks. We'll have lots of time together."

I hadn't told Libby I'd now be leaving after my program ended Friday, unable to take the additional time off. This wasn't something I wanted to bring up when I'd just arrived, especially after discovering she was pregnant.

I laid my head on Libby's shoulder, and my eyelids grew heavy as I gazed at the impressionist mural covering a section of the far wall—two young girls dressed in pink, holding hands by a flower garden. Several meandering cracks in the plaster gave the painting an aged, authentic feel. Large bows held back the girls' long, blonde hair, how Mom used to style Libby's and mine when we were young.

Libby had to come home with me to Milwaukee at the end of the week. Yet convincing Libby to leave Paris was probably going to be more challenging than persuading a group of beer distributors to sip champagne while watching men in tights perform *Swan Lake*.

⁓ ❦ ❧ ⁓

The next thing I knew, Libby was shaking me awake. I blinked the groggy haze from my head, pushing myself up on the futon, massaging the cramp from my neck.

"You have to leave for dinner in an hour," Libby said.

"An hour?" I sprang up, glancing at my watch. Five-thirty p.m. I'd slept *seven* hours? I rummaged through my purse for my iPhone. "I can't believe my assistant, Hannah, didn't call. I was supposed to meet her at one."

"She might have. I turned your phone off. It was so loud I was afraid it would wake you up."

"You turned it *off*?" I said, as if I didn't even know that could be done. I turned it on to discover five missed calls. I'd have to listen to the messages on my way to the restaurant.

I flew across the room to my suitcase and whipped out my new black cocktail dress. "Where do you keep your iron?"

"Don't have one."

My gaze narrowed in disbelief. "You don't have an iron?"

Libby shook her head. "I don't ever iron."

How could someone not own an iron?

Libby had exchanged her kimono robe for a long, green gauze dress, and she stood admiring my dress. "Ooh-la-la, sexy."

The sleeveless dress had a halter neckline with a full, flirty skirt. A tad unconservative compared to what I usually wore, but what the hell, I was in Paris. I could walk down the Champs Élysées nude and not turn heads.

I hung the dress on a hook next to the bathroom curtain, hoping to steam out the wrinkles. I grabbed my toiletry bag from my suitcase and whisked into the bathroom. The entire room was done in avocado-colored ceramic tiles. The shower consisted of a silver nozzle on the far wall and a drain in the floor. No shower curtain, so a large, plastic tub beneath the pedestal sink protected toiletry items from water damage.

God, please let there be hot water.

My prayers were answered, but rather than enjoying the steady stream of hot water, I showered in five minutes flat. I stuck pieces of tissue on several cuts marring my hastily shaven legs. After squeezing the water from my hair, I snagged a thin, yellow towel from the rack by the door and wrapped it around me. I went out and grabbed my hair dryer from my suitcase.

"Ah, you can't use that." Libby smiled apologetically. "The electrical wiring is too old. It could blow a fuse."

Water dripped from my hair and trickled down my back. What was I going to do with my hair? I tried to remain calm, not wanting to send Libby into premature labor.

"Sorry, I'm so used to not using one I didn't think of it." Libby removed the bright orange clip from her hair and twisted my hair up on top of my head, securing it in place. "There, that looks *très* elegant."

I smiled faintly.

"Have a great time tonight." Libby planted a kiss on my cheek. "I gotta run. Have a funeral to go to."

"Who died?"

Libby shrugged. "No clue. My friend Sophie's a medium. Funerals are a great way for her to practice her psychic skills."

"So she goes to funerals of people she doesn't even know?"

"It's not like anyone even realizes we're there. Except for the deceased, hopefully. She's made a lot of contacts through funerals. I'm meeting friends for a drink afterward."

"Should you be drinking?"

Libby rolled her eyes, groaning. "Yes, Mom, one glass of wine is fine."

Not wanting to pry into her life my first day in town, I let it go for now, along with the funeral crashing. I gave her a hug. "Be safe. Love ya."

"Love ya back. *Ciao.*" Libby breezed out.

I turned and stared at my cocktail dress hanging against the wall. I could live with a few wrinkles, but my hair was another story. I'd just give my bangs a quick blow-dry on low.

I grabbed the blow-dryer and zipped into the bathroom. No electrical outlets. Undoubtedly to prevent electrocution while standing in a water puddle. The only mirror in the place was on the medicine cabinet bolted to the wall. I found an outlet in the kitchen and improvised, using a stainless steel teapot for a mirror. I turned on the blow-dryer and finger combed my hair.

POOF. The kitchen light went out, and the small, dorm-sized refrigerator stopped humming.

I peeked from behind the rice-paper divider into the living room to find no lights on. Shit. Had I blown a fuse or fried the apartment's entire electrical wiring? Hopefully I could ask Luc or the landlady to fix it.

The evening of my big promotion definitely wasn't starting as planned.

Chapter Two

As dusk settled in, the Mercedes taxi whisked me across Paris. Rather than enjoying the sights, I squinted at my reflection in the teeny mirror in my lipstick case, attempting to do my hair. I rarely wore my hair up, so I hadn't packed hair accessories and had no choice but to use Libby's orange clip. I tucked the clip under my hair, hiding it as best I could. My phone's earpiece allowed me to multi-task, returning phone calls while finishing my makeup. I called my assistant, Hannah, and apologized for no-showing.

"Thank God you're alive. I filed a report with hotel security, but the police wouldn't do anything since it'd only been two hours. I told them you'd have to be dead before you'd not show up to—"

"Sorry, I've only got a minute. I'm almost to the restaurant. Does Roger Darwin's suite have the thousand-thread-count Egyptian cotton sheets and Siesta Springs coconut water in the minibar?" Unlike the down-to-earth multimillionaire distributors, some of Brecker's executives were total divas, especially their wives.

"Yep. And the minibar is free of competitor beers. No Bud girls hanging out anywhere. Everything's super." Hannah sounded overly confident.

"What's wrong?"

"Nothing. I'm on top of everything. It's going super."

Two supers in a matter of two sentences. Something was definitely wrong. This job had made me totally anal and neurotic, not to mention pessimistic.

"I'll be there by seven. See you in the morning."

I had plenty of time to troubleshoot whatever the hotel had

screwed up. Hannah would let me know if there was a major issue.

I returned Natalie Darwin's call, reassuring her I would make a reservation for her and Roger at Jules Verne. When I'd mentioned in one of our many recent phone conversations that I was indebted to the hotel's concierge for pulling some strings to get me a reservation only a week in advance, *Bat*alie—my secret nickname for Natalie Darwin—had said it was too bad they weren't going to be in early or they could have taken my reservation. She was totally serious. Even worse, I'd have given her the reservation even if it meant celebrating my big promotion at some crêpe stand. I'd be sucking up to the hotel's concierge big-time to get them in.

The taxi stopped in front of the Eiffel Tower. I paid the driver and hopped out. I zipped past a crowd of spectators oohhing and ahhing at a street performer riding a unicycle while juggling flame torches. The aroma of hot dogs wafting from a vendor's cart made my stomach growl for escargots. I paused briefly, peering up the center of the tower at the amber lights dancing against the gridwork like celebratory bubbles in a champagne flute. Thoughts of toasting my promotion with a glass of Dom Perignon brought a smile to my face.

I spied a beige-colored awning that read *Jules Verne*. I bypassed the throng of tourists herding through a ticket queue, making a beeline for the restaurant's private entrance. I flew through a set of glass doors and slipped inside the elevator. Upon exiting the elevator and entering the restaurant, I let out an appreciative sigh, the tension slowly easing from my body. The panoramic windows encompassing the restaurant provided a phenomenal view of the entire city.

The host led me past tables topped with cream-colored linens and flickering candles, surrounded by chocolate-colored chairs that made me crave a decadent dessert. Evan sat at a window table glancing at his Rolex. I was almost five minutes late. Usually, I was fifteen minutes early.

I touched the back of my head, ensuring Libby's orange clip was hidden beneath my upswept hairdo. I tucked an unruly strand behind my ear. Of course, Evan looked polished as usual, not a short, dark hair out of place, and his French blue oxford and matching tie made his blue eyes even more piercing.

"Bonsoir," I said. He stood, and I placed a fleeting kiss to each of his cheeks, feeling like a native after only twelve hours in Paris. Then I brushed a kiss across his lips.

He admired my dress. "You look gorgeous."

I smiled. *"Merci."*

The dim lighting provided ambiance and a better view of the city. It also helped hide the wrinkles in my dress. I gazed down, zoning in on several pieces of white tissue still clinging to the cuts on my bare legs. Lovely.

I sat, discreetly plucking the pieces of tissue from my legs, peering out at the city's lights illuminating the evening sky and at the trail of boats lit up along the Seine. Off in the distance, a large church sat perched majestically on a hill, washed in a yellow glow of lights, keeping watch over the city. Sacré Coeur. I recognized it from my travel books. On a platform directly below our window, tourists swarmed, elbowing their way toward the guardrail for an unobstructed view of the city.

Evan poured my glass of wine. "Hope you don't mind, I went ahead and ordered a nice little Bordeaux. You'll love it."

"Sounds great," I purred. Anything was better than beer, which I'd be forced to consume over the next few days.

The waiter, decked out in a black vest, slacks, and a crisp, white shirt with a black bowtie, materialized with duck foie gras.

Evan smiled. "Thought we'd start with a pâté."

The waiter removed the linen napkin from the table and, with a snap of his wrist, unfolded it and draped it over my lap.

"Merci," I said.

He nodded diligently then whisked off to the next table.

Evan gazed over at me, reaching across the table, taking my hand in his. "I have something to ask you. I was going to wait until after dinner, but seeing you now, I can't."

Heart racing, I attempted to relax, raising my wineglass and inhaling the aroma of vanilla and blackberries, preparing to toast my new position.

"Being in Paris for this program I thought would be the perfect time to ask you." He gave my hand a squeeze. "Will you marry me?"

I smiled brightly. "Absolutely. I would love..."

I stared in confusion at the signature blue Tiffany ring box in Evan's hand, showcasing an oval-cut diamond, around two carats. Wait a sec, he was offering me the position of *wife* rather than director of corporate events? This was the important discussion he wanted to have before the meeting started?

My hand slipped from Evan's and onto the table. "Marry you?" I muttered.

I apparently wore my disappointment like a bad Versace knockoff, since Evan's smile slowly faded.

"Ah, most women would get a bit more excited about a ring from Tiffany." He snapped the ring box shut. "So what, you don't like platinum, or you don't want to marry me?"

Both. Maybe. I for sure didn't like platinum, but did I want to marry Evan? I'd never bought a bridal magazine in my life. Had never even window-shopped for an engagement ring or a wedding dress. I'd never seriously considered marrying *anyone*.

I took a drink of wine, trying to ease the tension twisting every muscle in my body. I felt bad. Here Evan was proposing, yet all I could focus on was my promotion. However, we'd often discussed my future with Brecker but had never discussed *our* future together. "I'm sorry. It's just...we've never even talked about marriage." And if I didn't become director, working more with marketing promotional events, I wouldn't be in line for director of North American marketing when the current director retired in three years. And I could forget making VP of North American marketing.

"That's why I *thought* it would be a nice surprise."

"Oh, I'm surprised." My voice was so high-pitched every poodle within a half-mile radius was undoubtedly yipping. "I can't believe you just asked me this out of the blue."

"That's how it usually happens, Sam."

"No, it doesn't," I said, shaking my head for emphasis. "People have *usually* at least touched on the subject. We talked about moving in together for six months before we finally did it. We looked at a couple dozen bedroom sets before we bought one. I test-drove eleven cars before deciding on a BMW. So yeah, I'd have thought we'd have at least talked about marriage before...this."

"Are you saying you want to test-drive some more men before you make a commitment?"

"That's not what I'm saying." But I obviously needed to reevaluate our relationship if this was the reaction a wedding proposal evoked. I leaned in. "We haven't had sex in..." The fact that I had to stop and calculate how long it'd been since we'd had sex made me question just how much I'd missed it. Our relationship had been strained for a while. I couldn't believe Evan was so clueless.

"We haven't had sex," he said, lowering his voice, "because we've both been gone so much."

"Exactly. We've hardly seen each other lately."

"We've been together almost three years. I'm thirty-eight, you're thirty-four, it's about time we started thinking about having a family, having kids."

Kids? We'd certainly never discussed having kids. Even if I did want to marry him, Evan wanting kids was a definite deal breaker. I didn't want the responsibility of another family.

I took a huge gulp of wine, followed by a calming breath. "Since when do you want kids?" I finally managed.

He shrugged. "Been thinking about it lately. And we're a good match. Why not get married?" His tone was matter-of-fact, as if he were trying to match a tie with a shirt.

Gee, what a way to woo a girl.

Were we a good match? We were both passionate about our jobs, wine, and the theater. But that didn't mean we were passionate enough about each *other* to get married. I glared at the pâté. Typical Evan had ordered that and the wine without even asking my opinion.

"Curt seems so happy," he said.

"This is about your brother? When is this competitiveness going to end?"

"I don't want a family just because he had a kid. It made me realize what I'm missing."

"You *missed* the fact that Curt is a hands-on father, changing dirty diapers and up for two a.m. feedings. I can't see you trading in your Porsche for a minivan, or leaving work early to attend soccer and Little League games. What kind of a family life would it be with both of us working long hours?"

"If we were married, you wouldn't need to work so much. You could cut back on your travel."

"Cut back? With my promotion, I'll be working even—"

"Roger offered you the promotion?" Evan's eyes widened with surprise.

"Well, not yet, but..." My gaze narrowed. "Why would you be surprised if he *had* offered it to me?"

He pressed imaginary creases from his starched tie. A nervous habit. "Because he hadn't mentioned it to me." The muscle in his jaw twitched. A telltale sign he was also lying.

"I'm getting the promotion, aren't I? I mean, who else would get it?" Evan's gaze skittered around the restaurant as if he were searching for a viable candidate. "Who else would get it?" My voice rose, and he glanced apologetically at the other diners. God forbid I attracted attention.

"I don't know," he said, lowering his voice. "A decision hasn't been made."

"How hard of a decision is it?" I demanded. "I put in sixty hours a week. I'm on the road a hundred plus days a year. I've worked there for thirteen years. I've helped build that department. You'll never find anyone more dedicated to their job than me. Who else is being considered for it?"

He shook his head, removing the linen napkin from his lap and whipping it on the table. "Christ, I ask you to marry me and all you give a damn about is your promotion. Why do you even want the position? You work best on your own. You're not a big team player. You're the best planner in the department, but you might not make the best director." He snapped his mouth shut.

Eyes wide, mouth gaping, I stared at him, stunned. "You didn't recommend me for the position, did you?"

"Yes, I did. Roger's on the fence about giving it to you, and I think he might be right, although I didn't tell him that." His teeth clenched, preventing his jaw from twitching. My gut told me he was lying. I didn't believe for a second Roger questioned my management skills, and my consumer promotion plan had to have blown him away. I did, however, question Evan's motives. This spoke volumes about our relationship.

"You're trying to sabotage my promotion. You want me to stay home and plan family dinners rather than luaus in Hawaii."

"This isn't personal, Sam," he said in that condescending tone that made me want to go berserk and dump a two-hundred-dollar bottle of Bordeaux over his head.

"Bullshit," I said, slamming my hand down on the table, rattling the fragile china and crystal. "You know I'd make a great director. I should be a shoo-in for this position."

"It's not like I'm the only one making the decision here."

"No, thank God you're not, or three years from now I'd be stuck making babies rather than director of marketing. Which you can bet your ass I'll make without your help."

I surged from my chair, eyeing the wine bottle, dying to drench Evan's Armani suit in Bordeaux. I snagged the bottle. Panicked, Evan snapped back in his chair, his body going rigid. I raised the *très* expensive bottle of wine, enjoying the priceless look on Evan's face, suddenly feeling in control of the situation. Wanting to embarrass Evan in the worst possible way, I raised the bottle to my mouth and began drinking. Gasps of horror and disbelief erupted from the surrounding tables, as well as Evan. Our waiter expelled an indignant puff of air from between his lips, in a manner only the French had mastered, and shook his head at us crazy-ass Americans.

For the first time in my life, I felt a little wild and crazy. I came up for air and slammed the bottle on the table. "I've wasted three years on you. Sure as hell not wasting a great bottle of wine."

I stormed across the restaurant, hopefully looking more

confident than I felt. If I didn't get this promotion, I could kiss a VP position goodbye. I *had* to get it.

Just had to figure out how.

Chapter Three

I sat at the outdoor café on the corner next to Libby's apartment building, surrounded by couples kissing and fondling each other. Okay, not everyone was a couple, but it sure seemed like it. Actually, we were all rather intimate, our small, round tables lined up in rows, practically on top of each other, making maximum use of the sidewalk space. Those who weren't engrossed in foreplay discreetly glanced my way, debating whether I was a classy hooker in my black, designer cocktail dress or an eccentric wino, now on my second demi-carafe of Bordeaux. Consumed in a haze of cigarette smoke, lost in rapid conversations in French, I felt like a damsel in distress in some foreign film noir.

The front door of Libby's building was locked. It apparently was secured at night, which made me feel better, yet now even *I* couldn't get in. I'd called Libby's apartment, but no answer. Of course, she didn't own a cell phone. Hopefully she'd be home before long. I should have been reviewing my program binder rather than Café Balzar's menu. Starving, I'd polished off a cheese tray—even the pungent one that tasted like shower mold—and was debating a chocolate mousse.

I'd read sixteen new e-mails on my iPhone. Not too many, but then again, it was Sunday, and I'd checked it that morning. If I called Hannah to go over tomorrow's agenda, she'd know something was wrong since I wasn't at dinner with Evan. That I lived with Evan was the extent of her knowledge on our relationship. I preferred to keep it that way.

My co-worker Rachel and I occasionally did lunch, but she was busy working a consumer promotion in Miami. Desperate to tell someone what an ass Evan was, I called and got Rachel's voice mail. I left a message, merely asking her to call me.

Evan hadn't called apologizing. I couldn't believe he was sabotaging my career for his own personal gain. The fact he thought there was even a chance I'd give up my career to have kids showed we were so not in tune.

But what if he'd offered me the promotion and a lifetime of marital bliss, sans kids? Would I have accepted his proposal? Did I love Evan? At least, had I before he'd tried to screw me out of the promotion? What if he had gone to bat for me with Roger? A sick feeling said he hadn't.

We rarely ate dinner together, unless you counted being in the same office while we ate at our desks. We didn't do everyday chores together like grocery shopping. Our laundry was done separately. My whites never touched his. The last time we'd been to the theater together was *A Christmas Carol* last December. Had we been too busy with work to realize that work was possibly the only thing we even had in common anymore?

My phone rang. Mom. She was calling to drill me about Libby, no doubt. If I ignored her, she'd continue calling until I picked up. I took a deep breath and answered.

"How's Libby?"

"She's—"

"Have you convinced her to come home?"

"I—"

"I'm sure you'll convince her. I painted her room orange, her favorite color, I shopped online and got her a daisy bedspread, matching lamp and rug, all kinds of stuff, and I'm baking all her favorite foods...."

Omigod. Excessive shopping, mind racing, rapid speech...

My stomach dropped.

Was she off her medication again?

It had taken doctors most of my childhood to get Mom's medication right. Diagnosing her illness had been difficult because her symptoms were all over the place. She'd showed signs of several mental health disorders, including a form of schizophrenia.

The correct meds finally enabled her to live a better life, except she'd gone off them twice. The last time was three years ago when Libby had moved to Paris. I lived in fear she'd go off them again. But if she'd gone off them, her boyfriend, Ken, would have contacted me. Unless he was no longer around to tell me.

She was still rattling off things she'd bought for Libby. The last time she'd racked up her credit card shopping online, I'd ended up paying for the non-refundable items because she'd been out of work. And after Libby had moved to Paris, she'd painted the walls white, covering up the vibrant colors Libby had painted the house. In the process, she'd painted all the windows shut.

"Mom," I interrupted. "Are you off your medication?"

"What, just because I'm excited, you think I'm off my medication? I'm just happy. Can't a mother be happy?"

Click. She disconnected.

I couldn't deal with this right now.

I knocked back the last of my wine.

A scooter jumped the curb and zipped down the sidewalk in front of the café. Its motor hummed, causing my chest to vibrate along with the wineglass on the table. The driver parked on the sidewalk in front of Libby's apartment building and removed his helmet. It was Libby's neighbor Luc. Hoping he might have a key to Libby's place, I left money to cover my bill then strolled over to him.

He placed a fleeting kiss to each of my cheeks, causing a warm sensation to rush up my neck and across my cheeks. I made a feeble attempt at air-kissing his cheeks. He stepped back, his gaze slowly traveling down the length of my dress and back up. The corners of his mouth curled into an appreciative smile as he raked a hand through his hair. "You look...*incroyable.*"

His accent, more so than the compliment, made me blush. He could have been saying I looked like a total skank, and it would have had the same effect.

"*Merci,*" I muttered.

He opened the scooter's back compartment and exchanged his helmet for a black fedora. The hat's band secured one lonely cigarette. He plucked the cancer stick from the hat and lit up, inhaling a deep breath. The cigarette dangled precariously from his lips while he chained his scooter to a metal pole. He took a leisurely puff and blew a slow, steady stream of smoke out the side of his mouth, away from me. Considerate, yet my nose scrunched in protest.

"Libby met some friends for a drink," I said.

"I ran into them. She should be back soon."

"Do you have a key to her apartment?"

"No. But I received the note you left on my door, and I had Madame Gerrard let me in to fix the fuse."

I smiled. "Thanks."

"Would you like to wait at my place?"

Was that a subtle way of getting me up to his apartment? No, guys didn't try to pick me up and take me back to their places. Guys had always approached Libby, not me.

I tried to remember the last time I'd gone home with a virtual stranger. I never had.

I stared at the photo of a pregnant Libby wearing merely a pair of pink sunglasses, standing next to the Seine buck naked.

My gaze darted to the kitchen, where Luc searched the cupboard for clean wineglasses, then back at the small photo album I'd taken off the cocktail table. I flipped to the next page to find a photo of Luc and Libby with a group of people, all of them nude. A full frontal of Libby, a rear shot of Luc.

I zoned in on his butt. His incredible butt. And his back. My God, the muscles, for being so lean and—

"That was taken this summer," Luc said, peering over my shoulder. His breath smelled faintly of wine and felt warm against my neck.

Leaning back a mere inch would have my bare back flush against his chest. I swallowed hard, my heart thumping like I'd just sprinted up the building's six flights of stairs. I flipped the album closed, unsure if I felt more awkward having been ogling Luc's butt or looking at nude pics of my sister. I took a step forward, putting enough space between us so I could turn and face him. The dim lighting from a small table lamp gave his brown eyes a lustful gleam, and they held a hint of mischief. A slow, crooked smile quirked the corners of his mouth, and his gaze remained locked with mine.

He handed me a wineglass and set his glass on the cocktail table—two beat-up wine crates nailed together with bricks for legs. He slipped the album from my hand. "You didn't see the best one."

"Yes, I did," I muttered in a breathless tone. "They're all very good." As if I'd been admiring every one of his butt shots, for God's sake.

He opened the album and thumbed through photos.

"Really, I don't need to see any more," I assured him.

"Here it is."

He held the album in front of me, and I couldn't avoid looking at a photo of Luc and some chick naked and in handcuffs. Far from kinky since a cop was slapping on the cuffs and they stood next to several people holding signs. In the background, a cop was chasing a naked guy down the quay.

"What do the signs say?" I asked, acting like *that* detail in the photo had caught my eye.

"Liberty, equality, fraternity, and the right to bear butts and breasts. But see what's so funny? The guy running away. They never caught him." Luc laughed.

"So, this was a protest?"

I doubted nude sunbathing was the first time Luc had protested for or against a cause he believed in. It certainly wasn't the first time Libby had. In second grade, she'd rallied her classmates together, organizing her first protest when the school debated eliminating afternoon recess. When the recess remained intact, she became a hero at Marston Elementary School.

"*Ouais.* It's now illegal to sunbathe topless along the Seine. Women can't wear thong bikinis." His gaze traveled down below my waist, where it lingered, as if he were envisioning my thong. My inner thighs throbbed. "What's next? Will they outlaw kissing in public?" He raised his gaze to my mouth, and I instinctively licked my lips, thankful I'd reapplied my Risqué Red lipstick before coming up. He peered into my eyes. "Or smoking on the streets, now that it's not allowed in restaurants, or..." He went off on a passionate tangent, and I could barely keep up. Conviction filled his eyes, and outrage reddened his face. "*Putain de merde!* This is crazy. If I want to show my butt to everyone, I'll show my butt, *non*?" He looked to me for confirmation.

I nodded slowly. *Yes, please show your butt.* My nodding became more vigorous. "You're absolutely right. You should be able to show your butt."

It was the two demi-carafes of wine talking. I sounded like this was the most unjust law ever. As if I'd lost my right to the freedom of speech. He watched as I took a sip of wine. I slowly lowered the glass while his gaze remained fixed on my mouth.

Was he going to kiss me?

My mouth went dry with anticipation.

He placed a warm hand on my bare shoulder and gently massaged his thumb against it, gazing deep into my eyes, as if we were one, in this together. "You're as passionate as Libby."

His finger grazed my cheek, brushing back a stray hair. His hand lingered against the side of my face. "You have to stand up for what you believe in. It's your right."

My blood was racing. I *believed* I wanted to kiss Luc.

After just breaking up with Evan, and only twelve hours in Paris, I was suddenly open to making out with some guy I barely knew? I was looking at Luc through wine-colored glasses. He was not my type. But I was tipsy. Vulnerable. A scorned woman...

I didn't really want to sleep with Luc, right? He just had me fired up. Hell, I was so psyched right now I'd strip and picket outside Hôtel de l'Opéra for the deportation of Natalie Darwin. Something I truly believed in. However, I'd never protested anything in my life. At least not in public, where I could have been arrested or fired.

A rap sounded at the door, jarring me back to reality.

Luc frowned, dropping his hand from my face. "Libby."

Neither of us moved to answer the door. Inches between us, we stood staring into each other's eyes, our heavy breathing the only sound in the room. We were definitely on the same page.

Should we answer the door?

What if we ignored Libby? Then what?

Libby rapped again, calling out our names. We'd left a note on her door telling her my whereabouts.

My gaze darted to the door, breaking our trance. I glanced back at Luc. He shrugged off his disappointment and strolled over and opened the door.

"Why aren't you with Evan?" Libby asked, waddling in, hand on her lower back as if to keep herself from falling over.

"It's a long story." I stared into my wineglass, unable to meet her gaze, like she'd caught me having wild sex with Luc. "It's late. Let's get you to bed." I thanked Luc then fled as fast as I could with Libby waddling alongside me.

The light in her apartment flicked on. *Thank you, Luc.* Libby didn't mention the blown fuse, so I wondered if Luc had told her or if it was our secret.

We stayed up talking. I told her about Evan possibly screwing me out of the promotion and his proposal. Surprisingly, she didn't tell me I was insane for not accepting his proposal. She mainly listened, not talking much about herself or the baby.

"Who's the father?" I finally asked.

Libby let out an exhausted sigh, as if I'd been pumping her for info nonstop. "You'll never know him, so it really doesn't matter." She pushed herself up from the futon. "I need to get to bed." She leaned over and gave me a kiss on the cheek.

Usually Libby was so open. She used to tell me everything. My stomach tightened as I realized just how far apart we'd drifted. Even so, when had *Libby* become so secretive, and why?

Chapter Four

At six-thirty a.m., Paris was a ghost town. The city workers cleaning the streets and dog poop off the sidewalks were about the only ones around. Not having a taxi right at my door, and not wanting to wake up Libby to call one, I'd left my luggage for later. Good thing. After a half hour and trekking a dozen blocks, in my new cream-colored heels and suit, sweating up a storm, I finally flagged down a taxi that wasn't whisking tourists off to the airport. Taking the *Métro* was a last resort. Besides not knowing the stop nearest to the hotel, the antibacterial wipes in my purse wouldn't even get me through the station and to the train. The Center for Disease Control would have a field day with the germs festering in a subway. I couldn't afford to get sick on this trip.

I arrived at the hotel fifteen minutes late. Not quite three hours before eight executives and regional managers, along with twenty distributors and companions, began arriving.

If it weren't for everyone speaking French as I zipped through the lobby, the hotel would have felt no different than a Ritz Carlton in the United States. I'd expected a Parisian hotel to feel more exotic...French...something. It looked like dozens of other hotels I'd stayed in with its crystal chandeliers, elaborate floral arrangements, and dark wood. Guess it took a lot to impress me at this point in my career.

The hotel's best features were air conditioning and a Starbucks. I ordered a double espresso and slammed it. "Futon" was obviously the Chinese term for torture apparatus, and Libby's apartment was as cool as an Amazon hut. I was lucky if I'd gotten two hours of sleep. The seven-hour catnap yesterday hadn't helped. I glanced in a gilded mirror on the wall, adjusting my damp hair held up in Libby's clip.

My phone rang out. I took a deep breath, praying it wasn't Mom. I planned to talk to Ken before talking to her again. It was Rachel. After one a.m. in Miami and the poor thing was just now returning calls and e-mails.

I answered with a perky, *"Bonjour."*

"Samantha?"

"Oui. I'm trying to get into French mode this morning."

"I'm trying to get *out* of Miami mode. Thank God this was the last day. Anyway, I won't whine, what's up?"

"I didn't get the promotion last night as I expected."

Silence filled the line.

"Oh, that sucks," Rachel finally said, not sounding the least bit surprised.

"What? You don't think I'll get it?"

More silence. "No, I don't." She sounded apprehensive, as if debating being honest. How much more honest could she be? "I mean, I think you deserve it. Believe me, more than anyone, you deserve it. I just don't think you'll *get* it." She let out a heavy sigh. "Shit. I shouldn't tell you this. Sherri could get in a lot of trouble, but..."

Sherri was in Human Resources.

"What is it?" I started pacing, my heels clicking against the mosaic tiles. "You can't not tell me now."

She let out another sigh. "Sherri's getting divorced, and we were talking about men being jerks, and she slipped up and told me she was blown away that Evan was strongly against you getting the promotion, and he said..."

"He said what?" I practically shrieked.

"That he doesn't think you're a people person, and this position involved more client schmoozing and employee managing than your current position. That the department might lose employees if you got the job."

My grip tightened around the phone. Evan had lied right to my face saying *he'd* recommended me and *Roger* was on the fence.

Those had been his exact words. I wanted to cram them down his throat.

"He thinks you're too professional for the position, and Roger agreed he might be right."

I stopped pacing. "*Too* professional?"

And Roger agreed? A sense of betrayal tossed my stomach. Roger had assured me I'd go far in the company. But even more than being my boss, he'd been a father figure to me.

"That you don't relate to the distributors on a social level."

"Because I don't drink, smoke, and party with them? Like Lori used to." Lori the Lush would party until three in the morning and then be massively hungover, forcing me to pick up the slack for her the entire next day. But when Matt Davis, Brecker's largest distributor, needed someone to mentor his daughter in event planning, he chose me over Lori. Too professional, my ass!

"Yeah, if you at least partied, then being a woman in a good ole boy company wouldn't be such a major strike against you."

"They can't not promote me because I'm *too* professional. That's insane. A company can enforce a no drinking and smoking policy, but it can't enforce a *pro* one. And not being a man is just plain discrimination." Lori had been the only woman to hold the director position.

"Have Sherri photocopy any e-mails or documents in case they go missing." I clenched my fist. "Can't wait to see how Evan's gonna get himself out of this one."

"You can't say anything to him. He'll know it came from Sherri. She'll get canned. Her husband just left her, she has a little girl, she can't lose her job...." Rachel was sounding more hysterical than me.

"All right. I won't say anything. I gotta go. Thanks."

I placed a hand to my stomach, which was on fire. How many other times had Evan lied to me over the past three years? How could I not confront him? Yet if I did, he'd probably lie and say it wasn't true and then turn around and can Sherri.

Too professional. It was my professionalism that ensured all of the attendees' ridiculous demands were met and a program was flawlessly executed. And had Roger not read my consumer promotion plan? It was way better than any of Lori's.

A barely audible growl vibrated in the back of my throat. I wanted to rip the impressionist paintings of perky flowers off the walls and maul them to shreds. As I stalked toward the front door for some fresh air, prepared to annihilate anything in my path, a bellman advised a guest as to the nearest establishment selling liquor, since the hotel lounge was under renovation. It was only seven a.m. About the time my attendees would start knocking back beers tomorrow morning!

This had to be what Hannah wasn't telling me. She was obviously thinking there was nothing I could do about a closed lounge and I should enjoy the day with my sister. Well, there *was* something I could do.

When Lori wasn't hungover onsite, she was too good of a planner to have overlooked something like this. Had she known she'd be leaving the company on bad terms and booked a hotel without a lounge on purpose?

What else had she done to sabotage the program?

Although no further Lori issues surfaced throughout the morning, I had plenty of problems to troubleshoot. Like persuading the hotel to open the lounge two weeks ahead of schedule, to designate our ballroom a smoking venue for a *beaucoup* cleaning fee, and to get a minimum of one hundred cases of Brecker for our small group. I'd also endured the wrath of *Bat*alie Darwin. Ticked at the concierge for correcting her French, Natalie demanded he be fired. She'd alienated the one man who could get her into Jules Verne. I tipped the concierge to smooth things over and sent a box of Fauchon truffles to Natalie on the concierge's behalf.

I was so busy I managed to ignore Evan rather than cracking him upside the head with a bottle of Brecker beer. I had no clue how I'd survive the week working so closely with him. Or rather, how *Evan* was going to survive. By the end of the week, authorities would be dredging the Seine, searching for his body.

By noon, everyone had arrived, and the executives were off to Maxim's for lunch. Libby called asking me to meet her for lunch at the Luxembourg Gardens. Feeling bad about sleeping all day yesterday then having dinner with Evan, I promised to meet her for a quick lunch. I also needed to pick up my luggage.

When I arrived at the garden, I found Libby sitting on a green metal chair, her feet propped up on the edge of a large, stone fountain. Dressed in a long, orange gauze skirt and white knit shirt hugging her tummy, Libby was enjoying the sunshine and a sandwich, watching the children sail toy boats in the fountain. Kids and adults were everywhere. It was Monday. Shouldn't people be at work and in school?

"How did everything go with Evan?" she asked as I sat.

I was barely holding it together, and if I got started, I might lose it. "It went fine." I slipped off my suit jacket.

Libby groaned, dropping her head back against the chair. "I feel kind of funky."

I eyed her sandwich, my top lip curling back. "I can see why. What is that?"

"Brie, apricots, black olives, and salami."

Just the sound of it made my stomach lurch. "Thought we were going for lunch?"

"It's just a snack. We need to go see Luc first," Libby said, gathering up the remains of the picnic lunch.

Thoughts of Luc and me in his apartment last night kicked my heart rate up a notch and caused a flutter in my stomach as we headed into the garden. We came across a wall of high shrubs and an iron gate with an archway blanketed in ivy. Inside, a small, green shed displayed a red velvet curtain on the top half and brightly painted designs on the side and bottom panels. Kids scurried to claim their seats on the wooden benches lined in front of it.

A little boy ran up to a blonde girl with ringlets and swiped the doll tucked under her arm. Little brat. Reminded me of how nasty I was to Libby when we were younger. I'd resented no longer being an only child so I wouldn't let her play with my toys and refused to babysit her. My naughty behavior worsened as I grew older. Mom couldn't deal with my troublemaking, so Dad had frequently gone to school and discussed my disciplinary problems. He hit it off with Ms. Duran, my fourth grade teacher, and they ran off together. My mom's worst fear had finally come true, even though it was her illness that gave her delusions that every woman wanted my dad. We'd once had to move because she'd constantly accused a neighbor lady of trying to take away not only Dad but her children.

After Dad left, I never misbehaved and started taking responsibility for my actions, caring for Mom and Libby. I thought if Dad was proud of me, he'd come home. When I never heard from him again, I was determined to prove we could take care of ourselves. Despite Mom's emotional problems, I'd spent my childhood blaming myself for Dad leaving, rather than blaming him.

Libby sat on a back bench by the parents, and I joined her, welcoming the shade. The shed's red velvet curtain opened, revealing a whimsical backdrop of a sunny mountain village.

"Where's Luc?" I asked, glancing around.

"Up there." Libby nodded toward the shed.

Luc was a puppeteer?

A young girl came by requesting three euros per person, and I paid her. A soundtrack blared out French music, and the kids bounced up and down, anticipating the puppet that suddenly appeared on stage. It resembled Pinocchio, dressed in lederhosen and suspenders. Squeals of delight filled the garden. The puppet addressed the audience, and kids shrieked *"oui"* and *"non,"* responding to its questions, as did Libby.

A little girl puppet materialized, and the boy puppet waggled his brows with interest. He trailed behind her as she skipped along singing. He became more daring, cozying up alongside her. He took her coquettish glances as an invitation to peek up her dress. The kids giggled. The girl puppet smacked him on top of the head with her doll, and the kids laughed harder. The boy did a few flips through the air and landed on his face.

Fantasizing about doing this to Evan, I joined the kids in laughing. They quieted, but my laughter grew until it was almost bordering on hysteria. Rather than being embarrassed, Libby watched me with amusement and a bit of surprise. I couldn't stop laughing. Before long, tears streamed down my cheeks, and I clutched my side. The kids glanced at me with bemused curiosity, and the parents looked ready to gather up their children to protect them from the crazy woman. I dropped my head to my knees to avoid watching the show and because I was lightheaded, on the verge of passing out. I couldn't remember the last time I'd laughed so hard. I didn't think I ever had.

"You remind me of Mom that time I knocked over my milk at dinner," Libby said. "She laughed hysterically, knocking over Dad's milk, yours, and her own. 'Better to laugh than to cry over spilled milk,' she'd said. Remember that?"

I reined in my laughter. Yeah, I remembered. Dad had wiped up the milk without saying a word while Mom laughed. I lived in fear that I'd inherited Mom's emotional disorder and would one day start exhibiting symptoms of the illness. I couldn't believe Libby had just compared me to our mother.

Twenty minutes later, the show ended, and parents rounded up their children and dispersed into the park. Luc closed up the theater and strolled over. He had on jeans, a white T-shirt, an open jean vest, and a blue flannel shirt tied around his waist. A Celtic cross hung around his neck. He plucked a cigarette from his brown fedora, swept it under his nose, then slid it behind his ear rather than lighting it. He removed a roll of cinnamon mints from his vest pocket and popped one in his mouth.

He kissed my cheeks, and I responded in return, a warm feeling igniting my cheeks. He held up the boy puppet still on his hand, speaking French. I clamped down on my lower lip, stifling a laugh.

"Sam loved your show," Libby said.

A pleased smile curled the corners of his mouth. "I like to make people laugh."

"You're very good," I said.

"It's not so difficult. Here." Luc held out the puppet.

I stared at it. "I can't work a puppet."

Luc took hold of my hand and studied it, lightly massaging my palm with his thumb. The hairs on my arms shot up. "Why not? You have a hand." He removed the puppet from his hand then slipped the girl puppet onto mine, pulling the knit material beneath her dress up my forearm. Sitting next to me, he used the boy puppet to talk to mine. "So, how was your morning?"

When I just sat there, Libby nudged me with her elbow. And Luc's brown eyes seemed even softer, more compassionate, like he was urging me to open up.

"Evan's an ass. He didn't recommend me for the promotion," I blurted, moving my fingers in an awkward attempt to move the puppet's hands. "He even strongly recommended I didn't get it."

Luc and Libby exchanged surprised glances.

"I'm sorry." Luc now peered at *me* instead of my puppet.

Gazing deep into his eyes, I recounted every sordid detail. "He said I'm too professional. Not a people person. That my co-workers would quit because of me. That we'd lose clients. Like I'm some awful tyrant."

"He's an idiot," Luc said.

I'd been so focused on Evan screwing me out of the promotion, I hadn't really thought about his actual personal cuts. Sure, I rarely had time to chitchat with co-workers about their personal lives, but it wasn't like I was a total bitch and would cause the department to dismantle. I was a type-A personality, so was Evan, and he managed a lot more people than I did. Evan claiming I had all these issues was merely a cover-up for the discriminatory and selfish reasons he didn't want to promote me.

Libby slipped a comforting arm around my shoulder. Rather than looking freaked out by my behavior, as most men would, Luc placed a hand on my bare leg, flirting with the hem of my skirt. I discreetly eyed his hand, relaxing slightly.

"It'll be okay," Libby said.

"Why don't you come home with me?" Seemed like a good time to play the sympathy card.

Libby shook her head regretfully. "Paris is my home. I couldn't leave."

I should have come to Paris three years ago. I'd have had a better shot at convincing her to come home before she'd settled in here. But Mom had been a complete wreck. I'd had to cancel a work trip because Mom had been upset, certain I was abandoning her also. And honestly, I never dreamed Libby wouldn't return. I'd even promised to get off her back about quitting college, even though I'd helped with the tuition. I needed a strategy to get Libby to come home. Not just because it was the best thing for her, but because I missed her.

"I have my friends, my jobs..."

What about your family?

Libby glanced at her watch. "Which reminds me, I have to go to the café for a few hours." She let out a heavy sigh, pushing herself up from the bench. "Let's go grab lunch, and you can see where I work." Libby slipped her arm through mine.

We started walking away, and I turned back around, realizing I still had the puppet. "Don't forget this," I called out to Luc, waving the puppet on my hand, walking over to him.

He placed a hand over the puppet, preventing me from removing it, then swept his hand down the length of the knitted material on my forearm, resting it against my bare skin. My heart raced.

"You keep it," Luc said. "I can buy another."

Not to be unappreciative, but I really didn't want to walk around Paris with a puppet on my hand. I was already getting a reputation as a psycho American, and I'd only been here twenty-four hours. But he looked like he really wanted me to have it. Maybe I could fit it in my purse.

"Thanks. I mean *merci*."

A smile curled the corners of his mouth, and his brown eyes gazed deep into mine. *"Avec plaisir."*

The words wrapped around me like a warm embrace even though I wasn't sure what they meant.

"With pleasure," he translated.

"Ah, *avec plaisir*." I loved the way that sounded.

Especially the way Luc said it. Yet I was beginning to like more about Luc than his brown eyes and incredibly sexy accent. He had passion. One minute he had me so fired up I wanted to protest for nudity on the Seine when I preferred everyone remained clothed, and the next he had me walking around with a puppet on my hand, laughing harder than I ever had.

When I was with Luc, there was this part of me that somehow felt more...more everything.

It made me wonder how long I'd been feeling so much *less*.

Chapter Five

When Libby mentioned she worked at a café, call me crazy but I assumed it was a charming little outdoor café that sold croque monsieurs and crêpes. Although the Venus Café served a limited selection of sandwiches, they specialized in items such as palm and tarot card readings and aura photography. Libby was a gemstone therapist. So if a woman was in a funk, Libby advised her to go buy a pair of diamond earrings to feel better? No clue. After meeting Libby's co-workers, I gracefully excused myself with a tofu veggie sandwich and promised to pop in another time.

Another *life*time.

Libby gave me her extra key, and Luc was nice enough to help me haul my luggage down to the sidewalk and call a taxi. Upon returning to the hotel, I disinfected my room with antibacterial wipes, showered, styled my hair, and slipped on my black pencil skirt and white blouse. I had to exude confidence when I spoke to Roger about my promotion and reminded him that I was a dream employee who would help fulfill the company's minority status, being one of the only female executives in a male-dominated company. They'd be hard-pressed to find a woman my age willing to make the sacrifices I did. I'd also inform him Evan had sabotaged my promotion for his own selfish reasons. And knocking back a few beers with the distributors would show just how seriously I wanted the promotion, as long as I didn't vomit on the ballroom carpet.

I headed down to the ballroom. Hannah was seated outside the door at the hospitality desk, dressed in a lime green, mod print skirt and blouse. Her blonde hair was cut in a bob, and her bright blue eyes were wide with enthusiasm.

"Ballroom looks super," she said with a perky smile. "And we have twenty cases of backup beer."

"Great. I'll check it out."

The ballroom resembled dozens of others I'd held events in with its gilded woodwork, shimmering chandeliers, jewel-toned, patterned carpet, and tables draped in cream linens with gold organza silk overlays. Only difference, the waitstaff looked like they'd just walked off the movie set of *Marie Antoinette*, dressed in white wigs, long, blue jackets, and pantaloons. Lori had paid extra for the costumes as well as the fountain in the middle of the room where Brecker beer cascaded down crystal champagne glasses. Lori had blown the budget with all the froufrou décor and costumes. Precisely her intent, no doubt.

I was about to hunt down the banquet captain and review the menu when my cell phone rang out. Rachel. Thank God it wasn't Mom. I'd been putting off calling her boyfriend, Ken, all day.

"You aren't going to believe this," Rachel said. "Just talked to Sherri, and the director's position has already been filled. They hired some stupid yahoo sales rep from a hotel in Dallas. He only has twelve years in the hotel industry and has worked for four different hotels. No company loyalty, which is supposedly so important to Roger. We women need to stick together, or we're never gonna get ahead in this company."

What the hell? I wasn't surprised he was a good ole boy from Texas. The state boasted Brecker's largest market and concentration of distributors. Although hotel sales reps were big schmoozers, they often didn't have a background in logistics outside of the hotel. So I'd be expected to train my own boss. No way was I picking up the slack for another Lori! As fast as I'd moved up in the company, Roger had led me to believe I had a great shot at being the company's second female VP. Why pay for part of my grad school if they didn't plan to promote me any higher than a stinking manager?

"He starts in two weeks," Rachel said.

The week after I got back in town. They wouldn't want to make the announcement while I was onsite with the group in case I went postal and dumped out all the beer.

"Don't tell Evan I told you this. Sherri can't afford to lose her job. Her husband just left..." She once again rambled on about Sherri's personal problems.

I wasn't sure if Rachel had told me this because we were sort of friends, or if she was merely hoping to rally together the small percentage of women in the company, like she'd attempted to do over a sexist marketing campaign six months ago. I hadn't gotten involved. Rather, I'd been inspired to develop a campaign for marketing to women, an untapped consumer demographic despite the fact that women comprised twenty-five percent of U.S. beer consumers. Brecker didn't want to be known as a "chick" beer. I'd been jotting down ideas but hadn't put together an actual plan.

Time for a marketing plan that would guarantee a ten percent increase in sales and make Roger eat crow!

"Don't worry, I won't say anything. And you'd better believe I'm still getting this promotion." Even if I had to blackmail Evan. I had the ammunition if needed. "Thanks."

I disconnected, fighting the urge to hurl my phone at the champagne fountain, plowing over the glasses like bowling pins in a carnival game. I marched over to the bar and slammed a beer, drinking it too fast to gag on the taste. I'd almost polished off my second one when attendees began straggling in. I waited for Evan to walk through the door so I could drown him in the beer fountain.

A half hour later, the reception was in full swing, but still no Evan. However, Natalie Darwin was sashaying up in a slinky black dress with a red shawl and black stilettos, her short blonde hair bouncing against her shoulders. She was way overdressed compared to the distributors in jeans.

I was so not in the mood for this woman.

"Guess the concierge realized how rude he was this morning," Natalie said. "He sent a box of Fauchon truffles to my room. They're the best, you know."

Precisely why *I'd* had them sent to her.

"They are *très* French. So are dogs. Have you noticed all the dogs here? They're like an accessory. Women look even more chic walking down the street with a cute little dog prancing along on a leash. Walking a dog is soooo Parisian." Natalie's contact-enhanced bright green eyes lit up. "Samantha, you have to rent me a dog."

Sure, let me cruise on down to the doggie rental agency and pick her out the cutest little froufrou dog on the lot. Where was I supposed to rent a flippin' dog? This was the type of ridiculous demands I'd catered to for the past thirteen years with a smile, anticipating one day being director.

Roger Darwin strolled over and slipped an arm around his wife's shoulder. A tall, distinguished-looking man in his sixties, Roger was affluent, successful, and a prominent figure in the community. Everything I'd always wanted in a dad.

He eyed the beer in my hand, a surprised yet proud look on his face. "Glad to see you're having a good time."

Why did you give some Joe Blow from Dallas my job?

I bit back the words, envisioning Sherri and her daughter camped out at a homeless shelter, or worse yet, at my place.

I plastered on a smile. "Just let me know when you have time to go over my consumer promotion plan."

"Absolutely." Roger looked past me, waving at a distributor. "We'll have to try to make time for that this trip."

He'd been *trying* to make time for the past month and promised me an hour while we were in Paris. He hadn't even read it. If he had, he'd have given me the promotion.

"If you'll excuse me, I'll get right on finding you a dog," I told Natalie. By the end of the week, the concierge would have made enough in tips to buy a villa in Provence.

I marched out to Hannah sitting at the desk. "I need you to look into renting Bat... Natalie a froufrou dog."

A burning sensation ignited in my stomach like a flare gun going off. While riffling through my briefcase for antacid tablets, I pulled out the puppet Luc had given me. I smiled, the burning in my stomach subsiding.

"What's that thing?" Evan asked, walking up.

My grip tightened around the puppet. "A puppet."

"What do you want with a puppet? They're for kids."

If Evan had attended the puppet performance, he'd have been embarrassed by my laughing. He'd have demanded we leave. Or he'd have just left me. I couldn't remember the last time he'd made me laugh.

"We need to talk," he said.

I stepped away from Hannah. "So when do you think a decision will be made on the director's position?"

Evan leaned in. "I'd rather talk about *us* than your job. Do you think you can manage that?"

My cell sang out in my purse, stopping me from knocking Evan flat. Seething, I answered it to find Luc.

"Libby's at the hospital. She's in labor."

My body kicked into panic mode, my stomach clenching, my breathing becoming rapid and shallow, as if I were the one in labor. "Labor? But she's not due for six weeks."

"The baby is coming."

"Omigod." He gave me the hospital's address, and I disconnected. "Libby's in labor. I have to go."

Evan looked confused. "Since when is Libby pregnant?"

"Since seven and a half months ago. I just found out."

He took a moment to process this information then said, "She could be in labor for twenty-four hours. You don't need to leave right this minute, do you? This is a very important reception. You really need to be here."

"The reception's going fine. Hannah can handle it," I said with more confidence than I felt. "Libby's not due for another six weeks. This is bad." Hannah hung up the phone, and I turned to her. Having mentioned earlier Libby was pregnant, I got straight to the point. "My sister's in labor. I have to go. Can you handle the reception?"

Hannah popped up from her chair and stood at attention, reporting for duty. "For sure."

Evan shook his head in disbelief.

Whatever. I bolted inside the ballroom to find Roger.

"They're out of bloody beer," a distributor boomed in a fake British accent, standing at the bar.

I waved Hannah over. "Thought you verified they had twenty cases of backup?"

Hannah paled, a deer-in-the-headlights expression on her face. "The banquet captain promised he'd gotten them. I should have counted the beer myself. I know better than to trust the hotel...."

"Go get whatever Brecker beer is available in the lounge. I'll let banquets know they need to send staff out to buy more."

Hannah nodded diligently as she turned and made a beeline for the door.

Natalie Darwin sashayed up. "Evan told us about your sister. My cousin just had a premature baby and had a stroke during the delivery. She still hasn't regained any movement. And my friend's baby was premature and had bleeding on the brain, which likely caused his cerebral palsy. It was all those martinis she drank while she was pregnant."

Visions of Libby drinking wine flashed through my mind. Flexing my fingers, I fought the urge to strangle this bitch with her diamond choker.

I had to get to the hospital!

Evan walked up and grasped hold of my elbow, propelling me off to the side. "Seriously, Samantha. You need to stay here. Hannah isn't competent enough to handle this on her own. You don't want to jeopardize your promotion, do you?"

I practically crushed the puppet in my hand, realizing I was still holding it. "*Jeopardize* it?"

"You need to be here."

"Maybe I'd be more appreciated if I weren't around at all. Maybe you'd realize just how good of a job I do and that this program doesn't run itself like you seem to think it does."

A panicked expression flashed across his face, and for the first time, I felt appreciated.

"Fine, go to the hospital," he said, as if I needed his permission. "You're obviously all emotional about your sister, but really, be a little more professional."

My eyes widened, about shooting out of my head. "Be *more* professional? Why don't you make up your mind?" I envisioned Luc and Libby protesting nude along the Seine, sticking up for what they believed in. I believed in myself! Grasping hold of the puppet's dress, I hauled off and clubbed Evan in the arm with its wooden head and then walloped him one again. "I quit." I marched out of the ballroom, gripping the puppet at my side.

Vive Samantha!

Chapter Six

When the taxi stopped in front of the hospital, I hopped out and dashed through the gate in the massive concrete wall surrounding the facility. Worries of having just quit my job without any savings flew from my mind as a white van with a blue cross on the side sped past, blue lights flashing on top. Its shrill *wrrring* siren vibrated through me, kicking my panic mode up a notch.

What if Libby lost the baby?

What if she had a stroke?

What if she went into a coma?

What if she died on the delivery table?

A wildfire was raging out of control in my stomach, burning a path through my upper chest to my throat. The four antacid tablets I'd popped on the way there were doing little to extinguish it.

I'd just seen Libby a few hours ago, and she'd been fine. Except she'd complained about feeling a little funky and tired. And I'd refused to stay at the café and join her for lunch because duty called. I shouldn't have left her.

I zipped down the main road, searching frantically for building number five. The hospital complex was huge. I finally came across the building and flew inside. The stark white walls, buffed tile floor, and unearthly cry of pain carrying down a corridor conjured up thoughts of straitjackets and lobotomies. Behind the overwhelming scent of antiseptic lurked the musty smell of an aged, tired building. My sister was in an asylum!

I was about to run up to a woman manning a reception desk when I zoned in on Luc, sitting on a wooden chair, nervously twirling a cigarette between his fingers. As I rushed toward him, he spotted me and stood.

"Is she all right?" I blurted out halfway across the lobby. "What did the doctors say? She didn't have a stroke, did she? Is she in a coma? Is she—"

"She's doing fine." Luc grasped my hand reassuringly.

I let out a gasp of relief, slapping a hand over my mouth, stifling a meek sob. I could count on one hand the number of times I'd ever flat-out bawled. This wouldn't be one of them. I had to keep it together for Libby's sake.

Yet when Luc took me in his arms, I molded against him, planting my hands on his chest, curling my fingers into his T-shirt, choking back a sob.

"It'll be okay," he said softly, smoothing a hand over my hair. "The baby and Libby will be fine."

"What if they're not?" I clutched his shirt tighter. "I can't lose Libby, she's all I got. I want her to come home with me. I want her to be all right, I want..." to stop rambling like Mom had last night. Rapid speech, racing thoughts, impulsive and reckless behavior—like quitting my job—all signs of Mom's illness. Luc hadn't been there when I'd quit my job, but I'd been thinking about him. Hopefully it was merely Luc heightening my emotions. My heart raced faster.

Get a grip. I took a calming breath, loosening my hold on Luc's T-shirt.

"They'll be fine," he said.

Between the relaxing scent of Luc's cinnamony breath, his caressing my hair, and his voice's soothing calmness, I began to relax. The fire raging in my stomach had dwindled to mere embers. I reluctantly drew back, not wanting to leave the warmth of his arms. I released my grip on his T-shirt and smoothed a hand over the wrinkles. His rock-solid chest felt strong, reassuring...incredible. I continued smoothing a hand over his shirt even though the wrinkles had vanished.

He cupped the side of my face and tilted my head up, staring into my eyes with his soft, brown eyes. "Libby will be fine," he said firmly. *"Oui?"*

I nodded faintly. *"Oui."*

Smiling, Luc continued gently massaging my cheek with his thumb. "She'll be fine."

I tried to look convinced and to not appear disappointed when Luc removed his hand from my cheek.

"I should be in there with her. She shouldn't be alone. She needs support." Although I might pass out flat at the first sight of blood or whatever else came out of her.

"Sophie is with her."

"The medium, funeral-crasher Sophie?" That was hardly reassuring.

"She took classes with Libby for having the baby. She'll be able to help her."

A part of me was relieved I didn't have to be involved in the birthing process, yet it should be me in there with Libby. But if I hadn't come to Paris on business, I wouldn't have even known Libby was pregnant. If I weren't here and Libby had lost the baby, would she even have told me she'd been pregnant? She'd claimed she wanted to tell me in person, but it didn't make sense that she hadn't at least called.

But she *had* called, in July when I was at a meeting in Seattle. Had she wanted to tell me the news then? I'd forgotten about her call and hadn't returned it for several weeks. Maybe she'd been upset and decided not to tell me.

My phone beeped, announcing the arrival of a text. Evan had resorted to texting, since I wasn't answering his calls. His message said he realized I was upset over Libby, and he didn't take my quitting seriously. I wrote him back.

I'm more serious than a worldwide shortage on barley.

Luc and I sat in the maternity ward's waiting room along with a couple in their early fifties and their grandson. I was reading through an e-mail from Hannah assuring me everything was *super*. Evan probably hadn't mentioned I'd quit because he figured I'd be back in the morning. Not unless they offered me the promotion. I had to check out of the hotel and stay at Libby's to prove I was serious.

I was confident they'd be begging me to take the promotion by the end of tomorrow. They'd soon realize I'd been doing the job of two planners, troubleshooting all of Lori's mistakes. And when Roger read my consumer promotion and marketing plan, he'd realize the mistake he'd made hiring that other idiot. Most importantly, Matt Davis would blow a gasket when he discovered I'd been passed up for a promotion and quit. Thanks to my mentoring, his daughter had landed her dream job—an event planner position at an art museum—and we still kept in touch. Matt had told me he owed me one. This would be the time to cash in the favor.

Since Hannah would freak when she learned she was in charge, I decided to wait until morning to tell her and let her get one last good night's sleep. I e-mailed her back and gave her the skinny on the Loire Valley tour the next day and asked her to escort it, stating I had other work to do.

What the hell was I going to do all day tomorrow?

"Regarde-moi, regarde-moi, grand-papa," the little boy demanded for the dozenth time, proudly sitting in the chair as his grandfather had repeatedly requested.

The grandparents smiled.

I, on the other hand, glared at him. Luc didn't appear the least bit annoyed, which I found irritating.

Attempting to ignore the kid, and make better use of my time, I opened the notepad on my phone. "Libby might have taken Lamaze classes, but that's all she did to prepare for this baby. I need to figure out what she needs." Making a list of baby items was an optimistic thing to do.

Libby and the baby would be just fine.

"She needs...stuff. Lots of...stuff." I tapped a finger against the phone, clueless.

An hour later, the little boy lay zonked out on a small couch, which had enabled the woman to help Luc and I compile our extensive list of items required for a baby. Even if I extended my stay a few days, I'd be lucky to put a dent in the list. Not to mention, I'd have serious credit card debt.

Shipping this stuff back to the United States would be outrageous, but Libby wouldn't be coming home with me at the end of the week. Being premature, the baby would likely be in the hospital for a while. It might be months before it could fly. I hated the thought of leaving Libby here by herself to care for a baby.

I added "hire nanny" to the list.

I had to get this promotion.

A nurse came in and informed us Libby had a baby girl and both were doing fine. I let out a relieved sigh. When we walked into the room, Libby was lying in bed holding her baby, who was swaddled in several blankets with a white cap on her head. Libby kissed her baby's forehead. I smiled. Although Libby was a free spirit and not real reliable, she was compassionate and caring.

Libby would make a good mother.

Tall, thin, and thirtyish, Sophie stood next to the bed wearing a short, black skirt with knee-high, black boots and a tight, purple sweater. Her short, blonde hair had jet-black roots. Having met her at the Venus Café, I nodded hello.

"Her aura, it is very good." Sophie gazed lovingly at the baby.

A natural pink glow flushed Libby's cheeks, and sweat matted her blonde hair against her forehead. She glanced over at me and smiled brightly, patting the bed beside her. I slid onto the bed, remembering how she used to crawl in bed with me after a bad dream. She'd had a lot of bad dreams after Dad left.

Libby placed a hand gently on my arm. "Do you want to hold her?"

I shook my head. "She's too tiny. I don't want to break her. Besides, I didn't disinfect my hands."

"What will you name her?" Luc asked.

Libby shrugged, her smile fading. She slipped the cap off her daughter's head and gently brushed a finger over the thick, dark hair, a longing expression on her face. "You look just like your daddy. Yes, you do." A tear slipped down Libby's cheek, and she wiped it away.

This should have been a happy occasion. Libby wasn't in a coma, and her baby appeared healthy. She obviously still cared for the baby's father. Or maybe the miracle of birth and holding her daughter for the first time had merely made her emotional.

I gave Libby's shoulder a comforting squeeze. "Everything will be okay, Lib. I love you, and I'm here for you." Unlike the baby's deadbeat dad.

What exactly was wrong with the guy that Libby wouldn't consider him father or marriage material? Being a destitute artist or street performer wouldn't be a valid enough reason. If Libby was this upset over him, it must have been his choice, not hers, to not be involved in their lives. What sort of jerk wouldn't want anything to do with his own child?

Our dad.

Chapter Seven

At seven a.m. the following morning, I breezed into Libby's apartment, wired from two double espressos, licking the remnants of chocolate bread from my fingers. I'd gotten zero sleep. After Luc helped me haul my luggage over from the hotel, I'd stayed up all night freaking out over having quit. Planner jobs were few in Milwaukee. Besides, I wanted to get into marketing. Less travel and stress. No company was going to hire me for a management position without a marketing degree. My undergrad degree was in business.

Now in the light of day, I felt confident Roger and Evan would offer me the promotion by nightfall. The best strategy for getting the promotion was to sit tight and do nothing. Something I seriously sucked at. But not troubleshooting all the problems behind the scenes was the best way to sabotage the program. I now had time to finalize my marketing plan. I needed the director of corporate events job just long enough to impress the VP of marketing with my consumer promotion plan, so I then could swoop in with my women's marketing plan. It would involve marketing to women's core values, friendship and family, instead of objectifying and degrading them like Brecker often did.

I'd e-mailed Evan my twenty-two program folders and thousands of e-mails. That should be a shot of adrenaline to the heart. Or maybe I'd stopped his heart, since I hadn't heard back from him. No e-mails or calls from Roger either, or Sherri in HR with my exit papers. A good sign Evan was keeping my quitting hush-hush until we worked things out.

I glanced over at my puppet propped up against the vase of

daisies in the middle of the table. "So what do you think? Will I get the promotion?"

It seemed to give me a knowing smile. Women's intuition.

Hopefully it was right.

I headed toward the bathroom to shower and noticed the light on the answering machine flashing three messages. Two were new. Either from yesterday or when I'd run out this morning. In French, the only thing I caught was all three were from some Bruno guy. I saved the messages to have Luc translate them.

I showered and tossed my hair up in Libby's orange clip. In my undies, I riffled through my suitcase filled with business suits in muted tones. Dressing for work wouldn't help me ignore my job. Not to mention, all my outfits were in major need of ironing. I walked over to the armoire. Libby and I were the same size, just didn't share the same tastes. I slipped on a pair of Levis and spied a pair of pink flip-flops on the floor that looked comfy. My new black mules had given me a blister on both little toes last night.

A *ding* signaled the arrival of an e-mail. I raced over to my laptop. Evan. My body tensed with anticipation. I took a deep breath and opened it.

How's Libby?

That was his response to all the files I'd sent him? Had he not gotten them? Or was he toying with me? After being such a jerk about me going to the hospital, I should appreciate his concern. If it was legit.

I also had an e-mail from the dinner cruise for later that week, asking if one case of beer was enough for a group of twenty. Lori had under-guaranteed the group, and they'd blow through a case of beer by the time the boat left the dock. If there was even enough room for them on the boat.

I went to reply but clicked delete instead. The e-mail vanished. An evil grin curled the corners of my mouth.

An e-mail from Rachel popped in my inbox.

> *Sherri and I think you should sue Brecker if you don't get the promotion. Remember that VP at National*

Tobacco Corp who sued cuz she was turned down for a promotion because she'd quit smoking? She won. Besides being female, one of the reasons you didn't get the promotion is because you don't drink enough. It's only been twelve hours, and you already have 217 Likes on your Facebook fan page! Women of the world unite! Go, Samantha!

On *my* Facebook fan page? I didn't have a Facebook page, let alone a *fan* page. Rachel had created a fan page under my name? Omigod. Rachel was speaking out on my behalf? What the hell was she saying? I didn't want my dirty laundry out there for everyone to read about. Not getting the promotion was a major ding to my self-esteem.

What did Rachel think a fan page would accomplish, besides venting her frustration toward the company and pissing off Roger if he found out? Roger would go postal, thinking I'd taken this public. Hell, Roger probably didn't even know I'd quit. I prayed Evan hadn't told Sherri in HR because she'd tell Rachel, and my quitting would be posted on Facebook before Roger even knew!

I called Rachel and left a message telling her to take down that fan page. Stat!

I didn't want to be a martyr fighting for women's rights.

I just wanted my promotion.

And I would get it.

A rap sounded at the door. Probably Luc picking up Libby's suitcase, which I hadn't yet packed. I hadn't told her about my quitting, wanting to maintain the joyous atmosphere.

I snagged a fuchsia, satin camisole from a drawer. I slipped it on then noticed the elderly man Libby had waved at the other day sitting on his balcony across the street. His squinted gaze glued on me, he didn't bother glancing away in shame. Pervert. I'd have to hang a sheet over the doors.

I opened the front door to find a dark-haired guy, thirtyish, dressed in jeans and a green Heineken T-shirt. From his bloodshot eyes and eau de booze stench, he'd obviously put away a case of the beer last night. He leered at my low-cut cami and rattled off something in French.

"Je ne parle pas français," I said.

He smiled. "Ah, you are American, like Libby. Is Libby here?" He glanced impatiently past me, into the apartment.

"No, she's not." Something warned me not to tell him where Libby was. "Who are you?"

"Bruno. We are friends. I just returned from a trip. I came by to get..." He trailed off, the capillaries in his eyes about bursting. *"Fils de pute!"* He pushed past me and flew inside, his gaze skittering frantically around at the walls, a crazed look on his face. "Where are my paintings?"

"I, ah, don't know. I'd have to ask Libby." I kept the door open in case I had to make a run for it.

He pounded a fist against the impressionist mural on the wall. A large chunk of plaster fell to the floor. He stalked over to me, backing me up against the door, his breath about knocking me out. "Where is Libby? I want to speak to her now!"

My gaze darted to the balcony doors. The elderly man on the balcony was preoccupied with activity below rather than preparing to call the cops about the raving lunatic in my apartment. Unbelievable!

Flattened against the door, heart thumping in my chest, I strove to keep the shaking in my knees from finding its way to my voice, trying to appear in control. "She's out. I'll tell her you stopped by. Are you one of her students?"

"I am Bruno. I want my paintings." His gaze narrowed. "I think you know where they are. You are screwing me."

"I am not screwing *with* you. I have no clue where—"

Luc suddenly appeared, shoving Bruno away from me, giving him a verbal lashing in French. I peeled myself off the door and backed away from them. They were in each other's faces, yelling, and before I knew what was happening, Luc had the psycho pinned against the door, his forearm pressed against the guy's throat. Gasping for air, Bruno apparently muttered uncle, and Luc cautiously lowered his arm from Bruno's larynx, set to pounce if he made one false move. Luc pushed him out the door.

"Tell Libby I will be back for my paintings," Bruno hollered as Luc slammed the door.

Luc's gaze assessed me for damage, lingering on my camisole. An intrigued gleam softened his angry look, causing my body to stop trembling.

"Are you okay?" he asked, meeting my gaze.

I nodded, swallowing the lump of fear in my throat. "Do you know him?"

"I've seen him once or twice, but I don't know who he is. What are these paintings he's talking about?" Luc reached for one of the cigarettes lining the front of his brown fedora but then decided against it and popped a cinnamon mint in his mouth.

I gave him a palms up. "Some stupid paintings Libby had. I'm guessing he's a student. His name's Bruno. I'll have to ask Libby what it's all about and where this psycho's paintings are, because I'm sure he'll be back."

Luc smiled at the puppet resting against the vase, appearing pleased it was on display. Disheveled from his scuffle with Bruno, he rolled up the sleeve on his oversized, white cotton shirt, exposing a small Celtic cross tattoo on his forearm and several necklaces wrapped around his wrist as bracelets. He adjusted the lightweight, brown patterned scarf draped loosely around his neck several times. I could spend an hour without success trying to get a scarf to hang perfectly. Luc had this quirky fashion sense most guys would be hard-pressed to pull off and not be confident enough to even dare to try. Not to mention, he made a pair of Levis look much sexier than a crisp Armani suit.

"So what made you decide to be a puppeteer?" I said, trying to divert my attention from Luc's Levis and thoughts of psycho Bruno.

"Does it seem strange to you? A grown man playing with puppets?" He sounded defensive. As if he'd had to justify his career choice before.

I shook my head. "Not at all. It just doesn't seem a common thing to do. Like, was your father a puppeteer?"

"My father is a doctor. He thinks I'm wasting my life. He doesn't understand."

"Making people laugh isn't a waste of your life."

Although it couldn't pay great. Like Libby's art. I always told her it was okay as a hobby, but she'd never make a living at it. Dad had never made a living at his music. And the temp jobs he'd worked had barely supported us.

"Why'd you quit your job?" Luc asked.

"Someone else got my promotion because he's a man and a party animal. Total discrimination."

I walked over to the mural and carefully slipped my hand under the fragile chunk of plaster lying on the floor. The edges crumbled away. I wanted to kick Bruno's ass.

"He's an animal that parties?" Luc asked, confused.

"Means he drinks a lot."

I carefully slid the piece of plaster back in place on the wall. At least it didn't look like the girls had gotten their hands whacked off. Hopefully Libby could repair it.

"This is good." Luc smiled approvingly, a sparkle in his eyes. "You're protesting. Standing up for your rights. For what you believe in. You should always believe in yourself. If you don't, who will?" Luc's eyes dimmed, like people hadn't always believed in him.

"Guess I am protesting."

He nodded encouragingly. "That's right. Liberty, equality, fraternity." He gazed expectantly at me.

"Liberty, equality, fraternity," I muttered.

"You don't sound sure."

"Liberty, equality, fraternity," I said louder.

"That's good. You have a fire inside you."

Yeah, and for once, the burning sensation hadn't originated in my stomach.

—◦◦ ◦◦—

Twenty minutes later, I stood in a total panic next to Luc's scooter, holding Libby's packed duffle bag. "I don't think I can ride that with this bag." Sounded better than confessing I couldn't ride the bike period. The thought of roaring down the street unprotected scared the hell out of me.

Luc took the bag and slung it around his neck, resting it against his front. He opened the bike's back compartment and exchanged his fedora for a helmet then produced another helmet from under the seat and handed it to me. He started the bike, and it hummed to life.

It sounded cute rather than dangerous. Cute and safe. Cute and safe...

Heart racing, I slipped on the helmet and secured the strap under my chin. I lifted my leg over the seat, my flip-flop catching on it, throwing me off balance. Luc gripped the handlebars, steadying the scooter while I righted myself. I straddled the seat then shifted around, attempting to get comfy. Once I was settled, we eased into traffic.

"You want to hold on to me," he yelled over his shoulder.

No, I really didn't. Touching Luc wasn't a good way to keep my emotions in check. I placed my hands on my thighs.

As we picked up speed, cars raced past, and motorcycles weaved through the lanes of traffic. Panicked, I slid my arms around Luc's waist, resting my hands on his rock-solid stomach, feeling the warmth of his body through his cotton shirt and my thin camisole. I fought the temptation to allow my hands to meander up and explore his chest like I'd done at the hospital last night.

Luc swerved around a woman stepping into traffic. I buried my face in his back, the scent of musk infiltrating my senses, my arms tightening around his waist. Despite the cars whisking past, and having no protection other than a helmet, being molded against Luc gave me a calming sense of security.

Luc and I rode up the hospital elevator with a woman and a baby in a stroller. I smiled at the baby, who had on a pink dress and a white lace hat. The stroller was a heavy-duty contraption with a tan plaid, cushioned seat, a familiar pattern.

"Is that a Burberry?" I asked. I might not know my strollers, but I knew my designers.

"Yes, it is," she said with a British accent.

Who'd have thought Burberry made strollers? I made a notation next to stroller on my list of baby items.

We stepped from the elevator, and Luc turned to me. "So do you like children, or *non*?"

My gaze narrowed. "Why do you ask that?"

"You didn't like the little boy in the hospital last night."

"I don't like bratty kids."

Like when a kid acted up in a restaurant. And I didn't like it when women at work played the kid card so I and others picked up the slack because she couldn't travel because of her kids. It was fine to put family first, but then it was time to find another job. This job was all about the travel. This didn't make me a bad person; it made me a good manager.

The receptionist desk was unmanned. Nurses zipped in and out of rooms, not bothering to ask if we'd popped by to visit a mother or swipe a baby. Security was nonexistent, unlike in the United States where you had to be buzzed into most maternity wards, and if you tried to take a baby from the ward, the minute you encountered an exit, the baby's anklet caused the entire ward to go into lockdown. France obviously didn't have the need for such security. However, I did.

We entered Libby's room to find the bed made and no Libby. A nurse walked into the room. In her early fifties with dark hair and solid, angular features, she was built like a tank. She belted out something in French, her stern voice nearly causing me to stand at attention. I cringed at the thought of this woman caring for my niece. I told her I didn't speak French. She looked far from pleased but switched to English.

"You look for Libby Hunter?" she asked.

"Yes, I'm her sister, Samantha."

"She left an hour previously. There was a death in her family."

"A death?"

"How did you not know this if you are her sister?"

Good question.

"The doctor was not happy. She said it was urgent she leave. She asked me to give you this." She slipped an envelope from her uniform's pocket and handed it to me.

My name was scrawled across the front in Libby's handwriting, and the envelope was sealed. I was shocked the nurse hadn't opened it. I tore open the envelope and read the note.

I have to see my baby's father.

I showed Luc the note.

Libby probably figured she had a better shot in person convincing this guy to be with her and her baby. Or the guy was a destitute artist without a phone. Maybe she hoped once he saw the baby, he'd want to be involved in their lives. What if he got caught up in the excitement and was suddenly a proud father? Libby's hormones were seriously out of whack, and she was an emotional basket case after just having a baby. It would be just like her to do something irrational, like running off and marrying this guy she knew wasn't father or marriage material, only to have him dump her in a few months.

I had to figure out who the hell the father was.

Then it hit me. A destitute artist. The psycho looking for his paintings wasn't the father, was he? I prayed not. If Libby was out looking for Bruno, I certainly didn't want her finding him in his flipped-out state.

Nurse Nasty was glaring at me. I gestured to the note. "Her boyfriend's father died. He was like a father to her. We didn't have one."

"This year previously, a woman at a hospital in Paris only stayed a few hours after having a baby. She left and never came back." Suspicion filled the woman's steel-gray eyes.

I gave her an incredulous look. "I assure you, Libby didn't *abandon* her baby. Just because she's not here right now doesn't mean she abandoned her baby." To someone who didn't know Libby, it might appear odd she'd left, but she was too caring and compassionate to walk out on her daughter. No way. She loved her baby. I'd seen it in her eyes last night.

"I take full responsibility while Libby's gone. You can call me anytime." I handed her my business card. "But I guarantee you, she'll be back."

"A new mother should stay in the hospital four or five days," she said.

"In the United States, women sometimes leave the hospital twenty-four hours after having a baby." Still, I couldn't believe Libby had left! "Can I see my niece?"

I dropped Libby's bag on the bed. Nurse Nasty led us to the nursery, where my niece slept in a crib, looking fragile and helpless. The nursery was as bleak as the rest of the hospital with its white walls and floors and utilitarian furnishings.

My niece was alone in an asylum without her mother.

Nurse Nasty marched out, and the room temp seemed to shoot up ten degrees.

"Why did Libby tell the hospital someone died?" Luc asked.

"Nurse Nasty doesn't look like a hopeless romantic who would understand Libby running off to be with the baby's father. *I* don't even understand it." I smiled at my niece and lowered my voice. "How are you, sweetie? You don't know your mommy is gone, do you? I sound just like her; maybe you think I'm her. I'm going to go find her. Yes, I am." I glanced over at Luc. "Do you know the father?"

Luc shook his head. "When Libby was once upset, she told me she cared about the father but it didn't matter."

Libby must have meant it didn't matter to *him,* because that would be *all* that mattered to her. She was always thinking with her heart rather than her head. What had she been thinking *period* leaving her baby at the hospital?

Chapter Eight

We headed to the Venus Café, hoping Libby had gone to see Sophie, or maybe Sophie knew my niece's father. I didn't want Libby agreeing to marry this guy on a whim. Or what if he was a total jerk and told her to get lost? She wasn't emotionally capable of handling rejection right now. And she was in no condition to be running around Paris on her own. There was no way Libby had abandoned her baby, yet even the mere thought of it sent me into panic mode.

I had to find Libby.

The café was located in the heart of the Latin Quarter. With its narrow, winding, cobblestone streets it felt like a quaint, French village, except for the mix of spices and incense wafting from a Moroccan restaurant and the Italian guy trying to lure us into his restaurant with the promise of superb Chianti. I inhaled the aroma of fresh-baked baguettes, café au lait, and...cigarettes.

My nose instinctively scrunched as Luc plucked a cigarette from his fedora. He held it under his nose, inhaling a deep breath. He went to slide it behind his ear and realized there was already one there, and also one behind his other ear. So he twirled it between his fingers rather than lighting it.

He glanced over at me. "I'm trying to quit. I put a half a pack in my hat a day."

Seven cigarettes still lined his hat. "What were you smoking?"

"Two packs a day."

My lungs about collapsed at the thought of smoking two packs a day.

My phone rang, and it was Hannah. I had to tell her I'd quit and that she needed to go to Evan about the group.

"The concierge got Natalie Darwin a dog," she said. "Two hundred bucks a day. It's a cute little Yorkshire terrier with brown fur and a collar with a diamond K for Katsumi."

"Katsumi? What kind of a name is that?"

Luc gave me an odd look.

"According to Natalie, it's some Asian French designer. She brought it to the Valley with us. I can't imagine how we're going to work this into the budget."

"I have to tell you...I quit last night."

"Quit what?"

"My job. I'm having a few contract issues. I'm sure we'll work things out, but I quit."

Hannah gasped for air on the other end. "Think I'm gonna puke."

"You'll do fine. You know the program as well as I do."

"I won't do fine. Omigod. Natalie Darwin is heading toward me. What's she gonna want?"

"Don't tell anyone I quit. Only Evan knows."

"Okay." Hannah disconnected.

"What was that about Katsumi?" Luc asked.

"Hannah rented this nightmare woman a froufrou dog named Katsumi, after some fashion designer."

Luc broke out laughing, and I smiled faintly, not getting the joke. "Katsumi isn't a designer. She's the top French porn star. She's always in the news because she's dating the president's son."

An evil grin spread across my face. I imagined Natalie Darwin sashaying down the prestigious Rue du Faubourg calling out a porn star's name to the dog. The concierge knew precisely who Katsumi was. That probably wasn't even the dog's real name. A bit of retribution, no doubt.

I liked this guy, and I hadn't even met him.

We encountered the Venus Café, painted purple with gold, celestial symbols. A cat snoozed on the inside windowsill, snuggled up next to a flyer advertising Internet access and Sophie—psychic *extraordinaire*. Inside, New Age flute music played, and several people lounged on deep purple and gold velvet chairs and couches, reading books and sipping chai tea. A young, impressionable girl sat at a table having her cards read by Sophie. But no Libby.

A girl with short, red hair, dressed in jeans and a Lady GaGa T-shirt, stood behind a glass counter selling gemstones. She eyed Luc like he was a *pain au chocolat* in a pâtisserie display case. I half expected her to take a bite and lick her lips. Luc appeared unfazed by her flirtations, undoubtedly used to women hitting on him.

"*Salut,*" Sophie said, walking over from the table where she'd just finished her reading. She had on a brown suede minidress, knee-high brown boots, and a brown tweed pageboy hat. She kissed my cheeks then proceeded to kiss Luc's.

"Libby isn't at the hospital," Luc said. "She checked out. Have you seen her?"

"Checked out already? She told me she stays until Friday. Why would she leave?"

I shrugged.

Sophie winced, bracing a hand on the back of a couch, like she'd just been stricken with a migraine. "I had a bad feeling earlier something was wrong. I should have gone to see her."

Oh boy, a psychic with a bad feeling. If she was so in tune with the cosmic forces, why couldn't she just tell me where Libby was so I could go find her and haul her butt back to the hospital? I had zero confidence in psychics. Libby had gotten into New Age methods while working a temp job in Milwaukee, answering phones for a psychic hotline. Her two-day training period had consisted of learning to read tarot cards.

"Do you know where the baby's father lives?" I didn't admit I didn't know *who* he was. Since I didn't live there, maybe she wouldn't find it odd. I thought it was. I felt like an outsider. Luc and Sophie knew Libby better than I did.

Sophie shook her head. "Libby did not work here until finding out she was pregnant, and she never talked about the father. I could tell she was hurt, you know? I think he left her. What is the father's name?"

I reluctantly shrugged.

"I will call Sabine and Odette and ask if they know." Sophie left the room and returned minutes later pushing an antique wicker baby stroller with large metal wheels and a white lace umbrella. "Sabine and Odette have not seen her and do not know the father. I told them to call me if they speak to Libby. You should go to where she worked before. Maybe someone knows the father." Sophie gave Luc the names and locations of a Serbian art gallery and a boutique. She gestured to the stroller, smiling proudly. "I bought this for her baby."

"Libby will love it." She'd have thought the designer stroller was pretentious.

"I hope it makes her happy. She was so sad last night." Sophie tapped a long, gold nail against her lips, her gaze narrowing. "I know one more place Libby worked. I will take you to see her boss. She was to go there today. Maybe she is there."

"Are you taking the *Métro*?" Luc asked.

Sophie nodded. *"Ouais."*

"I'll splurge for a taxi," I offered.

Sophie's top lip curled back. "They drive crazy and charge much money. I do not ride taxis."

"I'll meet you at the train," Luc said. "I have to get something from my bike."

If I could ride a scooter, I could ride the *Métro*.

Right?

I followed Sophie down a set of stairs and into the cool cave of the *Métro*. I'd ridden the subway in Washington, D.C. once, and it had been quite clean, but I knew that wasn't the norm. It was dirty, but I was pleasantly surprised when the aroma of baked bread filled my head. We passed by a boulangerie selling bread and pastries and a flower vendor.

We encountered a mother and her two daughters making roses out of discarded straws and squares of tissue paper from baguettes. The mother wore a blue dress and a blue scarf wrapped around her head. The little girls had on matching dingy yellow dresses. The oldest girl, maybe seven, was helping her younger sister make her flower. Sophie contributed to the coins scattered across their worn, wool blanket. The little girls peered up at me with big, brown eyes, and one presented me a rose.

At least Libby and I hadn't resorted to begging after Dad left. Dad had sent a pathetic amount of child support annually, and Mom received disability. I'd contributed to our family income by babysitting and doing odd jobs. I'd lived in fear of losing our house and living on the street. One time, Libby gave away her lunch money, and I yelled at her until she cried. She'd likely given it away because she sympathized with people, knowing what it was like to not have money. She never seemed to worry about where money would come from. Much easier to give it away when you weren't the one earning it.

I handed the youngest girl a two-euro coin. Her eyes lit up, and she graciously thanked me, as did her mother, who handed me another rose. I smiled, thinking of Libby. We continued on, and I stuck the flowers in my purse.

Five minutes later, Luc joined us on the train platform, carrying a backpack and a short, metal tube. He watched with amusement as I scrubbed my hands with an antibacterial wipe.

"Would you like one?" I asked.

He shook his head. "I prefer to live dangerously."

A train pulled up, and we boarded. Luc headed straight for the rear of the car to two opposing sets of seats.

Sophie and I went to sit, and he stopped us. "Maybe you would like to watch."

"Watch what?" I asked.

Luc directed us to sit facing the back section of the train. He slid apart the metal tube, lengthening it, and wedged the rubber-tipped ends between two poles on opposite sides of the aisle. He pulled a small, red sheet from his backpack and draped it over the pole, disappearing behind it except for his lower legs. Accordion music filled the air, then two puppets popped up from behind the curtain.

Voilà. A traveling puppet show.

Sophie giggled and clapped, yelling out something in French. She smiled at me. "I adore puppets."

It appeared others did also. Adults and kids began snagging seats closer to the back, laughing, responding to the puppets' questions. I had no clue what the questions were, but I shouted out *oui* and *non* along with everyone else and laughed. It was a different show than yesterday, even better. My laughter quickly escalated, and I snapped my mouth shut, stifling it.

Stay in control.

I could see why Luc was so passionate about his job. Being his own boss and a one-man show, not having to worry about getting a promotion, was a pretty good gig. And he had flexibility, able to perform anywhere. However, it couldn't be great pay, at three euros a person for his scheduled shows and odd change for an impromptu subway performance. I was surprised he made enough to even make his rent. The financial instability would make me a wreck. Although I wasn't certain where *my* next paycheck was coming from.

Fifteen minutes flew by, and Sophie told me our stop was next. I peeked behind the curtain to find Luc smiling, fully animated, a small CD player by his feet. I told him I'd meet him at Libby's in a few hours.

A few minutes later, Sophie and I were walking through a mainly residential area of Paris. We encountered a cemetery surrounded by a concrete wall, and Sophie entered.

"Libby worked at a cemetery?"

"No, but her old boss is here. She was coming to his funeral today."

My first day of being unemployed and I was crashing funerals. Not promising.

A death in the family.

That's what Libby had told the hospital. And she'd told me she was going to see the baby's father. Was the father dead?

"Libby hadn't dated this guy, had she?"

Sophie shrugged. "Not that I know."

Libby would have confided in Sophie, and me, if the father of her baby had died. What reason would she have had not to?

We walked down a cobblestone lane, sunlight peeking through a thick canopy of trees filled with chirping birds. Lush foliage covered the inside of the surrounding wall, and green moss blanketed tombs and headstones. We came across the funeral. Five mourners, the mortician, and a priest. No Libby.

I placed a hand on Sophie's arm, leaning in and whispering, "If she doesn't come, I don't feel comfortable attending someone's funeral I didn't know." I rarely went to funerals for people I *did* know. I didn't handle death well. Too much emotion. And if Libby didn't show, this guy couldn't be the father.

A photo of a man sat on top of the casket. He looked fiftyish, with stern features and a strained smile that didn't include his dark eyes, which bore into me, causing the hairs on my arms to shoot up.

The mortician, a young, dark-haired guy dressed in black, gave Sophie a wave, and she flashed him a flirtatious smile. Obviously he was more than her funeral connection.

Three men stood together chatting, laughing. Sons or maybe co-workers? Upon spotting us, their conversation ceased, and they exchanged curious glances before continuing to talk. A guy texting on a cell phone stood off by himself. An elderly woman had her face buried in a romance novel. Sophie held a rosary in her hand, eyes closed, mouthing a prayer.

The priest began, in French, but I caught the deceased's name, Pascal Rochant. The guy texting stepped away as if annoyed by the priest's soothing words of comfort. The woman glanced up momentarily from her book. The mourners didn't appear distraught, unlike Sophie, who was dabbing her cheeks with a tissue. The lack of emotion made me uncomfortable. If they cared so little for the man, why'd they come?

Sophie's gaze suddenly darted over to the man texting then to the casket. She slowly approached the casket and touched her fingers to the photo on top. Everyone's attention was on her, even the guy texting. She closed her eyes. After several minutes, she stepped back by me. I didn't believe she'd actually channeled

Pascal, yet I wanted to ask if he was depressed over the poor attendance or if he didn't care.

Who would attend my funeral? Mom, Aunt Betsy, Libby...probably Rachel...Evan was debatable, Roger even more so at the moment, and Hannah would probably come to spit on my casket after what I'd done to her. I didn't stay in touch with any high school or college friends. I couldn't even come up with *five* people who would for sure attend. And besides my funeral, what if I inherited Mom's illness? Who would look out for *me* if I could no longer look out for myself?

The funeral ended. The guy with the cell phone marched over and swiped a hand across the casket's top, sending the photo sailing through the air before stalking off. The woman stashed the book in her purse. Everyone bolted without looking back.

Too weird.

Sophie introduced me to the mortician, Laurent.

"So how'd he die?" I asked.

"Libby did not say, but it was very sudden." Sophie winced, hand on her chest. "A heart attack, maybe?"

Laurent nodded.

Lucky guess. Although I'd have guessed a bullet to the head after attending this funeral.

"He worked too hard," Laurent said.

"What'd he do?" I asked.

"He owned several hair salons in Paris called Pascal Rochant."

If he was my niece's father, she could be set for life. Although she'd never get to know her father, which might not be a bad thing from the little I knew about him. But if he was the father, why had Libby no-showed for his funeral? Too emotional?

"Did he have family?" I asked.

"A son."

"The man on the phone?" Sophie asked.

Laurent nodded.

She had a one in four shot at getting that right. Although who was to say the son had even attended. She was a lucky guesser, I'd give her that. Even if Pascal only had one son, he must have had dozens of employees and hundreds of clients. Yet only *five* mourners at his funeral?

"Pascal forgives his son, and he is sorry," Sophie said.

My gaze narrowed. "Forgives him for what? Texting through his funeral? Murdering him? Embezzling from his salons?"

"Libby told me Pascal fired Alphonse because he shaved his head. Pascal told Alphonse it was not good for a hairdresser to have no hair. But Libby convinced Pascal to apologize and ask Alphonse to still work. I am so glad he did this before he died. But he must feel Alphonse has not forgiven him."

Libby must be glad that she'd convinced Pascal to apologize before he died. Not having closure when someone died, or a relationship ended, was difficult. I'd never had the chance to tell Dad how I felt.

"Libby tried to make Pascal realize money was not everything. She told him money cannot buy you happiness, but it can buy you misery."

Precisely what Libby used to say to me.

No way would she have dated this guy.

"It also cannot buy you life," Sophie said. "I wanted to talk to Alphonse, but he left so quick. I must find him later. Pascal will not cross over unless this problem is resolved."

So this was why Sophie crashed funerals. She truly believed she had the gift and chose to use it for the greater good. Her gift dictated her profession. She was destined to bring peace and harmony to the dead. Easier than bringing peace and harmony to the living. Something I'd been attempting to do for thirteen years.

We boarded the third train car from the back, same car we'd ridden on the way there, but no Luc. Likely a different train. Too bad. I could have used some serious cheering up.

Even if Evan were right I wasn't a huge people person and thus not many people would attend my funeral, my co-workers and the distributors respected me. I drilled this into my head on the ride back to Paris. When Hannah called, I tapped my finger against the phone. I needed to work on upping my funeral attendance, but helping Hannah wouldn't get me my promotion.

I let the call go to voice mail then listened to it.

"Katsumi just got bus sick. Projectile vomited all over Roger's shirt. He kept his cool in front of the group, but he's pissed. We're in a tiny, tourist-trap town, and the only thing we could find is a T-shirt that says I love France with a heart instead of the word love. Roger wants Katsumi off the bus. He wants me to hire a car to follow us. How am I going to find a car in the boonies?" She took a deep breath. "But I want you to know that I totally admire what you're doing. Standing up for our rights. Someone has to."

Our rights? At least I wouldn't feel so bad when the dinner cruise went to hell, knowing Hannah supported me.

"Hope your niece is doing okay."

Here Hannah was in the middle of a meltdown, yet she cared enough to ask about my niece. I wasn't even sure if she had any nieces or nephews. I didn't pry into people's personal lives because I didn't want them prying into mine. Old habits died hard. I'd had no close friends growing up. I never invited kids over. I didn't want them telling their parents that, while my mom was sleeping and we were playing Barbies, I had a load of laundry in and water boiling for mac and cheese for dinner. Or if she wasn't in bed, she might have been frantically bleaching down the house again because she could still smell Dad's cologne. She'd bleached her entire wardrobe to rid it of his scent. I'd lived in fear social services would come knocking on our door. Unlike Mom's delusional fears that everyone was trying to take away her family, mine were warranted.

I deleted Hannah's message, picturing Roger fuming. *Hannah, get me a fucking car, fucking now, before I kill that fucking dog.* I tried to ignore the burning in my stomach by losing myself in the Paris neighborhoods rolling past, hoping to catch a glimpse of Libby strolling down a street.

Suddenly, crashing funerals seemed like a much better way to have spent the past few hours than cleaning dog puke off Roger.

Chapter Nine

Upon returning to the *Métro* station by the Venus Café, Sophie and I came across the two little girls making roses. Their mother was nowhere in sight. The older girl had a protective arm around her sister. I couldn't believe the mother had left her kids alone in the *Métro* with thousands of people and derelicts passing by. And why wasn't the older one in school? Sophie asked the girls where their mother was, and they informed her she was buying lunch.

The older girl proudly showed us several drawings in her sketchpad. She was quite talented. One was of her and her sister playing with a dog in the yard, next to a house. She explained to Sophie that one day that would be her family.

Their mother returned a few minutes later carrying a baguette. That was their lunch? Reminded me of the time Mom was in such a funk she didn't go grocery shopping for a month, and Libby and I lived on condiment sandwiches until we ran out of mayo and ketchup. I'd used my babysitting money for groceries.

The mother didn't wear a wedding band, so I assumed she was the sole provider. I gave her a ten-euro bill. She attempted to hand me the four paper roses lying on the blanket.

I shook my head. "Please, give them to another customer."

Looking hurt, she glanced down at her daughters then said something to Sophie.

Sophie peered over at me. "She says she taught her daughters they do not accept charity. It is important they take care of themselves. You should take the flowers."

I accepted two flowers, not wanting to take away what little self-respect she had.

As we walked away, Sophie said, "That was very kind of you. You are very much like Libby."

Rather than claiming Libby and I were nothing alike and admitting that I'd never before given money to a needy person on the street, I smiled, thinking maybe I should have given them twenty euros instead.

I sat at Libby's dining room table waiting for Luc or Libby to appear, perusing the website for Pascal's hair salons. His bio said he'd grown up the son of a poor farmer in a rural village. His mother had died when he was five. Humble beginnings for such a successful man. I couldn't help but admire his drive and ambition. He'd owned six salons, including one in the prestigious Balzac Hotel. He'd built quite a name for himself with a long list of accolades. Very impressive.

Why had everyone hated him so much? Why did I care? Libby would never have dated a man like Pascal who stood for power and money, everything she was against. Unless he'd been her latest project. She seemed to have made him a better person in the very end. But why wouldn't she have told anyone about him? Because she'd been ashamed to have dated a man like Pascal.

A man kind of like me.

I'd received a few more e-mails on Lori's screw-ups. I shot them off to Evan. Welcome to my world.

I glanced over at the puppet lounging against the vase, which now also held my paper flowers. It seemed to be wearing an approving smile. I smiled back.

Still no response from Evan regarding all the e-mails I'd sent him. And Roger hadn't called. Did he know I'd quit?

Rachel had sent an e-mail an hour ago, excited that I had 286 Likes on *my* Facebook fan page. She obviously hadn't taken down the page. She said women had some great stories about their personal experiences with sexual discrimination. Curious, I went on Facebook and registered for an account under my mom's maiden name, Marshal. I searched out Samantha Hunter, Brecker, and every key word I could think of. I found several Samantha Hunters, but none were me. I e-mailed Rachel, asking her the page name. If the page wasn't under my name, I wasn't in a rush to take it down. I'd like to read these women's stories.

I thought about e-mailing Ken. If he and Mom had separated, I'd have heard all about him abandoning her like everyone else had. I couldn't flat-out ask Ken if she was off her meds, unsure if he was even aware she was on them. It wasn't my place to tell him. I'd never even told Evan about Mom, not wanting him to constantly be looking for signs of her illness in me. I did that enough. Especially lately.

A rap sounded at the door. Expecting Luc, I answered it to find Bruno, the psycho painter. He blew past me, stalking into the apartment before I could slam the door.

"Have you talked to Libby?" he demanded.

Heart racing, I remained by the open door. "No, I ended up not seeing her."

"Liar!" he yelled, causing me to cringe. "You are in this with her. If the paintings are not here, you sold them!"

He stripped the cushions off the futon then turned and swiped an angry hand through the air, somehow missing the vase of daisies but catching my puppet, sending it sailing through the air and landing on the floor with a thud.

First the mural, now my puppet. "What the hell?" I rushed over and picked up the puppet, assessing it for damage, not finding any. I glared at Bruno. "You need to leave right now."

"I am not leaving without my paintings."

Would Libby have sold his paintings for some extra cash? Maybe she'd thought he'd left town and was never returning.

"What were they worth? A couple hundred euros?" I snagged my purse off the table, willing to pay to get this psycho off my back.

He let out a sadistic laugh. "That is very funny. You are a comedian. I am sure Libby received several million for them. That was my best Pissaro. It was worth millions." He punched the air with his fist.

This guy was raking in millions painting copies of Pissaro? What person in his right mind would pay that much for a fake? Unless...

"You're passing these paintings off as originals?" I blurted.

Bruno's gaze darkened, telling me I was dead-on. "If I do not have my paintings or the money by the end of the week, Libby will be very sorry." He stalked out, and I slammed the door and locked it.

No way would Libby have sold forgeries. Besides respecting art, she wouldn't be living in this dump if she'd just sold paintings worth millions. Well, yeah, she would be living in this dump because she'd have donated all the money to charity. She couldn't have known Bruno was passing the paintings off as authentic. She'd never have condoned such a crime.

I glanced out the open balcony doors at the elderly man sitting on his balcony across the narrow street, craning his neck to see inside Libby's apartment, a concerned expression etched on his thin face. I stepped toward the balcony and gave him a little wave, forcing my trembling lips into a smile, assuring him I was fine. His features and narrow shoulders relaxed, and he turned his attention to a pot of purple flowers. A bit obsessed with flowers.

Monsieur Fleurs. The perfect name for him.

Forget covering the doors with a sheet. A neighborhood watch program was a must with Bruno on the loose. I just had to remember not to get dressed in front of the balcony doors.

I was still shaking five minutes later when a rap sounded at the door. I stood paralyzed. "Who's there?"

"Luc."

Relief washed over me, and I opened the door.

"Did you find Libby?" he asked, walking in.

I shook my head, letting out a ragged breath. "But that psycho was back looking for his paintings."

Luc's gaze narrowed in concern. "I wasn't home. Are you okay?"

I nodded. "He's a forger. Libby was holding on to a bunch of paintings for him. No way did she know he was passing the paintings off as authentic. He thinks she sold them, and now he wants the money. Millions."

"Libby would not sell forgeries."

"I told him that, but he didn't believe me. I need to call the police. He's crazy. What if he hurts Libby?"

"He obviously doesn't know where she is, so he can't hurt her. I'm more worried about you. But we don't know his last name or where he lives. The police won't wait here for him to show up. Besides, there are a lot of crazy people in Paris. Unless he threatens you with a weapon or harms you, the police won't do anything."

I let out a frustrated breath. "You're right. And I really don't want to tip off the police that Libby had any involvement with Bruno and his forgeries. What could she have done with the paintings?"

Luc shrugged. "Maybe she realized they were forgeries and she destroyed them."

I hoped not or this guy was really gonna snap. If it came down to protecting my family from this nut job or a few naïve art collectors from purchasing forgeries, I'd hand the paintings over to Bruno in a second.

"He said they were Pissaros."

"Libby had two Pissaros here until a few months ago. They were very good. I thought she'd painted them."

So what had she done with them?

I remembered Bruno's crazed messages and had Luc listen to them. They demanded Libby call him. Libby had played one of them, so she knew Bruno was looking for her. Had that had something to do with her leaving the hospital? I saved the messages in case I showed up dead, paintbrush through the heart, and the police needed evidence to put this lunatic away.

Luc zipped into traffic, and I held on tight, molding my body against his as we crossed a bridge over the Seine. I relaxed slightly, the wind against my face like a dog with his head out a car window. We turned off the boulevard and maneuvered down a maze of quaint, narrow streets lined with boutiques, art galleries, trendy hair salons, and no souvenir shops. The area had a more eclectic feel.

Luc slowed down in front of the Bozilovic gallery in the Marais area, where Libby had worked. The window displayed impressionist scenes of Paris, along with a sign reading *Fermé*.

"It's closed on Monday," Luc said. "We'll have to return tomorrow."

We continued on, turning down several narrow streets. We rounded a corner, about taking out a cluster of tourists loitering in the street, snapping photos. We parked by a café bustling with a late lunch crowd. I headed across the street toward the attraction being photographed—a large mural on the side of a building. A Picasso-esque painting of a nude woman, done in vibrant blues and reds.

I admired the mural. "It's beautiful."

Luc smiled. *"Merci."*

"You painted it?" I stared at the painting in awe.

"No, Libby did. That's Fiona. My wife."

Traffic skidded to a halt, and cameras stopped clicking. "You're married?"

He shook his head, his eyes dimming. "She died over a year ago."

"I'm so sorry." I reached out, touching his arm. I didn't usually do well at comforting people I knew, let alone someone I'd just met. Yet I wanted to comfort Luc.

He eyed my hand on his arm, looking a tad calmer. Whereas my heart was going berserk. After a few moments of us staring at my hand, I slipped it from his arm. He plucked a cigarette from his hat and lit up. Even after several long drags, his pained expression remained.

"She's very talented, *non?*" he asked.

I nodded, admiring the painting, a sense of pride welling in my chest. I snapped a picture with my phone.

"The week after she finished it, we closed the street and had a benefit for Fiona with painters, puppets, and clowns." Luc savored the last drag on his cigarette.

It made me feel good that, in a roundabout way, my monthly checks to Libby had made it possible for her to donate her talent and I'd contributed to Fiona's cause.

"Do you paint?" Luc asked, apparently not wanting to further discuss Fiona's benefit.

"No. I flunked finger painting in kindergarten."

"What do you do when you're not working?"

"I read travel industry magazines and..."

"That's still work. You must have a passion for other things."

My phone rang in my hand, and Luc eyed it.

"I guess maybe you work all the time."

I let it go to voice mail, planning on checking the message as soon as Luc turned his back. "I'm not working now."

He arched a doubtful brow.

He walked over to a vendor at a café window set flush to the sidewalk. The man took half of a small baguette and shot ketchup and mustard down the hollowed-out center then stuffed a hot dog inside. Luc handed it to me. "Paris hot dogs are almost as good as truffle-roasted chateaubriand."

My mouth watered at the thought of the chateaubriand I'd missed out on at Jules Verne. "Think you might be pushing it."

One bite convinced me it was indeed the best hot dog ever, even though the hot mustard would be like throwing kerosene on my stomach if it were acting up.

"I make a good chateaubriand but not a hot dog like this."

"You can make chateaubriand?"

"I was a chef."

I tried to picture Luc in a white apron and a tall, white hat with cigarettes lined up along the front, meticulously drizzling dill sauce over a salmon filet resting on a bed of asparagus. The vision was fuzzy.

"You were a chef? Why'd you quit?"

He shrugged, plucking a cigarette from his fedora. He lit up and inhaled a deep, suicidal drag. He eased a stream of smoke through his slightly parted lips. Cigarette smoke and awkward silence lingered in the air.

"One of my consumer promotion ideas is to have people submit their favorite recipes using Brecker beer, and the best recipes will be selected for the Brecker cookbook. And the top recipes will be chosen for a cook-off."

Luc took another drag on his cigarette. "My friend has a chefs' reality show in London. Maybe you could have chefs from one of those shows do a cook-off with Brecker beer."

"Excellent idea. They could all be women. Great for my women's marketing plan. Well, I'd probably need one guy or my boss would say it was a chickmercial."

An idea for a commercial started taking seed, involving a hot French chef cooking with beer and a female chef...

"You don't know any recipes made with beer, do you?"

He nodded. "Fiona's family was Irish. I created several Guinness recipes for them."

"How about Brecker uses *your* recipes in a commercial? That would be great money and exposure for you. And maybe you could be on the reality TV show."

Luc shook his head. "I haven't cooked in almost two years," he said firmly. "I'll never cook again. I prefer to be a puppeteer, not a puppet."

I couldn't picture a laid-back and free-spirited Luc having ever been a puppet. What had caused him to change roles?

Chapter Ten

We cruised down the street, passing by a black awning with hot pink lettering that read *Pascal Rochant*. One of Pascal's salons.

I tapped Luc's shoulder. "Can we stop?" Frazzled after the whole Bruno incident, I never mentioned Pascal's funeral.

He slowed down and maneuvered the scooter into a tight spot between a rusted-out Citroen and a shiny, black smart car.

"Libby used to work here," I said. "The owner just died."

"I didn't know Pascal died."

"You knew him?"

"I met him several times. He would come by Libby's."

"Why would he come by Libby's?"

"They were friends, I guess."

"Did he come by often?"

Luc shrugged. "I saw him a few times a month."

"Do you think Libby dated him?"

"He was a good-looking man, but I don't think he was her type. I don't know."

Luc waited by his scooter. I entered the salon, and techno music caused my chest to thump to the beat. A hip and trendy place with fuchsia walls and white leather furnishings, there were no white-haired ladies beneath dryers with curlers in their hair. The staff was sheathed in black. I didn't spot any of the men from the funeral. The receptionist, tall with dark, wavy hair and a goatee, smiled at me.

"*Bonjour,*" I said. "I don't have an appointment, but—"

"I'm sorry, nobody is available." He studied my hair with disdain. "But I can help you." He turned to a product display behind the counter. "This color, it would be very good for you." He selected a clear bottle containing shampoo the color of a Santa suit. "A nice auburn color like Brigitte Aumont."

"Ah, that looks kind of bright. Besides, I don't want—"

"It will not be so bright." He eyed my hair. "That brown color is not good for you. Your blue eyes, they look dull, and your skin yellow."

I glanced in a mirror. My skin did have a yellowish tint to it. Was that some kind of trick lighting?

He set the bottle on the counter, along with a conditioner.

"I'm actually wondering if you know Libby Hunter. I'm her sister. Just got into town."

He smiled. "Yes, Libby worked here. She is very *gentille*."

"I thought she might be here with Pascal's funeral and all, since I think they might have dated." Nothing like getting straight to the point.

He looked mortified. "Libby would never have dated such an awful man." His gaze narrowed with concern. "However, she convinced him to apologize to Alphonse when nobody else could. Pascal liked her very much. He did not like anyone." His gaze narrowed further. "And Libby was in his will."

"What did he leave her?"

"She will need to ask Alphonse. I know only she was in it."

Had he left her a year's supply of hair products? A salon? A college fund for their daughter?

He blew an indignant puff of air from between his lips. "I don't believe Libby would ever be with such a man. He was a beast. I cannot discuss him."

He grabbed another red hair product off the display and handed it to me. My total came to almost two hundred U.S. dollars. My gaze darted back and forth between the guy and the products. *You've got to be kidding me.* I glanced at myself in the mirror behind the reception desk. My skin did look yellow.

I handed over my Visa.

—☙ ❧—

As we cruised up a busy boulevard, a motorcycle zipped past, and I tightened my hold around Luc's waist. I managed to keep from squeezing my eyes shut, fascinated by the places we cruised past. *Sexy Show, Love Shop, Pigalle Peep Show...* The signs were all in English. Sex was a universal language.

"This is Pigalle," Luc yelled over his shoulder.

Paris's red-light district.

Luc pulled up next to a motorcycle parked on a wide, tree-lined pedestrian walk running up the center of the street. I slid off the scooter more gracefully than usual. He chained the scooter to a pole.

Besides tourists snapping shots of storefronts, there were plenty of seedy characters lurking around. A group of sleazy, middle-aged guys sitting on a bench leered at me as we walked past. I slipped my purse strap over my head and across my front. As if it would be my money they were after.

I checked my voice mail from Hannah. The bus driver's cousin ended up driving Roger around in his smart car. I could picture Roger crammed into the tiny car's front seat, his knees pressed against his chest. Hannah had informed Evan that, if I'd been there, Roger would have had a better car with all my connections. Very assertive for Hannah.

She went on to say that everyone on Facebook was rallying behind me. I had 372 Likes. She said the video was causing the Likes to explode. Video? I texted her asking what video Rachel had put on Facebook.

"You're predictable. I knew you'd check your voice mail soon."

Checking voice mail was a habit. I hadn't even realized I was doing it.

"Predictable? Excuse me, I just spontaneously quit my job last night." And I'd do whatever it took to get it back.

We walked down the street, and a guy called out Luc's name, prompting us to turn around. Apprehension flickered on Luc's face, and his gaze darted around like he was preparing to bolt. The guy was my age with dark hair. He walked up, and they exchanged an awkward hug, patting each other on the back, placing fleeting kisses to their cheeks. Luc plucked a cigarette from his hat and lit up. They chatted for a few minutes in French. Odd. Luc usually switched to English so I didn't feel excluded. Maybe the guy didn't speak English.

I peered around, trying not to feel awkward, and noticed a young guy staring at me. Our gazes locked, and he glanced away. He didn't look like a tourist but looked respectable for the area, clean-cut, dressed in jeans and an Oxford University sweatshirt. I peered across the street at a pink sign advertising *Go-Go Girls and Go-Go Guys* then back at the guy once again watching me.

He turned and bolted. Bizarre.

The guy Luc was talking to gestured to me, and Luc introduced me to Didier.

Didier smiled, giving me a curious look before kissing my cheeks. *"Enchanté."* He turned to Luc and switched to English. "I am going to Verte. You should come. Everyone will be there. They'll be glad to see you. It's been more than a year since..." He trailed off, shifting his stance, looking uncomfortable. "Since you moved."

Luc used to live around *here*? What "unmentionable" thing had caused him to move?

"I can't. I'm helping Samantha look for her sister."

Didier asked for Luc's new phone number, preparing to program it into his cell phone. Appearing a bit apprehensive, Luc gave him the number. Didier wrapped Luc in a big hug. Luc relaxed slightly, becoming more receptive to the man's display of affection. When Didier released him, Luc promptly excused us, and we continued on. Luc lit up another cigarette, little stress crinkles deepening around his eyes. I was waiting for him to torch his hat and OD on nicotine.

"Are you okay?" I said, breaking the silence.

Luc shook his head. "It's a long story." And apparently one he didn't want to tell. At the end of the block, Luc stopped. "This is where Libby worked."

We stood in front of a black-painted storefront with a purple neon sign reading *Carmen's*.

"I don't think so. There must be another Carmen's." A sign

advertised a transsexual specialist and four euros for a peep show. "No way."

"This is the address and store name Sophie said."

"She's wrong. I'd have known if Libby were a stripper." Just like I'd known she was pregnant, depressed, working at a psychic café, and involved with a forger.

Luc held aside the purple curtain covering the entrance, and I reluctantly pushed open the door with my elbow. Several slimy guys, along with two respectable-looking men in suits, trolled the aisles, ogling porn videos and sex gadgets.

Josette, a young, blonde salesclerk, knew Libby. "Libby sold her underwear here."

My eyes widened. "Her underwear?" Libby had been so desperate for money she'd sold her underwear? I'd heard about stuff like that happening on eBay but couldn't imagine Libby would do such a perverse thing.

"We still have a few pairs, I believe. They are next to the wigs." She gestured down an aisle. "How is Libby? I haven't talked to her for a while. We had coffee a few months ago."

I explained the situation. "Do you know her baby's father?"

"She was once seeing a man who I think worked at an antique shop, but that was all she said. She seemed to really like him, but I wondered if he didn't feel the same way, since she didn't talk so much about him."

"Did she mention where the antique shop was located?"

"No. Sorry. I'm not certain it was an antique shop, but I believe so."

I gave Josette my business card, and she agreed to call if she talked to Libby.

I found it very bizarre that nobody knew who my niece's father was. Why had she kept it such a secret?

Luc and I headed down an aisle in search of Libby's panties. "There are probably a hundred antique shops in Paris."

Luc nodded. "Or more."

Yet I was relieved Josette hadn't said he worked at a salon, confirming Pascal was indeed the father. If Libby did somehow love such a man, I didn't want her lover, my niece's father, to be dead. Although it was hard to know timing-wise who Libby had been dating exactly when.

We walked past an assortment of leather and lace costumes and brightly colored wigs. I came across *Lucious Libby's* thongs. The *new* thongs had candy hearts painted on them with sayings.

"*Mange-moi,*" I muttered, reading the saying on one with pastries and desserts painted on the front.

"Eat me," Luc translated.

Heat exploded on my face, and I scooped up the half dozen panties sitting there.

Luc raised an intrigued brow.

"I want to support my sister's...job." I couldn't bear the thought of Libby's name being attached to this place.

I bought the panties, and we stepped outside. I took a cleansing breath, wanting to bathe in antibacterial wipes. I slipped my white Valentino sunglasses down from the top of my head, and everything slowly came into focus, including Tom Meyers, a big, burly guy who owned one of Brecker's largest distribution companies. He had on faded jeans and a T-shirt reading *Dude, Where's My Beer?* There was definitely truth in the saying "Do what you love and the money will follow." Loving beer had earned these guys millions, but you'd never know it looking at them.

I slipped the purple Carmen's bag behind my back. Pigalle was a tourist attraction, so I wasn't surprised to see Tom.

"Hey there, little lady. So this where you've been hiding out all day?"

"You're back from the Loire Valley already?" I asked.

"Didn't go. Not into big, fancy houses." He glanced around, wearing a wide smile. "Don't got no area like this in Waco, that's for damn sure."

"We came here to get Moulin Rouge tickets," Luc lied, gesturing across the street at a white building with a red windmill perched on top, inside which topless girls performed.

"Think you could get me some tickets?"

"Actually...I quit." I had no clue what possessed me to tell Tom this when I wasn't even sure if Roger knew. Maybe I wanted to gauge his reaction, see if he cared. Maybe I wanted him to tell Matt Davis, so he'd confront Roger and demand I get the promotion I deserved.

"Shit." He slid back his Dallas Cowboys cap and rubbed his forehead. "How we gonna survive without you? Why'd you quit?"

"Contract dispute. Hope to be back soon."

"Can't believe Roger let you get away." He shook his head. "Sometimes I think that man is all foam and no beer."

At least Tom would miss me. And actually, I'd miss him, along with the other distributors, if I didn't get the promotion. At the farewell reception in Munich last year, they'd presented me with a purse by a German designer as a thank you for getting the hotel lounge to stay open until five every morning. They didn't care if I boozed it up with them, like Roger and Evan claimed. All they cared about was that I ensured *they* could drink.

Tom slid a beefy arm around my shoulder and gave me a squeeze. "Don't worry, little lady, you'll get your job back."

I smiled. With the distributors on my side, how could I not get the promotion?

Chapter Eleven

We swung by the hospital, and according to Nurse Nasty, Libby hadn't yet returned.

Libby had been gone almost *seven* hours.

She should have been back by now whether the father wanted to see his daughter or not. Why hadn't she at least called? She should have realized I'd be worried. I should be glad she'd at least left a note.

"She looks so...peaceful." Luc stared at my niece lying there asleep. "Let me take your picture with her."

I handed him my phone. I leaned over, my face next to hers. Luc snapped a shot. She cracked her eyelids, squinting at me through a sleepy haze.

"Oh...hello there, sweetie," I said softly. "I'm your Auntie Sam." Auntie Sam. I liked the sound of that. I massaged a soothing hand over her belly. "That's right. Auntie Sam. And this is Uncle Luc."

"Salut, ma petite puce," he said in a gentle tone.

She glanced over at Luc then back at me before stretching her tiny fingers and letting out a faint yawn.

I straightened. "What's a *puce*?"

"A flea."

"And calling her that is a good thing?"

"That's a common thing to say to babies or small children."

While I assured my niece she was as cute as a bug but certainly not a flea, Luc struck up a conversation with a proud father by the crib next to us.

Luc turned to me, gesturing to the other baby. "That is his daughter, Claudette."

I smiled at the man's daughter, who was nowhere near as cute as my niece. "This is my niece..." My gaze darted to Luc. "She needs a name, even if it's just temporary. We can't keep calling her baby or flea."

"You're right. What name do you think Libby will choose?"

I peered down at my niece. "Astroid, Moonbeam... Your mommy's name is Libby." I started singing the catchy little jingle from years ago. "If it's got Libby, Libby, Libby on the label, label, label, you will like it, like it, like it, on the table, table, table."

Luc laughed. "That is...fun. I like it."

"It was the brand name of canned fruits and vegetables. We should name her something French..."

"I want to name my daughter Amélie."

"You want kids?"

Luc shrugged. "Someday." He studied my niece. "She looks like a Dominique."

Nurse Nasty marched up, looking as unpleasant as ever. "She is not back. At least her baby is a good eater and is drinking a bottle good."

"The baby's father is a wreck over his dad's death. It was very unexpected and tragic. She needs to be with him."

"He lives in Le Havre," Luc lied.

"She is in no condition to travel so far," the nurse said sharply.

"I told her I'd be here if Dominique needs anything. I'm her guardian." I squared my shoulders.

"If she is not back soon, the doctor will contact the police."

Panic raced through me. "Libby will be back here before I am again, guaranteed." She sure as hell better be back before the police were here. How would I explain this when I had no clue where Libby was?

It killed me to leave my niece at the hospital with Nurse Nasty. That woman should not be the first person my niece saw when she woke up in the morning or the last person she saw at night. She'd give the poor little thing nightmares.

We stopped by Libby's apartment to make sure she wasn't lounging on her orange futon eating a brie, olive, apricot, and salami sandwich, clueless we'd been searching for her. But the apartment looked exactly as it had earlier, except hotter. I opened the balcony doors even though the only chance for a breeze would be if a flock of pigeons flew past. I gave Monsieur Fleurs a wave and had Luc check the answering machine. Four messages from me, two from Bruno, and one from an anonymous guy who told Libby to call him.

If, by chance, Libby wasn't out searching for the baby's father, she was probably freaking out about all the responsibility she now had and was avoiding it as usual. Maybe she was stressed and knew I was here to watch over her baby until she was forced to return. What if that wasn't until the end of the week when I had to leave?

Wait a sec, I never told Libby I'd be leaving at the end of the week. She still thought I was here for two weeks.

What if she hadn't returned by the end of the week?

I couldn't stay in Paris. I had a program in Vegas the end of next week. What would I do with Dominique?

I had to stop thinking the worst. It wouldn't come to that.

Libby couldn't have gone far without a suitcase or a credit card. She'd never believed in credit cards. I doubted that had changed. Determined to find clues on the father's identity, Luc searched the kitchen drawers and cupboards, while I paged through a photo album, hoping to find a picture of Libby and the baby's father. An affectionate person, she looked cozy with a lot of guys who were surely just friends. I came across the photos of Libby and Luc protesting nude along the Seine. My entire body went warm. After enjoying the view a moment, I turned the page to find a photo of Libby and me wearing matching pink lace dresses and white gloves, our long, blonde hair pulled back in bows. My gaze darted to the mural on the wall.

The picture had meant so much to Libby she'd painted it on the wall, yet I hadn't even remembered it. In my defense, Impressionism didn't clearly portray its subject matter; our features were a bit vague. And Libby had replaced my scowl in the photo with a bright smile that matched hers. Upset over Mom dressing us identically, I'd refused to smile.

I stared at the mural, the sound of Libby's giggles filling my head. Anxious to hunt for eggs, she hadn't been able to stop giggling while Dad took our picture by the garden, trying to bribe me with marshmallow chicks to get me to smile.

I walked over and gently placed my hand against our clasped hands in the painting, being careful not to disturb the loose piece of plaster. My chest tightened at the thought of Libby and me no longer holding hands, of us being separated, me being unable to help Libby with whatever had caused her to leave.

Now I *really* wanted to kick Bruno's psycho ass.

I riffled through the armoire drawers, finding nothing but clothes. I lifted the daybed's green, chenille bedspread and peeked under the bed to find several storage boxes. A montage of vintage Paris postcards decorated a pink hatbox, which held odds and ends, like theater ticket stubs and receipts. I unzipped a small, red velvet pouch to discover a bundle of euro bills and a savings book, noting a recent deposit of six grand.

"What the hell?" I glanced over at Luc. "There's like," I thumbed through the bundles, "a couple grand in euros here, and six grand in her savings account. Where would Libby get this kind of money?"

Luc walked over to where I sat on the floor. "Maybe she was saving the money you sent her to open her own gallery."

"How would she have been paying her rent?"

Luc shrugged. "She worked several jobs."

He snagged a cigarette from his hat and lit up. He'd been chain smoking since encountering Didier. One lonely cigarette lined his hat. "She'll be back. Or she would have taken the money."

Luc's optimism was getting quite annoying.

"Maybe there was a lot more, and she left this as an emergency stash."

Even though there was a lot I didn't know about Libby, she wasn't an art forger or any kind of criminal. There was a logical explanation why she was involved with Bruno. Maybe she was raking in the dough selling erotic panties at Carmen's.

I stuck the money back in the velvet pouch. I removed a stack of letters bundled with a red ribbon. Well worn, they looked like they'd been read often. There were no envelopes, so no postmark or return address. Love letters from the baby's father? I unfolded the top letter and began reading.

> *Dear Libby,*
> *It was so good hearing from you. I have wanted to contact you so many times. I can't tell you how difficult it has been not seeing you all these years...*

I sat paralyzed while my heart raced. After twenty-five years, I still recognized the sharp, angular, printed penmanship. My gaze flew to the bottom of the letter to the words *Love, Dad*.

I felt like all the oxygen had been sucked from my lungs, and I couldn't breathe fast enough to get more in.

"Oh...my...God," I sputtered.

"Are you okay?" Luc asked.

I shook my head, staring at the letter in disbelief. Libby had contacted Dad? How long had they been writing? Had he known Libby was pregnant, when I hadn't even known?

I popped up from the floor. "These are from my dad. I haven't seen him since I was ten. I had no idea Libby's been writing him. How could she do this without telling me?" Betrayal wrenched my gut, and my hand tightened around the letter, crumpling it. "I've always been there for her. Where the hell has he been? I have no clue, but Libby obviously does, she just didn't tell me!"

I whipped the letter on the floor.

Luc's mouth was moving, but nothing was coming out as he grasped for something to say.

There was nothing to say.

I bolted out the door.

The one person who needed to do some serious talking was nowhere to be found.

Chapter Twelve

I wandered aimlessly down the Latin Quarter's narrow streets, totally lost, more determined than ever to find Libby. I was going out of my mind, unable to confront her about the money, the forgeries, Dad's letters, and ditching her baby!

I kicked a large stone, forgetting I had on flip-flops. I yelled out in pain. It felt so good I yelled louder, feeling a sense of release. I didn't care that people were staring. I didn't care that my emotions were out of control.

Why did I care what those stupid letters said? Whether Dad had asked about me or explained where he'd been. Since the letters looked worn, and there were only a few, I clung to the hope they hadn't corresponded long. That Libby regretted contacting him, so she'd never told me. Except for when Dad first left, I hadn't once considered trying to find him. I would never forgive him for allowing me to blame myself for him abandoning us.

A sick feeling tossed my stomach. After everything I'd done for Libby, I couldn't believe she'd gone behind my back like this. And behind Mom's back. If Mom had known about Libby contacting Dad, she'd have demanded I put a stop to it. I wanted to hunt Libby down and demand answers. But I was at a dead end.

My phone rang, and my stomach tensed. I pulled it from my purse, but rather than Roger or Evan, it was Hannah. I let it go to voice mail then listened. The group was back from the Loire Valley. She couldn't believe I had 463 Likes on my fan page. *I* couldn't believe I had 463 Likes. Who were all these people? I checked e-mail, and Rachel had sent me the name of my fan page: *Promote Samantha—Down with Discrimination.*

I encountered the Luxembourg Gardens and realized I'd been walking in circles. Luc had a puppet performance in twenty minutes. He'd offered to cancel so we could continue searching for Libby, but we were out of clues. I should swing by and tell Luc I was okay after I'd bolted out of the apartment.

French music carried across the garden, inviting children and parents to the shed. It reminded me of the nostalgic, tinny music of the merry-go-round at the fair we'd gone to every year until Dad had left. Libby always rode a whimsical, white horse, while I'd ride a sleek, black one. She'd ride sidesaddle, like some princess in a fairytale. I'd crouch forward and pretend like the wind was whipping through my hair as I flew toward the finish line at the Kentucky Derby, in first place.

I walked through the ivy-covered gate and headed to the back of the puppet shed and knocked on the door. Luc opened the door and eyed me with caution.

"Sorry about before," I said.

A slow smile curled his lips, and he grasped my hand, giving it a reassuring squeeze. "Come." He ushered me inside.

He closed the door. I followed Luc down a few steps, the sunshine peeking around the edges of the closed, red curtain providing the only light. I stood below the stage. A row of puppets hung on hooks underneath the stage, including a replacement for the one Luc had given me. He turned down the volume on a boombox playing French music into a microphone.

"You can be Madame Souris," he said.

"I can't work a puppet."

He removed a gray felt mouse on a stick hanging alongside the puppets. "When I nod at you, the mouse runs onto the stage like this." He moved the mouse across the stage with a skittering motion.

After practicing a few times, I decided I could handle the role of Madame Souris. It was the same performance I'd seen yesterday, so at least I had a clue what happened.

"You can also do the thunder." He tapped a metal sheet lightly with a padded stick. "But harder."

"How will that queue be different than the mouse one?"

"I'll nod twice. I have to collect the money. Sylvie is not here today." He turned and headed outside.

A small accordion sat on the bench. Autographed photos of famous puppeteers filled the walls, along with one of Luc at a puppet festival. Would be nice to have a private office with nobody around to bug you. If I didn't get the promotion, maybe I could be Luc's assistant at ten euros a day. Or...I could help him expand his business. He could do private gigs. Like for Brecker. He could perform at receptions and gear his skits toward each specific company. He'd pull in five hundred a night easy. He was an incredible puppeteer. He deserved more than a shed in the gardens.

Luc walked back into the shed. "Are you ready to play Madame Souris?"

I nodded, feeling like I had little mouse feet scampering across my tummy.

Luc turned off the music and played a lively little tune on the accordion. A man of many talents. For as many times as he'd likely performed this skit, he wasn't merely going through the motions. His enthusiasm shone through in his puppets' performance.

My part didn't come up until the second act when Luc tugged a rope and the backdrop rolled up, revealing a dark and stormy night scene. Luc nodded at me, and I had the mouse scurry on stage. Laughter erupted in the audience. Luc's little boy puppet jumped with fright. The laughs grew louder. It felt strange yet good being the source of people's laughter.

Ten minutes later, the show ended, and Luc peered over at me. "You did very well."

"I feel better, thanks."

A suggestive grin spread across his face. "That's good. I like to make you feel better."

I about wilted into a puddle, imagining just how good Luc could make me feel. He stepped closer, a playful look in his brown eyes. He drew back slightly, apparently feeling my apprehension, gazing deep into my eyes.

"What are you thinking?" he whispered, his breath warm against my face.

Had he lived in Paris his entire life? What were his aspirations and dreams? Did he want to own a puppet shop someday? Could I not even kiss a guy without overanalyzing the situation?

If I lived in Paris, I'd have to worry that Luc and I were complete opposites and our relationship would be doomed from the start. That a puppeteer wasn't financially stable. That a hot French guy could never be faithful. I didn't have to worry about such things. I'd be gone in a few days. We could never get serious. No strings attached. No big deal.

Yet I quickly changed the subject. "You should work corporate events, like receptions for groups in town on business. You could gear the skits to each company. Make a puppet with the company logo. Like a beer can for Brecker. You could easily make five hundred a gig..." Staring at the puppet in his hand, Luc looked far from inspired, and he stepped back. "You could probably make more than five hundred. I could have Hannah book you for the farewell reception."

"Like I said, I prefer to be a puppeteer, not a puppet."

"You wouldn't be a puppet. You'd still be your own boss. Decide what gigs you did or didn't do."

"My job would become *all* I would do. I don't want that."

"You could just do a few events a month. Like—"

"I am happy with what I do." He slid the puppet off his hand and hung it on a hook.

Why did it bother me so much that Luc had no aspirations, no goals, no hunger for more?

"You'd be doing the same thing, just on a larger scale and for more money."

"No." His gaze sharpened. "You're happy being a puppet. I'm not. I won't let anyone pull my strings again."

I squared my shoulders and raised a defensive chin. "I don't let people pull my strings."

He glanced down at my phone in my hand. "You're still the puppet even after you quit." He grasped hold of my shoulders and gave them a gentle squeeze, his gaze softening. "You could be so much happier. I want you to be happier."

"I...am happy," I muttered.

He let out a defeated sigh and released my shoulders, slipping his hands down my arms. With a disappointed look, he turned and marched up the steps and out of the shed.

Luc didn't know me well enough to look at me with such disappointment. Why did he care if I was a puppet or not? And why did I care if he cared?

I marched across the garden, battling my emotions. Luc barely knew me, yet he seemed to genuinely care if I was happy. But who was he to rip on my job? As if anyone who had a boss was a puppet? At least I had a *real* job. Or would have a real job anyway.

Once I became director, I could implement all the changes I'd tried to get Lori to do, like contracting freelance employees to help execute programs so we weren't traveling a hundred plus days a year. I'd be in a better position to set boundaries with clients and demanding spouses like Natalie Darwin. Life would be better.

My phone rang. Roger.

"What the hell's going on?" he demanded. "We just got back from the Valley, and Tom Meyers laid into me, telling me I'd better hire you back."

"Matt Davis isn't going to be happy either."

Roger let out a frustrated sigh, undoubtedly realizing Matt would also soon be on his ass. "I can't believe Tom knew you quit before I did. Why didn't you talk to me before doing this?"

"I'm sorry. Honestly, I hadn't planned on quitting, it just sort of happened when I was talking to Evan last night."

"What's this about? Money?"

"The promotion. I know I'm not getting it," I blurted.

"Where'd you hear that?" Roger demanded.

"I confronted Evan." Better to get Evan's ass in trouble than Sherri's. "I questioned why I wouldn't have been offered the promotion immediately. Why you were waiting." At the back of my head, I'd always wondered this. Heart racing, I swallowed the nervous lump in my throat and continued. "I deserve the promotion, Roger. I do the work of two people. I picked up the slack for Lori the entire time she was here, and when she left, I took on most of her programs. I'm not picking up the slack for another director."

"Come back to the hotel so we can talk about this. We'll figure something out."

Did that mean I was getting the promotion?

"Jules Verne is tonight," Natalie yelled out.

"Shit, that's right," Roger muttered. "We have dinner."

"Is that Samantha?" Natalie yelled out again. Roger apparently nodded because she continued, "Tell her these aren't our sheets and pillowcases on the bed. Where are they? I mean, really, what did Samantha do all day while we were gone?"

My grip tightened around the phone.

"Come by tomorrow so we can talk," Roger said.

"Honestly, Roger, unless you're offering me the promotion, there's nothing to talk about."

He let out a disgruntled growl. "I'm not happy about this, Samantha. Not happy at all."

He disconnected without setting a meeting time and place. Did that mean I shouldn't come by to talk? That he wasn't offering me the promotion? What did this mean?

Maybe a sleepless night and chafed skin from two-hundred-thread-count sheets would do the trick.

The scent of hot dogs wafting from a food stand made my stomach growl. I headed toward the stand, yet the burning sensation smoldering in my stomach protested against the hot mustard. I'd ask them to hold the mustard.

I stood in line for a hot dog, and my phone rang. Evan.

"What the hell, Sam? I just got bitched out by Roger. I never said you weren't getting the promotion."

"You didn't have to. I could tell by the way you acted I wasn't getting it."

"You need to get back to the hotel so we can talk about this. You can't just up and quit while we're onsite. Christ, how unprofessional is that?"

"Unprofessional enough to get the promotion? Or do I need to get drunk and dance naked on the hotel's bar?"

"What the hell are you talking about?"

"Can you honestly tell me I've still got a shot at this promotion?" Silence filled the line. "What about us? If you get the fucking promotion, would we get back together?"

"Are you saying if we get back together, I'd have a shot at the promotion?" Was this bribery or extortion?

"I'm just asking."

"Roger didn't deny the position's been filled. Are you denying it?"

He let out a frustrated groan. "No, I'm not."

"I certainly hope this person is much more qualified than me. As you can see from all the e-mails I've been forwarding, I have a shitload of work going on right now."

"He's a good fit for the position."

The puppet music seemed to grow louder. I was the puppeteer, not the puppet.

"A better fit than you were for the position at Budweiser?" I blurted, not having planned to use the info against Evan.

I couldn't even hear Evan breathing on the other end.

More concerned about my promotion than Evan possibly stroking out on me, I pushed on, "Didn't think I knew about that, did you? You know how big Roger is on loyalty. He'd probably think twice about promoting you if he knew you weren't happy at Brecker. Hopefully he doesn't find out."

I disconnected.

Guess I didn't believe in suing but was fine with blackmailing. My heart was going berserk, yet I felt back in control. I was definitely the puppeteer. And Evan was dangling by a string right now.

I'd discovered Evan was interviewing with Budweiser six months ago when he'd been acting suspicious. Like flying to St.

Louis, the company's headquarters, to see an aunt he despised. And having two mysterious calls he couldn't take in front of me. I figured he was cheating, so I'd checked his recent calls and traced one to Budweiser's HR department. How sad. If we'd had a close relationship, he'd have confided in me about this. It had bothered me at the time, but I'd brushed it off. Like so many other things.

While focused on my conversation with Evan, two families had cut in front of me. I searched for a shorter line, noticing the guy in the Oxford sweatshirt from Pigalle staring at me. He glanced away. Pigalle was on the opposite side of the city. What was the chance this guy would be down here only hours later, standing in line next to me?

Why was I suddenly so paranoid?

Because I had a psycho forger on my back.

Was this guy Bruno's partner? If not, maybe he was my niece's father. Maybe Libby had called and asked him to meet her at the hospital and then changed her mind and bolted. So he was following me looking for her. That didn't make sense. Why not just come up and ask me where she was?

After ordering a hot dog without mustard, I escaped into the garden, heading for a heavy traffic area. A group of little girls zipped past, and my gaze followed them, an excuse to check behind me. No Oxford Guy. I speed walked toward the exit, trying not to panic, trying to convince myself this guy didn't want to hurt me.

So what *did* he want?

Chapter Thirteen

I sat safely at Libby's dining room table in front of my laptop, trying to get my blood pressure back to normal and to get Oxford Guy off my mind. My puppet lounged against the vase of daisies, watching me. I slipped the puppet on my hand and moved its arms around with ease. "Maybe next time," I said in a thick French accent, "I will get to play ze part of you rather zan a mouse. And I can kick your little boyfriend's ass." I tilted the puppet's head back, letting out a sadistic laugh.

I was losing it. At least puppet therapy was better for me than popping Xanax or a dozen antacid tablets.

My bright red hair products sat on the table. Pascal's will might answer whether he was Dominique's father. If he was, I knew Libby wasn't with him. I called Sophie to see if she'd contacted Alphonse. She'd left him a message. I asked her to inquire about Libby's inheritance when she spoke to him.

I signed in to Facebook and pulled up my fan page.

Promote Samantha—Down with Discrimination.

It now had 538 Likes. The profile pic was a generic beer bottle. It said that I worked for a brewery, but it didn't say where. There were over 5,000 brewers worldwide, including craft and microbrewers. I could be anywhere. It stated that I was about to be passed up for a promotion despite working sixty-hour weeks, not having taken a vacation day in five years, and being the most qualified person for the job. A lesser qualified *male* was likely getting my position at twenty-two grand more a year than what I made.

Twenty-two grand? I e-mailed Rachel, asking if she was serious about the pay. I scanned the posts, recognizing some of Rachel's friends' names. Numerous women had posted their personal experiences with discrimination. I came across the video Hannah had mentioned. The woman was in a police uniform, standing in front of her superior's desk, his back to the camera. Had she set up a teddy cam on his bookshelf?

"I'm sorry, but it's a fact that it's harder for women to stand out on the force," the man said.

"Stand out like how? Like this?" She thrust her shoulders back and her breasts out.

"I'm not saying that." But his low, suggestive tone said otherwise.

"But it would help?"

He shrugged.

"Would this help more?" She undid her top button. The windows and door blinds were closed, but couldn't somebody walk in?

He stepped from behind the desk toward her. He went to undo the next button, and she smacked away his hand.

"Exactly what I thought." She stormed out.

What an ass! It was not only sexual discrimination but sexual harassment.

The video had received seventy-three Likes and seven shares. I liked the video. So much for taking down my fan page. But it ticked me off that so many companies still got away with this. If I stayed in the beer industry, and even if I didn't, I'd continue to encounter discrimination. Besides, my page was anonymous. Even though that could change at any time since Rachel was a loose cannon.

I shut down my computer. I eyed the bed. As much as I was dreading seeing Dad's letters, I had to finish checking the info in that hatbox. It held a lot of personal items. I pulled out the hatbox from under the bed. I opened it, and the letters stared up at me. I wondered if they smelled like Aqua Velva. After Dad had left, I'd swiped his aftershave from the medicine cabinet before Mom could toss it out along with all his belongings. For months, I'd taken a whiff of it every night before going to bed.

It had taken me years to accept Dad was never returning. Why he'd left no longer mattered. I wasn't going to buy into his excuses like Libby undoubtedly had. I was old enough now to realize the issue had been with Dad, not me.

That was all that mattered.

I tossed the letters aside.

I sifted through receipts, notes, and business cards from restaurants and shops, including two for antique shops. Josette had mentioned Libby dated a guy who'd likely worked at an antique shop. I had to check these out.

I put everything back in the box. Not wanting Dad's letters in the apartment, I decided to stash the box at Luc's. Besides, if Bruno returned when I was gone, he'd likely tear the place apart and find the hidden cash. I marched down to Luc's and stood in front of his door, my heart thumping. I nibbled at my lower lip, unsure how to act after our first argument. Actually, it'd been more of a minor disagreement.

Before I could overanalyze it, I rapped on the door. Luc answered, smelling like he'd just doused himself in fresh, musky cologne. He had on a short-sleeved, black rayon shirt and clean jeans. A Celtic cross hung around his neck. Very spiffy for Luc. He'd replenished his hat's cigarette supply, obviously still stressed about running into Didier.

I held out the hatbox. "Can you keep this?"

"Of course." He took the box and set it on the wine crate table by the couch.

I followed him inside.

He turned to me and leaned in, kissing my cheeks, his lips lingering against my cheek for several moments, then his cheek rested against mine. "I'm sorry," he whispered, his breath warm against my cheek. "I know this is a difficult time for you."

I swallowed hard. "I'm sorry, too."

He drew back slightly, staring into my eyes.

Nervous, I glanced away. "I found business cards for two antique stores. Josette mentioned Libby dated a guy who worked at one. We should check them out."

"I'm sorry. I forgot I'm meeting...a friend."

A *friend*? As in a *woman*?

I stepped back. "Oh, that's okay."

"Maybe Sophie could go with you."

Wherever he was going was obviously more important than helping me find Libby. He wasn't offering to change his plans. It had to be a woman.

"I found my recipes."

He walked into the tiny kitchen. The counter barely had room to make boxed mac and cheese. Not the kitchen of a chef. Had Luc quit his chef job or been fired? It obviously had something to do with his whole *be a puppeteer, not a puppet* mantra. He removed a recipe box from a cardboard box filled with cookbooks and items wrapped in newspaper.

He selected an index card. "Lamb stew would be a good hearty dish for beer drinkers."

I smiled. "Thanks. I'm not so sure about the lamb though, maybe beef instead?"

Luc's brow crinkled.

"I'll need to taste test this using Brecker instead of Guinness. Although I'm sure it's excellent." I scanned the recipe. "Fourteen ingredients? I can't remember the last time I made something with more than *five* ingredients." And everything was in metric weight and volume. No woman in the United States had time to braise lamb for hours. The recipe was a nightmare. I smiled appreciatively. "Thanks."

"This is much easier than the pot pie."

"Easy for you. You're a chef, I'm not.... That's it! A commercial that's like a reality TV show with a beer recipe cook-off between a man and a woman chef. It could be a series of commercials. They start off competing but fall in love with each other's recipes and each other in the end. The recipes could be included on beer cartons."

"That sounds good."

"I just need to make the recipes with Brecker to be able to sell Roger on them."

Rather than offering to make the stew, which he could likely throw together in fifteen minutes with puppets on both hands, Luc kissed my cheeks goodbye. "I'll see you tomorrow. The gallery opens at ten. We should go see your niece first."

Definitely a woman or he'd ask me to tag along. Jealousy ripped through me like Hurricane Samantha barreling across a small Caribbean island.

So much for no strings attached.

I went back to Libby's and quickly typed up the reality TV show and commercial ideas in my marketing plan. I called the hospital anonymously, but Libby hadn't returned. Was it because things had gone well or poorly with her baby's father? Or the baby's father was dead, and she wasn't even with him? Either way, why wasn't she a bit more concerned about her daughter and back at the hospital?

She'd been gone *twelve* hours.

I called the two antique shops. The first one, I got a message. The second, a gentleman informed me they closed in two hours. I called Sophie to see if she'd heard from Alphonse. No such luck. However, she wanted to tag along to the antique shops. Like cemeteries, they were a good way for her to practice her psychic skills. She called the shop where I'd gotten a message. The message said the number was no longer in service.

I met Sophie at the Venus Café. We walked through the *Métro,* and the mother and her two little girls were gone. Sophie assured me they stayed in a very nice family shelter nearby. Their clothes had been in okay shape, and the family appeared to have access to a shower. Hopefully Sophie was right.

Le Temps Retrouvé was located a few blocks from the Louvre. I never understood what people saw in antiques. You paid way more for an item that was hundreds of years old than what a similar item would cost new. I could understand having antiques if they'd been in your family forever. I just didn't understand the idea of buying somebody else's old stuff.

We walked into the shop, and I spied a cradle that Libby would love. Paintings of small, white bunnies adorned the head and foot panels, and intricate carvings wrapped around the spindles. It cost nine hundred euros. That was insane. Had Napoleon slept in it as a baby?

I immediately ruled out the salesman as Libby's potential boyfriend. Monsieur Stick Up His Ass, a short, gray-haired gentleman who looked like he had twenty years on the oldest piece of furniture there. He was a bit peeved we were searching for a man who worked there rather than a nineteenth-century portrait of some homely aristocratic family or a fraying book written by an obscure French philosopher even the French had never heard of.

"Monsieur Beaufay works here also. But he is at his store in Rouen today."

"He's the owner?"

"*Oui, Mademoiselle.* Three shops."

I pictured the owner even more pretentious than this guy. Not to mention, he was likely much older than Libby to own three upscale shops, which also meant he was a stable businessman. So not Libby's type. Same as Pascal.

"Is there another man who works here, by chance?"

He shook his head. "Gerrard works at the shop in Rouen. He is retiring soon. I don't know who works at the shop in Dijon. That is new."

"Okay, thank you." So either the guy worked in Dijon or for the other antique shop that had gone out of business.

We started to walk away.

"Oh, Julien Chaffee used to work here. He moved to Venice a few months ago to be a gondolier." He rolled his eyes. "He was very bizarre. He didn't even speak Italian and decides one day to become a gondolier."

"Sounds like Libby's type." As if I had time to paddle around the canals of Venice searching for a gondolier serenading tourists in French. But this guy was a step up from psycho Bruno. Funny how everything was relative. Two days ago, I'd have thought a gondolier wasn't good enough for Libby and Dominique. Now, he topped my list of acceptable fathers. As long as he was alive, mentally stable, and made Libby happy.

"Libby Hunter?" the man asked. "You look much like her."

I nodded. "She's my sister."

He smiled at the thought of Libby. Libby made everyone smile. "She would sell us items from estate sales sometimes. I have not seen her since earlier this year. The last item she brought in was a dress. She seemed so sad to sell it. I priced it too high, hoping she'd return for it, but she hasn't. Such a lovely girl."

He walked us over to an ivory-colored satin-and-lace wedding gown then excused himself to assist a customer.

"Why had Libby been sad over selling a wedding dress?" The price tag read 1,499 euros. "Especially when she probably made over a grand on it."

"She must have been getting married and decided not to. She never mentioned she was engaged." Sophie gasped. "She sold it early this year. Maybe she sold it when she found out she was pregnant and her boyfriend did not want to marry her."

"Libby would have told me she was getting married."

"Maybe she wanted to know for sure before she told us."

A woman in her early thirties walked up and admired the gown. She spoke excitedly in rapid French to a friend. Sophie placed her hand against the gown, closing her eyes, a pained expression contorting her features. She opened her eyes and spoke to the woman. The woman's smile faded, and she walked off, shooting disturbed glances over her shoulder at Sophie.

"What'd you say to her?" I asked.

"I told her the woman who first owned this dress did not love the man she married. It was likely an arranged marriage. Everyone who wore the dress after her lived sad lives. I told her it would bring bad luck to her marriage."

I raised a skeptical brow.

"I lied. She cannot buy the dress if Libby wants it again."

I brushed my fingertips lightly over the smooth, satiny material. *Were you going to get married, Libby?*

"Ne touchez pas!" the salesman reprimanded me, scurrying over to us. I snapped my hand back from the gown, yet he went off on a tangent.

Sophie glanced over at me. "He would like us to leave. He says I am frightening his customers." She pointed at a tapestry cushion, her voice filling with conviction.

The man gasped in horror, looking freaked out.

I leaned toward Sophie. "What'd you say to him?"

"I told him an elderly woman died on that cushion, and he should not sell it. It has very negative energy. I am right, and he wants to know how I know this. I told him, but he does not believe me."

I studied the cushion for blood stains or other obvious signs of death but didn't find any. How *had* she known the story behind the cushion?

The man eyed Sophie in a similar manner as the townspeople of Salem had likely eyed a witch before burning her at the stake.

I didn't blame him for not believing Sophie. However, I feared Sophie was beginning to make a believer out of me.

Chapter Fourteen

Disheartened by another dead end, I needed to feel like I was accomplishing something. And I needed some serious comfort food. Sophie and I went shopping for the ingredients for Luc's lamb stew. I had to suck it up and learn to cook if I was going to pitch this idea.

Brecker wasn't real popular in France, so few stores carried it. I sent Sophie to Hôtel de l'Opéra to get some bottles from Hannah. Sophie didn't cook and had no clue where to buy spices, so I called Luc, happy to interrupt his little liaison. He gave me the address of a spice shop that catered to chefs. The shop was overwhelming with thousands of spices filling the shelves. Luckily, the salesgirl took pity on me and filled my order. I stopped at a charcuterie for a half a kilogram of lamb. I asked Sophie to stop by a produce stand and buy potatoes and carrots.

By the time we met back at Libby's, it was nine p.m.

We were getting organized in the kitchen when footsteps echoed down the hall and a door closed. Luc was home from his date, or possibly his date was home with him. Trying to focus on the recipe rather than what type of woman Luc might have in his apartment, I heated the oil and started browning the lamb. I opened the bottle of Bordeaux I'd bought for moral support.

Sophie opened a bottle of Brecker and took a drink. "Mmm. This is very good. Beer, it is getting much more popular here." She removed a scale from the cupboard to measure out the dry ingredients.

"Luc's recipe doesn't say if this bay leaf should be chopped, crushed, or what." This recipe had to be perfect, and I really wanted to see if Luc had brought a woman home with him. "I'll be right back. I'm going to go ask Luc."

I walked down to Luc's and paused in front of the door, preparing myself for who might be on the other side. What would I do if Luc answered the door half naked with a woman in his bed? No time for being neurotic, I rapped on the door, heart pounding. Luc answered. I gazed past him. No naked woman on the pull-out sofa. I breathed a relieved sigh.

"Looking for someone?" He raised an intrigued brow.

"Just didn't want to interrupt if you had company."

He smiled. "I'm alone. Did you find the father at the antique shops?"

I shook my head. "One is out of business, and the guy at the other one is old enough to be the baby's great-grandpa. But she sold stuff there, including a wedding dress. I wonder if it was hers. Did she mention possibly getting engaged?"

Luc shook his head. "Why would she have kept that a secret?"

She seemed to have been keeping a lot of secrets.

"I'm sure Libby will want to spend the night at the hospital. She'll be back."

I shrugged. "I'm making that lamb stew recipe and—"

"You're cooking?" A crooked smile curled the corners of Luc's mouth.

I regretted telling Luc I was a completely incompetent cook, but he was about to find out anyway.

I raised the bay leaf in my hand. "What do I do with this? Chop, crumble, what?"

"You put it in whole."

"Oh. Thanks. See you later."

I returned to Libby's, and the aroma of onion and garlic greeted me. I threw the bay leaf in the pot.

Sophie picked up a sprig of rosemary. "It says a few sprigs of rosemary and thyme. Is that a few of each?"

"No way am I going to ask Luc. He already thinks I'm a complete idiot. Let's do a sprig and a half of each to be safe."

A rap sounded at the door.

Bruno? I grabbed a pan and headed cautiously toward the door. "Who is it?" I demanded.

"Luc."

I lowered the pan and opened the door.

"I forgot to tell you that you remove the bay leaf before serving the soup. It's for flavor; you don't eat it. It would not be good to digest."

"Ah, yeah, I knew that."

He smirked. *Yeah, right.* He glanced cautiously toward the kitchen.

"Bonjour." Sophie gave him a wave then yelled out, *"Merde!"*

Luc and I flew into the kitchen. Sophie had sliced her finger with the knife, and drops of blood dotted the cutting board and rosemary.

We studied the cut, which wasn't deep at all.

"You probably just need a Band-Aid," I said.

"Yes, it is not so bad," she said.

"Yes, it is." I eyed the blood on the rosemary. "I don't know if I have enough rosemary."

Luc stared in horror at the rosemary. He swept the chopped rosemary in the garbage and washed the blood off the cutting board. "You don't chop the rosemary with the stem. You must remove from the stem first. Like this." He held a sprig at the top of the stem and ran his fingers in the opposite direction of the way the leaves grew. "And now you chop just the leaves."

"Ah," Sophie and I said in unison.

"That could make a difference in the taste, huh?" I said.

Luc looked at me like I'd just asked if I could use chopped grass instead of rosemary. "But of course. It wouldn't be good with the stem. You were serious. You don't cook much."

I shook my head.

Luc eyed the knife forever. He'd created this recipe for Fiona and her family. A lot of memories tied to one little recipe. I suddenly regretted involving him, not wanting to cause him pain. I was about to assure him I could chop rosemary when he hesitantly picked up the knife and slowly started chopping.

He tossed the knife on the counter. "This knife is no good. No wonder you cut yourself." He went to his apartment and returned with a block of knives. He selected one and began chopping with expertise. Sophie and I watched in awe.

"Go." He pointed the knife toward the living room.

I smiled. "Thanks."

Sophie and I walked out of the kitchen, and I paused at the dining room table to check my fan page.

713 Likes.

"Is that your Facebook page?" Sophie peered over my shoulder.

I explained my situation.

"I once lost my job as a waitress because the owner said men waiters made the restaurant more refined. I will like your page." Sophie glanced at Luc in the kitchen. "Have you seen Samantha's page?"

Luc walked out, wiping his hand on a towel. He scanned my page, smiling. "This is a good protest."

"See, I'm not a puppet."

He smiled wider and walked back into the kitchen.

Sophie and I pulled two dining room chairs onto the balcony. Ten minutes later, Luc joined us for a glass of wine. "The lamb must simmer at least an hour. Better it is two, but we will be eating stew for breakfast if we wait that long."

Luc and I drank wine while Sophie downed two bottles of Brecker. She'd be a great spokesperson for the beer. An hour flew by, and Luc added potatoes and carrots and more beef stock to the stew. The apartment was basking in the aroma of spices. It had to simmer another thirty to sixty minutes. Sophie had to open the café early, so she couldn't stick around.

"Do you have any recipes with beef?" I asked Luc.

"Shepherd's pie is another hearty dish."

He went to his apartment and returned with the recipe.

It had four sections. How to make potato filling, meat filling, gravy, and how to put it all together. "Four recipes to make one dish is never going to fly. It will have to be altered, like using a dry gravy mix and frozen veggies."

Luc looked like he was going to faint. "Frozen vegetables?" The timer on his cell phone went off. "It's done."

Luc dished up two bowls of stew. I took a spoonful. The lamb melted in my mouth it was so tender.

"Mmm..." I took another bite. "Ohh..." I moaned.

Luc smiled, taking the bowl from my hand.

"Hey," I said, my spoon following the bowl to the counter. "This isn't a taste test. I plan to eat it all."

He set down the bowl and stepped toward me with a playful look. He slipped the spoon from my hand, and I swallowed hard. He brushed a stray strand of hair behind my ear, and his hand lingered. He held my gaze, his look turning steamy. He swept a finger below my lip then slipped it in my mouth. I licked it, tasting stew, which I'd apparently dribbled on my chin. How romantic.

He eased me up against the counter, placing his hands on my waist. He brushed his lips against mine, slipping his tongue and the taste of garlic and spices into my mouth. Our tongues slowly got acquainted. He drew his head back slightly, gazing deep into my eyes as if gauging my reaction. In case he didn't see the green lights flashing in my eyes, I curled my fingers into his white cotton shirt and pulled him to me, seizing his mouth. He slid his hands around to the small of my back and drew me snugly against him. He deepened the kiss with a sense of urgency, and our hands were all over each other, neither of us coming up for air. Then Luc's hands suddenly stopped exploring my body and rested on my waist, and the fervor of his kisses slowed to a gentle caress.

Luc drew his head back slightly, and I slowly opened my eyes, gazing at him through a haze of lust.

"I should probably go," he whispered, his breath warm against my face. He traced a finger along my chin. "But this was very nice."

I nodded. "Thanks," I said in a breathless tone. "I mean for your help with cooking."

He smiled. "I'll see you in the morning." He turned and left.

I stood there leaning against the counter for several minutes, mind reeling, lips pulsating, my entire body ready to self-combust. Why had Luc left when he could have taken me right there on the kitchen floor? Was this about me, the date he'd had tonight, or Fiona?

Frustrated, and having lost my appetite for the stew, I pulled the chairs in from the balcony and dropped down on one at the table. Trying to get my body temp back to normal, I checked my Facebook page.

794 Likes.

The latest post was by a single mother who worked in IT, a male-dominated industry. She said being passed up for promotions was more about respect than money. She'd considered changing careers but didn't want her daughters to think she was a quitter. Women could succeed at whatever they wanted. She told me to never give up!

I commented on her post.

> *I know how difficult it is being a single mom. It's a lot of responsibility financially and emotionally. It's tough juggling a career and family, especially when you're the main provider. I respect what you're doing, and I'm sure your daughters do also. And I admire that you're in IT. I'm inept when it comes to computers. ☺ Hang in there!*

Technically, I wasn't a *mom*, but I'd raised Libby and been my mom's caretaker. And I knew how hard it was to have a career and be responsible for a family.

Another post was by a woman who worked for a brewery. Curious about where she worked, I went to her page. She lived in England. She'd posted the link to my fan page in her status, asking her friends to post it to their statuses. Besides that video, no wonder I was getting so many Likes, my fan page had become a chain letter.

My private life was going viral on the worldwide social network. However, nobody knew it was *my* life. Yet.

—◌ ◌—

My eyes shot open, staring into total darkness. I slid my lavender eye mask onto my forehead, and the apartment slowly came into focus, dimly lit by the ambient, yellow light of the streetlamps below. I lay on Libby's bed, my white cotton pajama top soaked with sweat, clinging to my body.

The phone shrilled, shattering the peaceful evening air. Bruno probably assumed if he called in the middle of the night, he was sure to get Libby. It wasn't Libby calling, since she didn't know I was here. I grabbed my cell off the nightstand and checked the time. Three a.m. I'd just gone to bed two hours ago after reading all my fan page posts.

I felt around on the pillow for the earplug that had fallen out. The machine picked up, and a dial tone blared out of the speaker. Even Bruno's dead air sounded sinister. I closed my eyes, trying to block out Bruno, and saw Pascal's face. My eyes shot open, but Pascal's stern features remained as I recalled the nightmare I'd been having. Pascal had fired his son for shaving my head. I felt my head, making sure I had a full head of hair. The dream had seemed so real.

I had no clue how to even begin analyzing it.

Something told me I was better off not knowing.

A flash of light from the apartment building across the street caught my eye. Monsieur Fleurs's TV washed his apartment in a blue glow. Why wasn't he in bed? Restless leg syndrome, insomnia, nobody to share his bed with? All those catnaps he took during the day undoubtedly kept him up nights. The TV sound didn't carry out his open balcony doors, so he either had the volume low or off. At least he was considerate of his neighbors. Unlike my neighbor Rod who'd installed a kick-ass sound system six months ago. Besides being rude, I couldn't tell you one other thing about Rod. I knew more about Monsieur Fleurs than I did Rod.

I squinted into his apartment. Although I didn't see him, knowing he was there, possibly awake like me, gave me a strange sense of comfort. Suddenly, I wanted to know my neighbor.

Chapter Fifteen

A rap sounded at the door.

Did that psycho ever sleep?

"Go away," I yelled.

"Not without you," Luc responded on the other side.

Talk about a shot of adrenaline!

I flew out of bed. "Just a minute," I called out, trying not to sound totally panicked about Luc seeing me after I'd just rolled out of bed! I zipped into the bathroom and peered in the mirror. Ugh. I threw my hair up in a clip and splashed cold water on my face. I grabbed Libby's red kimono robe and threw it on over my undies, tightening the sash. I opened the door with a perky smile.

Luc eyed my robe, an intrigued smile curling the corners of his mouth. I glanced down. I'd pulled the sash so tight the satin was molding against my nipples. Did Luc now regret not sticking around last night? I swallowed hard, recalling our steamy encounter in the kitchen. "Ah, what's up? It's kind of early."

Luc's gaze darted up, meeting mine. "This is the time to go to the market. The stew wasn't the best last night because the ingredients weren't as fresh as they should be. If you're going to make the shepherd's pie for your boss, you can't use frozen vegetables or a gravy mix."

"And we need to get those ingredients at six a.m.?"

"The market opens at seven. We have to leave in a half hour. I'll be at my apartment." He gave my robe another glance before turning and leaving.

"Ah, okay, I guess this means you're helping me?"

"I am *supervising* you," he said over his shoulder.

Suddenly, cooking didn't suck nearly as much.

I walked through the shower and threw myself together as best I could. A half hour later, Luc and I were walking down the streets of Paris. The swishing sound of a passing street sweeper and a cheerful exchange of *bonjours* between a produce deliveryman and a market owner filled the peaceful morning air. We walked in companionable silence, enjoying the Zen-like quality of the early-morning hours in Paris. It was as if this had been our daily routine for years.

We'd been walking for fifteen minutes when rows of yellow awnings came into view, lining the street ahead. Not yet seven, people were filtering into the market, the sound of lively chatting carrying down the street. As we neared, Luc's pace slowed, and he reached for a cigarette in his hat. He tapped a nervous finger against the cigarette then lowered his hand. He took a cinnamon mint from his pants pocket and popped it in his mouth. If he hadn't cooked in almost two years, he likely hadn't shopped at an open-air market either. Luc had undoubtedly been surviving on hot dogs the past year.

Feeling the need to break the silence and lighten his thoughts, I said, "This place is huge. Are they here every day?"

"Twice a week, but there are many markets throughout Paris. The food is brought in from around France, except for items that can't be grown here, like bananas."

"So the potatoes aren't from Idaho?"

He smiled. "Ah, no."

A petite, elderly woman behind a stand displaying jars of confit de canard and foie gras spotted Luc and threw her arms up in the air, smiling wide. The apprehensive look on Luc's face disappeared. She whisked out from behind her stand and greeted him with a kiss to each cheek. Luc introduced me to Madame Charron.

The woman's look softened, and she placed a gentle hand on Luc's arm. "How have you been?"

He nodded faintly, looking a bit uncomfortable with her compassion. "Fine. How have you been with the new grandson?"

Her brown eyes brightened, and she snatched baby photos from her purse and handed them to Luc. "He looks like his grandmother, *non*?" she asked proudly.

Luc smiled. *"Ouais."*

I nodded in agreement. The little guy had big, brown eyes and dark hair. He wore a wide smile, looking as bubbly as his grandmother.

While she showed off her grandson to passersby, Luc spread a sample of her foie gras on a sliced baguette and handed me a piece. I took a bite, the pâté melting in my mouth, same as the lamb the night before. He swept the bread under his nose, inhaling a deep breath, then took a bite and smiled. I'd already polished mine off. Luc bought a jar and slipped it into his green shopping bag.

"My grandson will be here in a few weeks. You can see him."

Luc nodded noncommittally and said goodbye.

We walked on.

"Madame Charron comes six hours from Toulouse every week to sell her confit de canard and specialties of that region." Luc stopped in front of a man selling a slew of olives. "There are more than forty varieties of olives here, all made in different ways."

"Don't tell me you make your own olive oil for this recipe?"

Luc's gaze narrowed. "You don't use olive oil in shepherd's pie. But Monsieur Fournier has twenty varieties." He selected a bottle and removed the top. "Close your eyes." He swept it under my nose. "What do you smell?"

I inhaled a deep breath and opened my eyes. "Vanilla?"

"Very good. Vanilla and truffle. It is *fruite noir*." He poured a dollop on his finger and raised it to my lips. I licked off the oil, and a rich, mushroomy vanilla taste filled my mouth. Luc's finger lingered on my lips, and I raised my gaze, meeting his. He smiled and slowly lowered his finger.

Who knew shopping could be such a turn-on?

Monsieur Fournier stopped talking to a client and glanced over at us. His eyes widened in surprise. "Luc!" He rattled off something in French, and they shook hands vigorously. Luc introduced us. The man had us sample a tapenade with a fresh baguette. Luc sniffed the spread, and I did the same before wolfing it down like I had the foie gras.

"Mmm. Sun-dried tomatoes?" I asked.

The man nodded. "It is good, *non*?"

"It's excellent," I said.

He gave Luc an enthusiastic grin. "So, you are working again?"

Luc shook his head. "Not at a restaurant."

"Chez Andre is looking for a chef. I think the man they have is English. He knows nothing about cooking." He clamped a hand down on Luc's shoulder, peering over at me. "This is the best chef in Paris. He knows olive oils."

Luc smiled. "I know you make the best ones."

"And this is the most important thing to know." The man let out a hearty laugh.

Luc bought the tapenade and the bottle of olive oil.

"I hope to see you next week." The man embraced Luc, giving him a pat on the back.

Luc nodded. "I'll see you soon."

We continued on.

"You know everyone here. I couldn't tell you the name of one person at my grocery store." But this was more than a shopping experience, it was a social hour. There was an art to shopping here.

Luc arched an intrigued brow like he wasn't sure if I was kidding, and then he looked like he felt bad for me.

It took Luc fifteen minutes to select the perfect carrots, onions, and potatoes. I pictured myself zipping through the grocery store and filling an entire cart in fifteen minutes flat. That was it. An idea for the second segment in my commercial series. The chefs, a man and woman, were unknowingly shopping at the same open-air market, selecting items for their famous dishes. Their next stop was a liquor store where they both reached for the last six-pack of Brecker for their recipes. Who would get the last six-pack? Stay tuned for the next commercial. I smiled.

After an hour at the market, we finally had the ingredients needed for *one* dish, along with a dozen other items we'd taste tested. I'd likely put on three pounds since starting our shopping expedition.

"So, this was nice, seeing everyone you haven't seen in a while?"

Luc nodded, smiling, all the cigarettes in his hat still intact. "I've missed them, and cooking. It was good for me to come here. I'll be back next week." He gazed off into the market. "Last night was the first time I cooked in almost two years. Cooking was my passion. I'm sure Fiona believed I loved it even more than her. When she became ill, I didn't believe it was serious. She was always so full of life. I thought she'd get better and nothing bad could happen to her."

He lit up a cigarette. "I was head chef at a new restaurant and worked many hours. This was my big chance. I missed out on so much time we could have spent together. I couldn't get that back. I quit my job to care for her. To perform puppet shows because she loved them but could no longer go to the park to watch them." He shook his head. "I'll never forgive myself."

A lump of emotion swelled in my throat. I reached out and touched Luc's hand. He glanced down at my hand on his, his eyes watering. "I'm sure she forgave you."

"I'll never let a job consume my life again. All I ever wanted to be was a chef, but it should never have been more important than Fiona."

"There must be a middle ground. Some way you wouldn't have to work so many hours." Although I hadn't found mine.

Luc shook his head, taking a drag on his cigarette.

Luc and I were more alike than I'd realized. But I couldn't imagine having a passion for one job, let alone two. Did Luc truly have a passion for being a puppeteer, or was it a way to keep Fiona's memory alive and to live with his regret?

I was sticking all the shepherd's pie ingredients in the fridge when my cell phone rang. Sophie.

"I know where Libby is," Sophie said excitedly.

"Where?"

"In a room someplace by herself."

"In a room *where*?"

"I am not certain. My dream, it was not clear."

Oh boy, a dream.

"There was a blue blanket on the bed and a rocking chair. The room, it was much warm. She was on the bed crying."

After the antique store last night, I had a tad more faith in Sophie's dreams. Just a tad. But the mere possibility of Libby alone in a room somewhere crying killed me.

"You should bring me something of Libby's. It would help me see more clearer."

"Okay." I recalled my disturbing dream, an eerie feeling creeping over me. Sophie could undoubtedly provide insight. "I had a dream about Pascal Rochant."

"He came to you in your sleep? What did he want?"

"He didn't *want* anything. I'm sure I dreamed about him because I found the funeral a bit upsetting."

I explained the dream in detail.

"Oh," Sophie said in a clipped tone. "He must have felt a connection with you and contacted *you* instead of *me*." She sounded put out with me, like I'd stolen her client.

"He wasn't contacting me. It was merely a dream."

"He will not cross over unless his issues are resolved. Libby would want him to cross. I will try to talk with his son today."

"Remember to ask Alphonse what Pascal left Libby in his will."

"Okay."

We said goodbye.

I noticed the piece of plaster had fallen from the mural. When I picked up the piece off the floor, the edges crumbled away. Afraid it would fall again and become even more damaged, I placed it on the table. After searching for glue and coming up empty-handed, I stared at the piece with Libby's and my hands clasped together. I should be with Libby, holding her hand, taking care of her. Like I had after Dad left. What if I hadn't been there for her?

What if *she* hadn't been there for *me*? Libby had made me feel loved and needed. If she hadn't needed taking care of, I might have been like Mom and never have gotten out of bed, especially since

I'd blamed myself. She'd given me a sense of purpose, of worth.

I stared at the mural.

Why didn't you tell me about Dad, Libby?

And where the hell are you?

Almost twenty-four hours since Libby had left the hospital.

I glanced around, as if searching for Libby, and noticed the flowers on the balcony limp from dehydration. Libby's pride and joy. I rushed out to the flowers. Across the street, Monsieur Fleurs sat smugly amongst vibrantly colored blooms, shaking his head. He picked up something and tossed it toward my balcony. The item fell shy and dropped to the street below. I ran down and picked up the small box containing round sticks. Plant food.

I peered up at Monsieur Fleurs gazing down at me and held up the box. *"Merci,"* I called out.

He nodded.

The florist next door was placing flats of colorful flowers on tables outside her shop. I needed to replace the dead daisies in the vase. I walked inside, and the petite, elderly saleswoman in a red floral dress gave me a friendly *bonjour*, which I returned. The small beagle at her feet barked *bonjour*, and the woman introduced her as Gigi. I scratched behind her ears, and she trotted behind me, assisting me in selecting a bouquet of daisies. Upon checking out, the woman introduced herself as Cecile and told me to come back and visit her and Gigi.

I went back to Libby's and replaced the daisies in the vase and stuck a plant food stick in each pot, giving the flowers a little pep talk.

I booted up my computer and opened my Facebook fan page.

1,312 Likes.

Wow! I'd had 847 Likes when I went to bed. One woman who'd sued her company for discrimination gave me her e-mail if I wanted to contact her for info. It wouldn't come to suing. I was going to blow away the VP of marketing and Roger with my new marketing plan.

There was an icon in the left corner with a number one on it. I clicked on it to find a message from Ella, the IT woman.

Thanks for your comment. I'm pretty much the sole provider for the family. My ex-husband is a total deadbeat. Even more so than the financial responsibility, it's hard being a role model and having two little girls looking up to you. Sometimes it's a lot of pressure. Sorry. Don't mean to whine. ☺

I'd always tried to be a role model to Libby, but rather than looking up to me, she tried hard *not* to be like me. Hopefully I'd be a good role model for Dominique.

I can relate to deadbeat dads. And it's hard when you try to be a role model yet the person wants to be the opposite of you. You wonder what you did wrong. Okay, guess I'm whining also. But thanks for listening. Will try to be more positive!

I wondered what her husband did to be a deadbeat dad but didn't want to pry.

I forwarded thirteen e-mails to Evan.

I glanced over at the puppet relaxing against the vase of daisies. "See, I'm not a puppet. I deserve this promotion."

Still no e-mail from Roger confirming the time and location of our meeting that day. With as crazy as I'd been acting, Evan had likely taken my blackmail threat seriously, and he and Roger were busy compiling my promotion offer. Roger would be contacting me by the end of the day. I could feel it.

I went into the bathroom and stared at myself in the mirror. Maybe it was the chestnut-colored hair or stress, but my skin did look a bit blah. I decided to try the shampoo from Pascal's salon. My hair turned out auburn, not flaming red. I tossed my hair up in the clip. I slipped on the *Mange-moi* thong from Carmen's, feeling a little sassy after my kiss with Luc last night. I threw on a pair of Libby's jeans and a lime green camisole. My oversized Marc Jacobs bag wasn't meant for riding on a scooter, so I decided to use Libby's orange backpack purse.

I walked out of the bathroom and noticed two calls had come in when I was in the shower or out running around this morning.

"I have some exciting news," Mom said. "I quit my job. Ken and I are going to travel around in his RV. We're going to Mount Rushmore. Can't imagine how they carved something so big in stone. We're leaving in two weeks. Tell your sister to call me when you see her. Love you." She disconnected.

How was she going to pay for all her online shopping? I couldn't fund Mom's retirement in addition to helping support Libby and my niece. Although I was upset, I was happy that things were going so well with Ken. She hadn't dated for ten years after Dad left. And then she'd dated one loser after another. Hopefully Mom wasn't off her meds but just on a high because everything was going so well with Ken. I'd worry about her finances later. I had enough to worry about.

Libby's soft voice was barely audible on the machine.

"I called the hotel, but you're not there, and I can't remember your cell number. I hope you get this message. I'm sorry I didn't call sooner. I didn't go to see the baby's father. I went to..." She started sobbing. "I can't..." She gasped a sob. "I'm sorry."

Click.

She went to what? And she can't what? Go back to the hospital? Come home, ever? There was a note of finality in her *I'm sorry* that I couldn't shake.

I couldn't believe she'd left me hanging like that. At least I knew she was alive, but she didn't sound all right. And she certainly didn't sound like she was on her way back to the hospital. What if she didn't return before I had to leave at the end of the week? Would authorities allow me to take Dominique out of the country? I couldn't take care of a baby. I also couldn't allow her to be placed in foster care. What if she ended up with someone like Nurse Nasty? Precisely what I'd always feared would happen to Libby and me. Libby wouldn't allow that to happen to her child. Besides not abandoning her child, Libby would never abandon me.

Except she had, when she'd come to Paris.

The responsibility of a baby had probably sunk in, and Libby had panicked. Yet I was realizing Libby wasn't as irresponsible as she used to be. She'd made a stable life for herself in Paris and had a lot of people who relied on her.

I needed to get to the hospital and see my niece. What if her doctor contacted the police as Nurse Nasty had threatened?

—◌ ◌—

Luc answered his door in a pair of Levis, sans shirt, and wet hair. I about fainted flat-out. I fought the urge to reach out and feel up his stomach rippling with muscles. He kissed my cheeks, and I air-kissed his in return. I told him about Libby's message.

He looked confused. "She can't *what*?"

"Exactly. What the hell is that supposed to mean?"

"I'm sure she'll call back." He snagged a white cotton shirt off a chair and slipped it on, leaving it untucked. Tendrils of hair fell over his eyes, and he finger-combed them back from his face. Thank God the electrical wiring was too ancient for blow-dryers.

"She sure as hell better. I'm worried sick about her.

She obviously isn't worried about Dominique or me. I have to find her. I could hire a detective, but if none of us can find her, how would a detective? What am I going to tell the hospital today?"

Luc placed a calming hand on my arm, gazing deep into my eyes. "We'll find her. I promise."

My shoulders relaxed slightly, and I nodded, even though I wasn't convinced.

Luc's cell went off. He eyed the number with apprehension. The phone stopped ringing. "Didier."

"You don't want to talk to him?"

"I saw him last night."

I was relieved that Didier had been his date, not some woman.

"Didier is my brother. He wants me to see my parents, but I don't know if I'm ready."

"You haven't seen them in a while either?"

"Not since Fiona died more than a year ago. When he called and asked me to meet last night, I wasn't going to go. Then I thought about Libby. I know she'll be back, but I realized how much I would miss Didier if he left France and I never saw him again."

My stomach tossed at the thought of never seeing Libby again. I wondered what Fiona's death had to do with Luc cutting ties with his family.

"I admire the way you take care of your family, and you are always there for them."

"I don't know if I'm *always* there for them."

But I couldn't imagine cutting ties with Libby and Mom for as long as a year. I spoke to Mom on the phone weekly and saw her a few times a month. I needed to stay in better touch with Libby, yet I never went more than a few months without e-mailing or talking to her on the phone. Granted, they drove me nuts sometimes, but they'd have to do something really awful for me to never see them again. Look at everything Libby had done behind my back. I was furious, yet I would never disown her.

"Libby told me you were like a mother to her growing up. I haven't been nearly as good of a brother to Didier as you have been a sister to Libby. I'm going to be a better brother."

"Why haven't you seen your family for so long?"

He shrugged. "A story for another time."

Luc obviously didn't want to discuss his family further, so I changed the subject. "I should go shopping, or Dominique won't have anything when she gets home from the hospital."

"That would be good." Luc selected a princess and a prince puppet from a shelf lined with puppets. "I'll put on a show in the children's ward." He traced a gentle finger over the princess's black hair. "I hope you didn't mind me talking about Fiona earlier. I haven't talked about her for so long."

"I'd love to hear more about her." Luc was opening up to me about his wife and his family. Nobody opened up to me.

"It's easier if I don't. Too many regrets." He took a deep breath, as if cleansing the thoughts from his mind.

Luc had obviously loved his wife dearly and felt a huge sense of loss over her death. I didn't feel a great loss over losing Evan. Besides material items, like his Picasso prints and elliptical machine, there had to be some things I would miss about Evan. Yet I didn't have that hollow feeling you should have when you break up with someone after being together three years. Probably because I had already been alone. As much as Luc mourned the loss of his wife, I envied him for having experienced a love so strong that losing that person was like losing part of yourself. I had *never* experienced such a love. My chest tightened.

What if I never did?

Chapter Sixteen

I browsed the toy section, toting a purple Barbie suitcase. Dominique was too young for it, but I'd had a similar one when I was little. After Dad left, my toys came from rummage sales, and Libby got my hand-me-downs.

While Luc marveled at the vast array of children's puppets, I headed for the baby section. I was debating between a bunny or giraffe blanket when Hannah called. I answered the phone to tell her she had to start contacting Evan.

"Natalie Darwin is super pissed at me. She called at midnight that the hotel wanted to stick Katsumi in the doggie jail and that it was inhumane."

"Doggie jail?"

"Some room away from guests because she was making tons of noise barking at Roger. She can't stand him. I could hear Roger yelling in the background. I haven't heard him so pissed off since firing that guy over drinking Budweiser. I offered to call the manager, and Natalie said she was useless and hung up on me. What did she want me to do? Post bail? What should I have done?"

"I'd have taken Katsumi in my room."

I'd rather have psycho Bruno calling and harassing me at midnight than Natalie Darwin.

"I'm glad I didn't. Katsumi spent the night in jail. Roger looks like shit. Serves him right for what he's doing to you. I don't think he slept all night."

Probably not, between the Katsumi ordeal and the hotel's sheets chafing his skin.

"Not like he can fire me while we're here. I so admire you for sticking up for our rights. After this, they'll think twice about screwing with women in this company. I can't believe all of your Likes on Facebook. It's awesome!" She disconnected.

Hannah was right. Although I wasn't trying to be a martyr, the stand I was taking wasn't just for me but for every woman in the company.

Ten minutes later, my arms and the Barbie suitcase were filled with blankets, booties, toys, and stuffed animals. Luc went pedaling past on a pink Hello Kitty tricycle, his legs spread wide, knees knocking against the handlebars. Mickey and Minnie Mouse puppets sat in the front basket, and I imagined them squealing *weeeeee* as they sped along. Luc smiled, waving as if in a parade, then disappeared behind an aisle of toys.

I laughed, glancing around at the people watching him, including Oxford Guy two aisles over, holding a doll. Only he wore a jean jacket today. Two times could maybe be a coincidence, but three times, no way. My heart raced.

What the hell did this guy want?

Luc walked up smiling, toting the trike in one hand, the puppets in the other. "This is a very good bike. It rides well."

"She's a little young for it." I glanced in the direction of Oxford Guy. He'd vanished. I told Luc about him, and he took off to find him.

Luc returned a few minutes later. "I didn't see him. I don't think you should go anywhere by yourself until we know who this guy is."

A great excuse to spend all my time with Luc.

Luc slipped the puppets on his hands and left a trail of giggling kids as we walked toward the checkout.

The clerk gestured to my purchases, speaking French.

Luc smiled, peering over at me. "No, we're not new parents. She's a new aunt."

"A very kind aunt," the clerk said.

"I don't have kids, so I get to spoil my niece."

Luc insisted on buying the puppets for Dominique. After packing what I could in the Barbie suitcase, I still had two bags to carry. I'd be taking a taxi to the hospital. Luc rolled the Barbie suitcase behind him. As we walked out, I realized I hadn't bought many practical items. No bibs, diapers, or bottles. I'd gotten so caught up with all the fun stuff, I'd never referred to my list.

"Do you want children?" Luc asked.

I shook my head. "I work too much. I'm never home."

"So work less."

"I can't afford to work less. Besides, it was always my dream to travel. To get out of the small town I grew up in. Even if I worked fewer hours, I still wouldn't want kids. Not wanting kids doesn't make me a bad person." I sounded defensive.

"Of course not. You're a very good person. I think you would make a good mother. That's why I wonder why it is you don't want children."

I slowed my pace, staring in disbelief at Luc. "You think I'd make a good mother?"

Nobody had ever told me that before.

"But of course. You're a compassionate person. You take very good care of Libby and now your niece." He glanced at the bags in my hands. "Even if you didn't know what you needed to buy, you learned. Parents don't know how to care for a baby at first. They learn."

Like I'd learned to take care of Libby. When Mom wouldn't get out of bed in the morning, I'd get Libby ready for school. I made dinner, even if it was only TV dinners or mac and cheese with cut-up hot dogs, Libby's favorite.

But these hadn't been maternal instincts that had kicked in when Dad left. They'd been survival instincts.

—◌ ◌—

As usual, nobody was manning the maternity ward's reception desk, and I didn't recognize any of the nurses scurrying around. I wanted to march up to one and demand she ask my purpose for being there. I waltzed right into the nursery. I slipped my hand through the small, oval opening in the incubator's side and gently massaged Dominique's tummy, wondering why she was no longer in a shallow crib. She peered up at me with soft, brown eyes framed with thick lashes. I smiled, not wanting her to sense my concern. Nurse Perky—short, blonde, and bubbly—was on the phone, so I couldn't ask what was up with the incubator.

I managed to stuff the giraffe blanket through the incubator's opening and smoothed it over Dominique. I pictured her at home where she belonged, me rocking her to sleep in the cradle from the antique store.

"Uncle Luc's gonna do a puppet show for you after he's done putting one on for the big kids." I brushed a gentle finger over her cheek, which felt a bit too warm. "You look just like your mommy. She'll be back soon. Yes, she will."

A tall, gray-haired doctor dressed in blue scrubs and a white jacket approached. His name tag read Dr. Bouliveau. "I would like to speak with you about your niece."

"Libby did not abandon her. I guarantee it. If she—"

"I didn't say she had." He looked confused and a bit impatient. "I must speak with her. I tried calling her house, but nobody answers the phone."

"She's helping the baby's father plan his dad's funeral. What did you need to talk to her about?" My gaze darted to the incubator. "It's about why my niece is in there, isn't it?"

"Maybe it would be best if we sat down and talked."

I swallowed hard. "What's wrong with her?"

"Come." He led me outside the nursery and sat me down in a chair in the hallway.

"She is running a slight fever. If the fever continues or goes higher, we will need to move her to ICU."

I placed a hand to my chest. "What do you think it is?"

"It could just be a virus."

"What else might it be?"

"We are running a few tests."

"What could it be?" I demanded.

"We'll check for spinal meningitis and a few other possibilities. We'll do a CT scan if needed. It could be hydrocephalus, water on the brain, which often resolves itself."

"That sounds awful. What if it doesn't resolve itself?"

"Then we operate and put in a shunt."

"Is this because she was six weeks premature?"

The doctor's gaze narrowed in confusion. "She was only two weeks early."

Why had Libby told me she was due in six weeks?

"Do whatever you have to. I don't care what it costs."

"It's not a concern about money. Her bills are covered. But I need to speak with Libby about how we are proceeding."

"I'll get in touch with her."

The doctor walked away as Bruno stalked down the hall toward me, looking as crazed as ever. He'd followed us shopping? I surged from the chair as Nurse Nasty marched up. I was happy to see her for the first time. If anyone could take out Bruno, it was this woman.

"Did the doctor speak with you about your sister's baby?" she asked.

Bruno stopped dead in his tracks.

I glared at her. "Yes, he did."

"Where is Libby?" Bruno demanded.

Nurse Nasty studied Bruno a moment then said, "Are you the baby's father?"

"Yes, I am," Bruno said, not missing a beat.

What the hell?

"I'm glad one parent is worried enough to return."

I didn't deny Bruno being the father. Not just because I wasn't certain, but because having the father here would keep Nurse Nasty at bay for a while.

She marched off.

Bruno got in my face. "I trade you my baby for the paintings."

"She's not your baby," I shrieked.

"Then why didn't you tell the nurse that? The baby is mine. I will not want the baby if I have my paintings."

I hoped like hell this was a scare tactic and Bruno wasn't seriously the father. Libby would never have been involved with this psycho, unless she hadn't known he was psycho.

"If I had the paintings, I'd give them to you whether you're the father or not."

Bruno's face lit up. "You don't know where Libby is. If she is gone, I know where she is. If you know where the paintings are, you better give them to me." He turned and stalked off.

My heart raced. Was he serious? Or did he think I'd hand over the paintings if I thought he was going to harass Libby? He didn't need to prove he was the father to take away Dominique. Hospital security sucked. If I alerted the nurses that Bruno might kidnap my niece, they might contact the police. But I couldn't risk her safety. I calmly explained to Nurse Perky that if Bruno returned, they'd want to keep an eye on him since this was his first baby and I was a bit nervous.

Luc returned, all smiles after his puppet performance. My hands were still trembling from the Bruno episode.

He obviously noticed my panicked state. "What's wrong?" He crouched in front of me, placing his hands on my knees.

I choked down the lump in my throat and explained Dominique's condition.

Luc enveloped my hand in the warmth of his. "It's probably just a virus." He placed a soft kiss against my palm, and I relaxed slightly.

"What if it isn't?"

"Even if it is more than a virus, they'll figure it out, and she'll be fine." He gave my hand a reassuring squeeze then stood. He snagged a cigarette from his hat and twirled it between his fingers.

I was seeing a pattern here. Cigarette behind the ear was low stress. Twirling it between the fingers meant medium stress or boredom. And smoking it meant major stress. He'd be lighting up right now if we weren't in a hospital!

"See? This is another reason I don't want kids. Besides disrupting your life, you have no control over their health, whether or not they'll do drugs, end up in rehab, run with the wrong crowd. No matter how hard you try, you never have total control over what they do or how they'll turn out."

Damn Libby! She should be going through this with me!

_⸙ ⸙_

I'd barely walked in the door of Libby's apartment and set down all the baby stuff when my cell went off. It was Sophie, wondering when I was popping by with an item of Libby's. I had no clue what Sophie was looking for, so I grabbed a few paintbrushes and a prenatal book—the only baby-related thing Libby had bought. I told myself I was humoring Sophie. Even though she'd been dead-on about the items she'd channeled last night at the antique shop. Maybe Libby had sold those pillows to the shop and told Sophie the story behind them.

I checked the answering machine, praying for another message from Libby. An older-sounding man spoke in rapid French, and I assumed it was Libby's doctor. Then I recognized the voice of the anonymous guy who'd called yesterday. A brief message, I assumed it once again asked Libby to call him.

Who was this guy?

I peeked out at the flowers on the balcony, assuring myself they already looked perkier thanks to the plant food. Monsieur Fleurs sat slouched in his chair on the balcony, sleeping.

Worried that, before long, Nurse Nasty would contact social services claiming Libby had abandoned her baby, I phoned the hospital, pretending to be Libby inquiring on her daughter's condition. Libby and I sounded alike in person; it would be impossible to distinguish between our voices over the phone. I was fairly certain I was put through to Nurse Perky. Since Libby was American, the nurse didn't seem to question why I was speaking English rather than French. I advised her that I—Libby—would return the following day after the funeral. The nurse seemed to buy it. If Libby didn't return tomorrow, I didn't know what lie I'd fabricate.

A *ding* signaled the arrival of an e-mail. It was from Roger. My heart pounded. Taking a deep breath, I opened it.

Meet me at 7 pm in the hotel lounge to discuss your job.
R.

Was it to discuss my promotion or the fact I no longer had a job? Or that every woman in the company was rallying behind me on my Facebook fan page and he was pissed?

I checked my Facebook page.

1,734 Likes.

I was averaging over seventy-five Likes an hour. One woman admired my dedication and work ethics and offered me a hotel sales position in Vancouver. It would likely be quite the demotion and thousands of miles from Milwaukee, but it was nice to feel wanted. Any job that allowed me to use transferable skills in the industry would likely entail a hefty pay cut. I'd worked hard to ensure I wasn't one of those women whose husband ditched her with two kids and no marketable skills right before her thirty-second birthday. Like Mom.

I stuck my phone in my purse. Luc was waiting for me. I glanced over at the bags filled with baby items and the Barbie suitcase. I'd gone a tad overboard. Dominique wouldn't be able to use the suitcase for several years. However, I knew two little girls who could use it now. I stuck two stuffed animals inside the suitcase then went to meet Luc. I was able to prop the suitcase on my knee while riding Luc's scooter with one arm wrapped snugly around his waist.

Luc and I popped by the *Métro* station near the Venus Café. I bought sandwiches and milk from a vendor inside the station. We walked down the dingy, yellow corridor, and I smiled when I caught sight of the blue scarf wrapped around the mother's head. She had on a different blue dress than yesterday; however, the little girls had on the same matching yellow dresses. When I was eleven, Holly Phillips had teased me that my mom shopped at her family's rummage sale and I was wearing her used clothes. I'd dreamed of one day owning a designer wardrobe. I should have been thankful I hadn't had to wear the same outfit every day.

We approached, and the girls' wide-eyed gazes locked on the

Barbie suitcase.

"I thought you could use this to carry your stuff." I gestured to the worn, wool blanket and supplies for making roses.

Luc translated for me.

The woman eyed the tattered plastic grocery bags she'd been using and smiled enthusiastically. *"Merci."*

The little girls giggled excitedly, latching on to the suitcase. Luc told them to open it, and the older girl hurriedly unzipped it. Their faces lit up at the sight of the stuffed animals. Luc asked them their names. The older girl was Gabrielle, the younger, Anouk, and the mother, Inès. I smiled and told them our names. Gabrielle anxiously opened her sketchpad and showed me a drawing of who I presumed to be me because of the orange clip in her hair, sitting with them at a table filled with food. I smiled and said it was very good.

I handed Inès the food. She smiled, and her eyes misted over. Afraid I was going to cry, I said goodbye. Inès grasped my forearm, stopping me, giving me two flowers.

The little girls gave us cheerful *au revoirs*, waving the hands of their stuffed animals at us. We waved back then headed down the corridor and exited the *Métro*. We headed to the Venus Café, where the gemstone salesgirl informed us that Sophie had gone to see Pascal's son. Crap. I could understand how people turned to psychics in desperation when a loved one was missing. They grasped at any thread of hope no matter how far-fetched.

I asked the girl to pass Libby's items on to Sophie. Hopefully Sophie would return before long. And hopefully she would remember to ask Alphonse about Libby's inheritance. Right now, it was the only possible clue I had.

Chapter Seventeen

When Luc and I arrived at the Bozilovic art gallery, the salesguy was assisting clients. He had that early Elvis Costello thing happening—short, dark hair and thick, black-rimmed glasses with purple-tinted lenses. He had on a purple mod print shirt and black leather pants. I instantly ruled him out as Dominique's father.

I admired a painting done in blue and red hues with a whimsical, airy feel to it. A bride and groom floated over Sacré Coeur, as if they'd drifted up from the basilica after being united in marriage.

"Close your eyes." Luc stood closely behind me, his words warming the back of my neck.

I closed my eyes.

He leaned in, speaking softly in my ear. "Imagine you're light like a feather, floating over the city, holding your lover's hand. Feel the warmth of his hand and the rays of sunshine against your face. Picture what you would see." He placed a hand lightly on the small of my back, as if guiding me on my journey.

I envisioned Paris, everything I'd seen the past few days from the back of Luc's scooter. Like Luc's back muscles rippling when he gripped the handlebars, maneuvering the bike through the city streets. Our first kiss...

"What scents are in the city below?"

Luc's cinnamony breath and musky cologne. A luscious hot dog stuffed in a freshly baked baguette. The aroma of spices in Luc's lamb stew. I instinctively licked my lips.

"What do you hear?"

Luc's scooter humming. His soft whispers in my ear. The

laughter of children, and me, at the puppet show. Luc and I laughing about Katsumi. I'd laughed harder the past few days than I had in years.

What if I never laughed again?

My eyes shot open, my body going rigid.

"Did you feel the painting, see it clearly?"

I nodded faintly. Suddenly, everything was quite clear. I would miss Luc something fierce. The way he made me laugh. His passion for Paris, cooking, being a puppeteer, life in general. How he made *me* feel passionate about things, like him, and fighting for my rights. I felt not only physically but emotionally connected to Luc.

"You look worried," Luc said.

I scrambled for something to say. "If Libby isn't back soon, I need to stay. I mean, how can I leave? Yet once I'm offered the promotion..."

"She'll be back. But you should stay a few days. You should spend time with Libby. I wish I were going to be here, but I leave Sunday for a traveling puppet show, visiting small towns."

Luc knew I might be staying, yet he still planned on leaving. It was unrealistic for me to expect him to give up his work for me. If Libby were back and he asked me to stay, I wouldn't, not once I received my promotion. If Libby weren't gone, I'd never have spent the past few days with Luc. I'd been forced into this situation and it had been some of the best days of my life.

A guy walked up behind us, speaking French, and I turned to find Elvis Costello, or rather Mirko as he introduced himself. I asked if he spoke English and if he knew Libby.

"Yes, I know Libby." From the guy's name, his broken English sans French lilt, and the gallery's ethnic focus, I gathered he was Serbian. He had an arm crossed in front of him, and he brushed his fingertips over the sleeve of his satin shirt. "How is she?"

"She just had a baby girl."

"A baby!" he practically squealed. "How precious."

"I think the father works at an antique shop. I was hoping you might know him."

"Why you not ask Libby?"

I explained the situation.

"Hmm..." he mused. "We bought desk from one man Libby knew, and I thought he might be more than friend." He walked over to an ornately carved, antique wooden desk and removed a Rolodex with business cards. He thumbed through them then removed one and handed it to me.

Le Temps Retrouvé. The antique store I'd gone to with Sophie. The card was generic without any names.

"Do you know if his name was Julien?"

Mirko shrugged. "I do not know."

All signs pointed to this shop.

I thanked Mirko and gave him my card should he hear from Libby. I glanced over at the bride and groom painting.

"Could you ship that to the U.S.?"

"Of course. You recognize sister's work."

I pointed to the signature at the bottom. Jakob Petrovic. "That's not Libby's painting." Yet the painting was cheerful and optimistic, like Libby.

Mirko's gaze skittered cautiously around the gallery. "We don't always have enough Serbian artists so sometimes is necessary to sell painting by someone who is not and put different name on it."

That wasn't as bad as being a forger, but I was still shocked Libby would do such a thing.

"If you don't believe me, I show you receipt for which I paid her." He left and returned moments later with the receipt. It was indeed Libby's signature.

"I'll take it." It was the first painting of Libby's I'd ever owned. Since I'd never been real supportive of her art, she'd never given me one. I'd gone to a few...maybe one...of her art exhibits when she was in college. That was it. "So do you ever sell art that isn't Serbian? Like, say, a Pissaro?"

Mirko shook his head. "Too much money to sell here."

He would likely have asked questions if Libby had showed up with valuable Pissaros. Besides, Libby wouldn't have helped Bruno sell forgeries. No way.

So why was I even asking Mirko this?

When we reached Luc's scooter, raindrops began falling. Clouds had moved in from nowhere, so I hadn't grabbed my Burberry umbrella. Sprinkles turned into a steady stream of rain within seconds.

"It's okay," Luc said. "I have raincoats."

He removed two large, black trash bags from the scooter's back compartment and handed me one. I'd bought a Burberry raincoat for this trip, and now I was wearing a trash bag.

Luc tore a section of the bottom seam away. I reluctantly did the same. We slipped the bags over our heads and punched our hands through the sides. The rain fell harder, and I blinked raindrops from my lashes, sweeping my tongue across the drops on my upper lip. Luc smiled, eyeing my lips. He reached out and brushed a finger gently over my top lip, wiping away the moisture. His gaze still fixed on my mouth, he traced the contour of my lips with his finger then leaned over and brushed his lips against mine, slipping his tongue and the taste of cinnamon into my mouth. I returned the kiss, sweeping my hands up over his chest and shoulders to the back of his neck, tunneling my fingers through his damp hair. He wrapped his arms around me, gathering up fistfuls of my trash bag in his hands, pressing my body against his, deepening the kiss.

Luc drew back slightly. He traced a finger down my cheek and along my neck, hooking it over the top of my trash bag, his hand resting against my breasts. My breath hitched in my throat. Luc leaned over and kissed me gently.

"The rain has slowed," he said. "We should go."

I nodded, licking the taste of cinnamon on my lips. Luc's finger was still curled around the neckline of my trash bag.

He smiled. "I'm glad you're here."

This was turning out to be my favorite raincoat.

We headed home to change out of our soaking clothes, and I had to get ready for my meeting with Roger, which I hadn't told Luc about. I didn't know why I hadn't told him. Not like he didn't know I was trying to land a promotion.

It was still raining when we pulled up in front of Libby's building. Cecile was struggling so hard to close one of the paneled windows she'd shaken her bun loose, and her white hair was about to tumble past her shoulders. The wind had picked up and was blowing rain into the shop. Luc secured the window shut while Cecile pinned her bun back in place and Gigi rubbed affectionately against Luc's leg. Luc's sex appeal transcended all species of women.

Cecile thanked Luc and insisted he accept flowers in return for his kindness. She chose a small bouquet of yellow daffodils. She handed them to Luc, speaking in French.

He glanced over at me, smiling. "These are for you, *Mademoiselle.*" He handed me the flowers, and my stomach fluttered like some goofy schoolgirl's.

Cecile placed her hands to her chest in the universal *Oh, how sweet* look.

Gigi let out a bark, jealous, no doubt.

"Merci," I said.

When Luc and I parted ways, I made up an excuse about Hannah having a meltdown and needing to meet her for a drink. I hated lying to Luc, but I also didn't want to tell him the truth and have him call me a puppet.

There were no messages on the machine from psycho Bruno. I preferred his crazed messages over none. None might mean he was no longer desperately searching for Libby, that he'd found her.

I prayed not.

I placed the daffodils in a yellow ceramic vase and set them on the table next to the daisies. I stuck the two paper roses in the vase with the rest. The baby items I'd bought were laid out on the futon. I introduced Monsieur Mickey and Mademoiselle Minnie Mouse to my girl puppet then set the puppets together on the table. I inventoried the rest of the items, including a mobile to hang over

Dominique's crib, which Libby didn't even have. If Dominique came home in a few days, she needed someplace other than the futon to sleep. I had to go back to the antique store and buy that cradle. Despite the price, I couldn't stop thinking about it. And after the shop had come up at the gallery, I had to check it out again.

I peered over at the mural on the wall, at the gaping hole where Libby's and my hands should be clasped together. The sound of Libby's giggles no longer filled my head. I craned my neck toward the painting, as if straining to hear her laugh. Why couldn't I hear her? Had something awful happened to her? I was suddenly panicked, and an eerie feeling raised the hairs on my arms.

I suddenly felt deathly alone in the world.

Like I had at Pascal's funeral.

I raced down to Luc's and borrowed glue. I hurried back to Libby's and carefully turned over the piece of plaster and squirted a spiral of glue on the back. I slipped the piece into place on the mural and gently pressed it against the wall.

Concentrating on our clasped hands, I placed my hand over Libby's in the mural, imagining myself holding her hand. Closing my eyes, I willed Libby to feel our connection wherever she was.

"I'm with you, Libby," I muttered. "Everything will be all right." After a few moments, the empty feeling inside me diminished slightly.

My phone rang. Sophie.

She enthusiastically recounted the visions she'd gotten from Libby's book and paintbrush. "Libby is in the same room from my dream. In a large, stone building, a chateau, I believe. And in the garden, there are dogs peeing in a pond."

That was her big clue? Dogs peeing in a pond?

"So how am I supposed to find this castle with dogs peeing in a pond?" I asked.

"Maybe my dream tonight will show me where she is."

Had I really expected Sophie to provide me with the GPS coordinates of Libby's location? Frustrated, I changed the subject. "So what did Pascal's son have to say?"

"Alphonse inherited the salons. Pascal told me he wants Alphonse to sell them, but now Alphonse is unsure if he wants to. I assured him his heart will tell him what to do, you know? Before I left, he cried. So Pascal should not contact you tonight."

Hopefully Sophie was right. I desperately needed a good night's sleep.

"Did Alphonse mention what Pascal left Libby?"

"No, he didn't seem comfortable talking about it to a stranger. He seemed shocked by whatever it was. He said he wished he'd known about it when Pascal was alive."

It being his half sister?

We said goodbye and hung up.

I checked Facebook quickly before heading out the door.

2,089 Likes.

Ella had replied to my message.

You have to believe you did the best you could as a role model, as I'm sure you did. We can't control other people's actions or choices in life. You're an awesome role model to women around the world. I so admire what you're doing!

Pride welled inside me. Libby might not think I was a great role model, but she'd admire what I was doing. I envisioned myself and more than 2,000 women picketing outside Brecker's brewery. For my rights.

For *women's* rights!

Chapter Eighteen

I walked across the hotel's lobby, smoothing a hand down the front of my black tweed dress and double-breasted blazer, attempting to press out the wrinkles. I adjusted the jacket's shoulders, trying to get it to lay better. It didn't feel right.

I noticed an assortment of jeweled hairclips in a boutique's window. I popped inside. They were made of a heavy metal but would go much better with my suit than the orange clip. I bought one with faux black onyx and exchanged my clip for it.

As I neared the meeting space, a flame flickered in my stomach. The air seemed to thicken. I took several deep, calming breaths. I rounded the corner and saw Hannah and a banquet server at the beverage station. Rather than her usual perky smile, Hannah's lips were pressed into a tight, thin line.

"I called for beer twenty-two minutes ago," Hannah told the guy. "If somebody takes these last two beers, I have none. Do you see the problem here? I need those beers now."

Whoa. I'd never heard Hannah talk to anyone like that. She sounded demanding, assertive...like me.

The guy looked ticked but took off after the beers.

Hannah snatched up the phone on the desk and punched in numbers. "I called forty-three minutes ago for a bellman to pick up these room gifts I need delivered before everyone gets back from dinner. Do I need to deliver them myself or what?" She slammed down the phone.

Omigod. In a matter of two days, Hannah had morphed into a Mini-Me. But did I really sound that bitchy?

Hannah spied me, and her face lit up. "You're back!" She rushed over and gave me a huge hug. I couldn't recall us ever having hugged before. "You have 2,146 Likes on Facebook. How awesome is that?"

"I'm here to meet with Roger. If things go well, I'm back."

She let out a massive sigh. "Thank God." She snatched a piece of paper off the desk. "Natalie got a ticket for not scooping Katsumi's poop off the sidewalk. Can I work that into the budget?"

"No way, the budget's already blown."

Hannah's eyes widened in panic. "But I told her I could."

I snagged the ticket and ripped it to shreds. It floated like celebratory confetti into the garbage can.

"Omigod. What if she comes back to Paris and immigration has her flagged with an outstanding ticket?"

"I'm not lucky enough to have Natalie Darwin sentenced to fifty hours of community service work, scooping poop off the sidewalks of Paris. I doubt she'll have a criminal record over an unpaid poop fine. We need to draw some boundaries."

"I like that policy. You're totally my mentor. I've learned so much from you I can't even tell you."

I felt honored she looked up to me, yet I saw a Mini-Me forming in Hannah that I wasn't real proud of. As I headed off to the lounge to meet Roger, I realized Hannah hadn't commented on my new hair color or asked how Libby was doing. Not like her.

Roger sat at a corner table in the dimly lit lounge, swirling cognac in a glass, no attendees in sight. They'd either drunk the bar dry of Brecker beer or were out to dinner. I approached Roger, placing a hand against my stomach, trying to calm the burning sensation.

"Samantha." Roger stood and shook my hand. He eyed my hair, smiling. "Nice color. Looks good on you."

"Thanks."

It *felt* good on me. No more boring brown blending into the background. For thirteen years, I'd done my job, much of it behind the scenes, and had received little recognition for it.

No more.

I sat in the stiff, wingback chair. With the brown leather

furnishings and dark woods, the place felt like a stodgy men's club. How ironic. Since Roger was drinking a cognac, I skipped the beer and ordered a peach Bellini to celebrate.

"I think you'll be happy with what I've come up with. It's a win-win situation for everyone. You've certainly earned it. And I'm throwing in an extra week's vacation."

Considering I'd accumulated over a hundred vacation days since starting, that was no bonus. He knew he'd never have to pay out on them.

Roger handed me the agreement. I scanned it, zoning in on the eight grand a year raise. What happened to twenty-two grand more? My gaze darted to the job title: director of corporate events.

"This is great, but I expected more of a raise."

Roger's smile tightened. "That'll come with the senior director position."

"*Senior* director?" There was no such position.

"You'll be the senior director's right-hand man without having to deal with the sales end of things."

"In other words, I'll be doing what I'm doing now, including picking up the slack for the director who has zero planning background." Roger arched a curious brow. How had I known this guy had no background? "Are you filling my current manager's position?" Technically, it wasn't my current position since I'd quit.

Roger shook his head.

"So in essence, I get a different title, a mediocre raise, but same job with twice the workload." I tossed the job offer on the table. Roger wore a ghost of a smile, and his gray eyes bored into me with a stern intensity that always made me wimp out and say whatever he wanted to hear, not wanting to rock the boat and hurt my climb up the executive ladder. *Well, I guess I could try the position and see how it works out.*

Luc was right. I was a puppet, and Roger was seriously pulling my strings. My jaw tightened, and I squared my shoulders, willing my voice to stay firm. "I want the senior director's position, Roger. Make this other person the director."

Roger's smile vanished, and his gaze sharpened.

My body went rigid, and I straightened in the chair.

"I just don't think you're ready for the position. It involves a lot of marketing and sales—"

"When will I be ready? When I have a sex change? I'm not the right *man* for the job, Roger, I'm the right *woman* for the job. Women make up twenty-five percent of the beer market. You're missing out on one of the biggest demographics. Stop turning them off from Brecker with sexist marketing campaigns. You work hard not to offend ethnic groups, so why do you want to offend women? Start by hiring a woman to market to women. I have a lot of great—"

"Is this about more money?"

"Everything isn't always about money." Had I just said that? "It's about respect. You don't even respect my ideas enough to consider them. How are my co-workers supposed to respect me when my boss doesn't? When he gives my job to Joe Schmo? It's about some guy getting my promotion. Some guy who doesn't even work for the company. Some guy who hasn't put in sixty hours a week here for the past thirteen years." As I surged from the chair, my voice rose along with me. "Some guy who's a fucking *guy*! It's called discrimination, Roger. It's illegal. Just ask your lawyer!"

Omigod, had I just threatened to sue Brecker?

Roger sat there, eyes bugging out, mouth gaping, as I bolted from the lounge, kissing my promotion *au revoir*. I stripped off my suit jacket, freeing myself from its constraint, and removed the weight of the hairclip from my head.

As I headed toward the *Métro*, I called Rachel and told her I didn't get the promotion and I was done with Brecker. I told her I was disclosing my full name and employer on my fan page. I asked her to retrieve my consumer promotion plan from Roger's office. His assistant, Beverly, would know right where it was. If I wasn't executing the plan, nobody was. Some beer company was going to want my ideas even if I didn't have a marketing degree. I'd make damn sure of it!

I flew up the stairs of Libby's building, still on an adrenaline rush. One minute, I was proud of myself for standing up to Roger, the next, kicking myself for quitting without having another job and for burning bridges. This was the only job I'd had in thirteen years. Roger wasn't going to give me a good reference. What the hell was I going to do?

Quitting or getting canned was something I'd never planned ahead for. It was so unlikely to ever happen. My savings would last six months max. I refused to dip into my retirement account. I'd built up a network of industry contacts over the past thirteen years. I would e-mail every one of them. Hopefully somebody was hiring.

Evan had to have known Roger wasn't offering me the promotion. A heads-up would have been nice. He owed me that. And Roger certainly owed me more. When I looked past all my anger over not receiving the promotion, deep down, I was hurt. The man I'd highly respected didn't respect *me*. I'd always been there for him and the company, and then the one time I really needed his support, he wasn't there. I rarely took things personally at work, but this felt personal. Same as it did with Evan.

I paused at the top of the stairs, in front of Luc's door. Needing a pep talk on how I would be much better off as a puppeteer than a puppet, I pounded on his door, about taking it off the hinges. Luc answered, dressed in a black T-shirt and faded jeans. He greeted me along with the aroma of herbs and spices.

He smiled. "You're just in time. The shepherd's pie is ready."

Our gazes locked. I stood there breathing heavily, a tear of anger slipping down my cheek. Luc took my purse and blazer and tossed them on the floor. He grasped my hand and drew me to him, shutting the door behind us. He cupped my face in his hands and gently touched his lips to mine. He slid his tongue across my lower lip then along my upper one before slipping it inside my mouth. The kiss deepened, growing more urgent.

I tugged his T-shirt from the waistband of his jeans and peeled it off over his head. His gaze followed his hands as they slowly swept up the front of my dress to my breasts, where they paused before slipping around to my back. Peering deep into my eyes, he inched down my dress's zipper. My stomach muscles tightened in anticipation.

I was going to orgasm before he even had my dress off. I'd always figured Luc for a wild, tossing-clothes-on-the-ceiling-fan kind of lover. Dress unzipped, he swept his hands up over my back, his touch heating my bare skin. He curled his fingers around the shoulders of my dress and slipped it down my arms. He grasped hold of the dress at my waist and slid it down my legs, kneeling in front of me. I stepped from the dress, standing there in my white lace bra and *Mange-moi* thong. Eye level to my thong, Luc smiled, his gaze eating me up. I swallowed hard, ready to explode just thinking about what was to come.

All thoughts of Libby and work flew from my head.

I woke up in a sweat. Disoriented, it took me a few moments to realize I was lying naked on Luc's pull-out couch. His body spooning mine, his arm draped over me. His breath warm against my neck, I recalled his hot body intertwined with mine like some Rodin sculpture. But rather than having hot and steamy dreams about sex with Luc, I'd had another Pascal nightmare. Having fired everyone in his salon, he offered to train me as a hairstylist. Was this telling me I had to think outside the box with my career, or that I should go to beauty school?

"What do you want?" I whispered to Pascal. "Sophie talked to your son today. Isn't that what you wanted?" I was so desperate for a good night's sleep I was talking to some dead guy. If he started responding, then I'd be seriously worried. "Tell me what you want from me."

Luc stirred and let out a soft moan. "What I want from you?" He kissed my shoulder, his hand slipping between my legs. "How about what I want to do *to* you?"

A sigh of ecstasy drifted up my throat, and my back arched.

Okay, my attempt at channeling Pascal had been a huge success. Just not with Pascal.

Chapter Nineteen

I awoke to find myself once again spooning with Luc. His warm, naked body pressed against mine, his arm draped over my side. I molded against him. It hadn't been a wild romp with clothes flying in all directions but rather a slow, sensual experience, unlike any other. I could lie there forever. Yet even if I stayed in Paris until Libby returned, Luc was leaving Sunday on his puppet tour. I had to act like this was merely casual sex and I didn't have any expectations, because I didn't. This was a fling. No strings attached. No strings attached....

I began slipping from Luc's arms, and he stirred. I froze. When he didn't wake up, I slid off the bed, snatching the red throw blanket off the floor and wrapping it around me. Luc could strut nude along the Seine in front of the entire city of Paris, and I couldn't even walk across the room while he slept. I slowly released the blanket, letting it drop to the floor as I strolled across the room, feeling liberated. First Luc, next the Seine. Baby steps.

I headed toward the bathroom, snatching my *Mange-moi* thong off the floor by the couch and my dress and blazer from in front of the door.

"You're beautiful," Luc said, his voice low and raspy from sleep. Way sexy.

I glanced over my shoulder at him, not confident enough to flash him a full frontal view. His stare ate me up, making me glad I'd dropped the blanket. He laced his fingers behind his head, causing the muscles in his chest to tighten. My gaze traveled down to his waist where the sheet flirted with his lower abdomen. Mmm...

"I wish I didn't have to go to work," he said.

"At the garden or on the *Métro*?"

"At a school. And then I need to work the *Métro* for a short while."

Luc slipped out of bed wearing a lazy, seductive smile and nothing else. He strolled toward me, and I tried not to gawk at his incredibly sexy bod. I turned and faced him, slipping into his arms as they wrapped around my waist. He rested his hands against the small of my back, drawing me snugly against him. I fanned my hands across the dark hair of his chest.

"Thanks for making the shepherd's pie. Sorry we didn't get to eat it."

The corners of his mouth slowly curled into a mischievous smile. "I'm not. We can have it for a late lunch. Although I feel inspired to create a new recipe. It's been a long time. Like...pheasant à la Samantha." He traced a finger gently down my cheek. "You inspire me. I never thought I'd feel inspired again."

Wow. I'd never been anyone's inspiration for anything.

"This is the season for wild mushrooms." His finger trailed over to my lips and brushed across them. "Girolles are the best ones. A rich, smoky flavor."

"I love it when you talk food," I whispered against his finger.

He placed a soft kiss against my lips. "I'll give you a key in case you get here before I return."

A key? I wanted to read more into it than it meant. How much could a key for two days mean anyway?

He kissed me again, sweeping his tongue inside my mouth, kissing me with the same hunger as last night. Maybe he wouldn't ask for the key back in two days, leaving the door open for me to return. Suddenly, a key meant a lot.

Upon entering Libby's apartment, my gaze locked on the mural. Our hands were once again missing, replaced by the gaping hole. The piece of mural lay on the floor, dusted with plaster. My breath caught in my throat. The fall had caused the plaster to break in half. Instead of repairing it, I'd made it even worse. I carefully slid a piece onto my hand and took it over to the dining room table. I gently turned it over to find merely the top of my hand and the beginning of my fingers; barely a trace of Libby's hand was visible.

We were no longer holding hands at all.

A lump of panic swelled in my throat. I told myself this was only a painting. It wasn't a sign something awful had happened to Libby or that Dominique's condition had taken a turn for the worse. Yet the lump in my throat had grown so large it was cutting off my breathing!

I raced over to the phone and called the hospital. The nurse guaranteed me Dominique was fine. I placed a trembling hand to my chest, managing to thank her before hanging up. The nurse didn't mention that the doctor had called the police. Had he? Libby had been gone almost *forty-eight* hours. And I hadn't heard from her in *twenty-four* hours.

The red light on the answering machine flashed two messages. I listened to them, praying one was from Libby. The anonymous guy had left another message; his voice now holding a sense of urgency and concern. Mom had left a message, upset that we'd put her on ignore status. No message from Bruno. I'd give anything to have him pounding on the door, harassing *me* rather than possibly Libby. Now not only did I have to worry about where Libby was but also about psycho Bruno. What if he'd found her? My heart raced, along with my mind. If he hadn't found Libby, he'd surely take my call.

I grabbed my cell phone and discovered it'd been turned off since I'd left the hotel last night. I turned it on to find three voice mails. Before checking them, I phoned Bruno and got his voice mail. Now I knew how Bruno felt when I ignored his calls. It made me berserk! I left him a message, sounding a tad psychotic myself, telling him to call me.

I checked my messages. One was from a panicked Hannah. She'd seen on my Facebook fan page that I didn't get the promotion and she thought this totally sucked. Sophie had had another dream with Libby watching dogs pee in a pond. Oddly, this gave me comfort that Libby was okay, wherever she was. The last message was from Evan, in a state of shocked confusion. He'd obviously spoken with Roger. He asked me to call him.

I didn't have a clue what to say to Evan. That I was suing Brecker or needing a reference? After what he'd done to me, he at least owed me a reference. And I had to face him at some point to discuss the separation of our things. Hearing his voice didn't make me feel the least bit guilty about sleeping with Luc and reconfirmed we should be separating.

I was unemployed for the first time since high school.

What would I do for income? Sue Brecker? How would I pay the legal fees? If I did sue, it wouldn't be just for myself but for every woman who worked at Brecker, or would work there.

Panicked, I perused the business cards scanned into my computer. I shot off my résumé to several planners in Milwaukee who I'd met over the years.

After showering, I threw on a pair of jeans and a short-sleeved, pink spandex T-shirt. I checked my Facebook fan page.

3,362 Likes.

My post about not getting the promotion had caused my Likes to skyrocket. People commended me for revealing my identity. Several lawyers posted their websites and offered to represent me in a discrimination lawsuit against Brecker. Even though I'd threatened Roger with suing, I hadn't made that public on my fan page.

Ella had posted.

I'm furious for you right now! I never had enough evidence to sue my company for discrimination, but if I did, I would have. I'm joining you in a cyber glass of the best Argentinean Malbec!

I could see us sitting at a café right now drinking a Malbec. Too bad she didn't live in Paris. Actually, I had no clue where she lived.

I sent Ella a private message.

Where do you live? You're not in Paris, by chance, are you? I could go for that glass of Malbec right now!

Several posts, from both men and women, offered me planner jobs around the United States, but nothing in Milwaukee. Although if Mom and Ken were traveling and in a serious relationship, she really didn't need me there. But I didn't know if I could leave her. Besides, I didn't want to be a planner unless it involved marketing, even though I needed any job for now. My fans didn't realize I was interested in being more than a planner, so I posted a new status to all brewery employees.

> *How would you like to increase your company's beer sales by 15 percent? I've developed a consumer promotion and marketing plan geared toward women that is sure to accomplish or exceed this goal. It takes a woman to market to women! (If you could repost this to your status that'd be great! ☺)*

If all of my 3,362 fans had an average of even 250 friends, my job posting would be viewed by 840,500 people. Where else could I get this kind of exposure?

I checked e-mail to find one from Roger's assistant, Beverly. She'd secured my consumer promotion plan, and she wondered if she should destroy it or return it to me. She said she couldn't *like* my page in case Roger found out, but that she'd had her nieces and friends like it. She wished me good luck.

If even Beverly knew about my page, it was only a matter of time before Roger found out. He was going to freak. Too bad I couldn't be there when it happened.

—⚬ ⚬—

Yesterday's rain, and the plant food, had resuscitated Libby's flowers. I owed Monsieur Fleurs. Before heading to the hospital, I popped into the flower shop and bought two packages of plant food. Cecile tucked a complimentary daisy in my hair clip on the back of my head. I thanked her and gave Gigi a pat on the head. I headed over to Monsieur Fleurs's apartment building, glancing up at the empty chair on his balcony.

I scanned the two dozen names on the intercom panel, wondering which one belonged to Monsieur Fleurs. No security access panel, so I opened the blue-painted door and walked inside, encountering a small entryway with a wooden door and a security code panel. I was about to leave when a young guy flew out the door past me. I caught the door and slipped inside. I hiked up the stairs to the sixth floor and down the hallway, counting off apartments until I was at the one directly across from Libby's.

The scent of greasy bacon filled the air. I debated whether or not to knock, not wanting to infringe on his privacy by showing up unannounced, especially during his breakfast. Even though he'd been infringing on mine since day one.

I had the urge to meet him face-to-face. Yet I was doubtful he spoke English, and he didn't appear overly enamored with me. However, maybe the plant food would elicit a smile from him. I wasn't sure why I cared so much whether some man I didn't even know smiled or not.

Because Libby would care.

Best that I imagined my gift brought a smile to his face. I set the packages in front of the door and left.

Chapter Twenty

When I entered the nursery, my gaze locked on my niece's empty incubator. Even her giraffe blanket was gone. My gaze darted frantically from the Asian baby in the incubator next to Dominique's, to Claudette in a crib, to the empty nurse's desk. Was she in ICU? Had Bruno taken her? On the verge of a panic attack, I heard soft, melodic singing coming from behind a drawn curtain. I raced over and whipped back the curtain to find Nurse Perky rocking my niece, who was wrapped in the giraffe blanket. I eased out a shaky sigh of relief.

"How's she doing?" I asked.

"Her fever is the same, but not worse, so that is good." She smiled. "Would you like to feed her? It would be good if you held her. She would like to hear your voice. You sound like her mother."

Did she know I'd been calling pretending to be Libby?

Unable to recall the last time I'd held a baby, I sat in the chair, ramrod straight. The nurse placed Dominique in my arms then handed me the bottle and burping towel. I draped the towel over my shoulder then touched the bottle to my niece's lips. She immediately suckled the nipple.

"She is a healthy eater. That is very good."

I gazed down at Dominique peering up at me wide-eyed, sucking away on her bottle like she hadn't eaten in a week. "A healthy eater, that's very good," I said in a cooing voice.

Nurse Perky walked over to Claudette, leaving us alone.

Dominique continued drinking, gaze glued to mine. My shoulders relaxed, and I adjusted her carefully in my arms, as if she were a fragile piece of Tiffany crystal. I could picture Libby sitting in a rocking chair, up for two a.m. feedings after working all day and playing with Dominique all night. She'd be exhausted. Being a single mom, she'd have no relief. I now hated the thought of hiring a nanny. Of a strange woman rocking my niece and feeding her. If anyone should be there to help Libby, it should be me. But I had to start a massive job hunt, and I couldn't convince Libby to move back home with Dominique if I didn't have a home.

I shoved the thoughts aside, not wanting my niece to feel my stress. I smiled. "You're going to like living in Milwaukee. You'll have a big yard with lots of toys. I'm going to buy us a nice house in the suburbs."

When had I decided to sell Evan the condo?

Besides not being able to afford it being unemployed, I wanted my niece to have a yard to play in. I also lived on the thirty-seventh floor. I couldn't take the chance of her climbing over the balcony.

"Your mom will be able to take you to the park every day. I can take you on the weekends when I'm home. We'll enroll you in ballet and French classes. Your mommy and I dressed up like ballerinas one year for trick-or-treating. She had a pink tutu, and I had a white one with sparkly rhinestones all over it."

Mom had made the costumes the year after Dad had left. She'd been going through a good spell. Times weren't all bad.

Dominique stopped sucking on the bottle. Her forehead bunched into a grimace.

"What's wrong? Time to burp?"

I rested her against my shoulder, gently patting her back. A big burp erupted from her, followed by a stream of puke, which landed next to the towel, on the shoulder of my pink shirt. I wiped off the puke with the towel.

"That was a healthy burp. Yes, it was." I continued rocking, massaging her back. "Your mommy will be here today. Yes, she will."

Nurse Nasty opened the door, and a cold draft whooshed into the room, sending a chill up my spine. She marched over. "She still has small fever, but she does very well. She may be ready to go home Saturday. The doctor will speak to your sister about this when she comes." Her look said she didn't believe Libby was *ever* coming back.

I tried to hide the panic zipping through my body. What if they wanted to release Dominique and Libby hadn't returned? Would they release her to me? Would it matter that I was family but not a French citizen?

Was I prepared to take care of a baby?

I approached *Le Temps Retrouvé*, checking my phone to make sure I hadn't missed Bruno's call when I was in the *Métro's* dead zone. No call. I'd left him a message almost two hours ago. However, my message hadn't really given him an incentive to call me back. So I called him and left a message claiming to have the paintings and told him to meet me at the fountain in the Luxembourg Gardens in two hours. I'd be lurking in the shadows, and if he showed up, then he obviously hadn't found Libby.

I checked my fan page.

4,093 Likes.

No reply from Ella.

A small microbrewery in Colorado wanted to discuss increasing its sales by fifteen percent. I doubted they could meet my pay requirements. However, if nobody else showed interest, my only requirement might be to get paid.

Upon arriving at the antique shop, I made a beeline for the cradle, relieved it was still there. I placed a hand on the cradle's side, gently rocking it, picturing my niece sleeping cuddled up with her giraffe blanket. Dominique could pass the cradle down to her children. Hopefully it would remain in our family forever.

A young, brown-haired salesgirl dressed in a gray suit walked up and spoke French.

"*Je ne parle pas français,*" I said.

"You like the cradle?" Her gaze narrowed, and her dainty nose crinkled faintly. I smelled like Dominique's puke.

I smiled. "Would you be able to hold it for a few days until I can find a way to pick it up?"

"Yes, of course, that is no problem. Where do you live?"

"I'm staying in the Latin Quarter."

"I have a delivery in that area in three hours. Would that be good?"

"Great."

She introduced herself as Evette and slipped a sold tag around a spindle on the cradle.

A middle-aged gentleman entered the store, and Evette waved. *"Bonjour, Monsieur Beaufay."*

Monsieur Beaufay, the shop's owner?

"Bonjour," he called out. He walked over to a man admiring a tapestry wall hanging.

In his early forties, Monsieur Beaufay had short, salt-and-pepper hair and brown eyes. His tailored suit screamed money in Italian, as did his loafers. However, he didn't have a snooty air about him like Monsieur Stick Up His Ass. He totally had that George Clooney thing happening with his charming, dimpled smile and sparkle in his eyes. Much more my type than Libby's. No way was he Dominique's father.

I paid for the cradle, gave Evette Libby's address, then stepped out into the sunshine. I spied an antique cuckoo clock in the shop's window and stopped to check it out, discreetly glancing in at Monsieur Beaufay talking to the customer. He let out a hearty laugh, not merely a congenial one. I had no clue why, but I found myself drawn back inside.

Evette was apparently in the back. After a few moments, Monsieur Beaufay excused himself from the customer and walked over to me.

"Bonjour. Parlez-vous anglais?" I asked.

"Yes, but of course I speak English. My name is Gilles Beaufay. May I help you find something?"

My sister.

"Actually, my friend Libby Hunter recommended your store."

"Libby," he said softly, as if it was the most beautiful name he'd ever heard. More than a mere glint of recognition shone in his brown eyes. He stared past me, off in Libbyland, before returning to the conversation. "She was...a good customer. I miss her very much."

He definitely missed more than her purchases.

"I have not seen her in some time."

Like nine months? Which reminded me Libby had claimed she was due in six weeks rather than two. Why?

"Has she moved back to Paris?" He wore a hopeful expression. "Are you visiting her here?"

Something told me he wasn't referring to Libby having run off two days ago. When exactly had she told him she was leaving and why? What motive had she had for lying to Gilles?

Was he my niece's father?

Why else would Libby have lied to him?

I glanced over at the satin-and-lace wedding dress Libby had brought in. "Your salesman mentioned Libby sold the shop her wedding dress."

Gilles's gaze darted to the dress. "Libby brought that in?" He looked like he was going to be ill. "Libby is married?"

This had to be her baby's father. Although he wasn't Libby's type, maybe it had merely been a fling for her. She'd met him while picking out Mirko's desk and suddenly had the urge to take a walk on the "tame" side. Yet I was starting to think maybe I no longer knew Libby's type.

"Libby is married?" he demanded again.

I shook my head.

"Where is she? Is she staying with her father?"

"Her father? You must be mistaken. Her father doesn't live in Paris." Guess he didn't know Libby as well as I'd thought.

He looked confused. "He lives in Montmartre. Or at least he used to. Her father is Derrick Hunter, *non*?"

No. *Our* father was Derrick Hunter.

Dad lived in Paris?

My stomach dropped to the hardwood floor, and the entire room was spinning. I was sure I was about to vomit in the five-thousand-euro oriental vase on the table. Had Dad moved here to be by Libby, or had she moved here to be by him? It suddenly dawned on me Ms. Duran was French.

Heart racing, I somehow maintained my composure and spoke as calmly as possible. "Oh, I didn't realize he was her *father*. Thought he was her *uncle*. I'm not sure if she's visiting him or not. I'm actually a friend of a friend in town on business. My friend mentioned maybe Libby was around." I was talking so fast, my pitch so high, I sounded on the verge of hysteria. *Stay in control.* "Where exactly does he live?"

"I'll write the directions for you." He pulled a business card and pen from his suit jacket. He scribbled on the back of the card and handed it to me, not appearing to notice my trembling hand. "It's north of the city. Please, ask Libby to call me." His eyes pleaded with me.

I was torn about whether or not to mention Dominique. After all, I wasn't sure he was the father, and if he were, it was Libby's place to tell him, not mine.

But Libby wasn't here, was she?

A phone shrilled, filling the awkward silence. A second later, Evette popped out from the back and called across the room to Gilles. I managed to catch the word *l'épouse*.

This guy's *wife* was on the phone?

Gilles glanced over at me, looking busted. I couldn't wipe the shocked expression off my face fast enough. He knew that *I* knew who he was. The fact he had a wife was why Libby thought he wasn't marriage or father material.

I wondered if his *wife* knew he wasn't.

Chapter Twenty-One

Libby not telling me about Gilles was one thing. She knew I wouldn't have approved of an affair with a married man after what Dad had done to us. But Libby living in the same city with Dad for three years without telling me might just be unforgivable. Had she planned on telling me before I left Paris? Libby wasn't here to give me answers, and I sure as hell wasn't going to ask Dad. But maybe his letters could tell me what I needed to know.

I arrived at Luc's, blood racing. I rapped on his door, even though his scooter wasn't parked outside, just to be sure. No answer. Using my key, I unlocked the door and flew inside. I glanced around the apartment, not wanting to riffle through Luc's personal stuff but wanting to find Libby's hatbox. There weren't many hiding spots. I started in the kitchen and, within a few minutes, found the box at the back of a cupboard. I dropped onto the worn, linoleum floor and began reading the letters in order, the sick feeling in my stomach intensifying with each page.

Libby had found Dad through a private detective. She'd known he was living here when she'd signed up for the study abroad program. Following the program, she'd obviously stayed with Dad rather than some art professor in need of an au pair. Dad's family was the one that had treated her like a daughter because she *was* a daughter!

One letter read: *And how is my ladybug doing?*

How dare he still call me ladybug after everything that had happened. Yet the word caused my chest to tighten, recalling how he'd given me the nickname because I'd loved capturing ladybugs. I stared past the letter at the contents of the hatbox, noticing the red velvet pouch was flat...empty. I unzipped it to confirm the two bundles of cash were gone. If Luc cared about money, he'd go back to being a chef. Besides, he wouldn't steal from Libby.

Libby had apparently come home when I was at the puppet show the other day with Luc. Before I'd brought Luc the box.

My stomach dropped. The money was gone, and so was Libby.

Had she cleaned out her savings account also? I had this sick feeling Libby wasn't returning. A week ago, I'd never dreamed she'd run off and abandon her daughter and me. However, if there was one thing I now knew, it was that I no longer *knew* Libby. How could she abandon her baby after what Dad had done to us? Wherever she'd gone, it'd likely been on impulse. She could be gone until the ten grand ran out. It could last Libby years if she shacked up with a band of Romanian gypsies.

If she sold Bruno's forgeries, she'd be set for life.

Somebody had to know where she was. Did Dad know?

I had to stay in Paris. If I didn't, what if Dad had a shot at temporary custody when Dominique was released from the hospital? No way would I allow that to happen. It would also kill me if she went into the foster care system. But not being a French citizen, did I have a shot at temporary custody? I needed to hire a lawyer. Needing Luc's help, I called his cell phone again, getting voice mail. He'd mentioned the line he'd be working on was packed with tourists, servicing the Louvre and the Champs Élysées. I took off for the *Métro*.

The closest stop for the orange line that serviced the Louvre and Champs Élysées, was Châtelet. According to the map at the *Métro* station, four lines ran through it. *Quelle* nightmare. I opted for the smaller Louvre Rivoli station serviced merely by the orange line. No clue which direction Luc would be heading, I stood on the westbound platform and scanned both westbound and eastbound incoming trains for a bright red puppet curtain.

Thirteen trains later, I was about to say screw it when a train pulled into the station and a streak of red cruised past at the back of car number four. I raced down the platform. The train's doors whooshed open, and I hopped on. I followed the lively music to the back of the car and stuck my head behind the curtain.

Luc smiled. "You came to help."

I threw my arms around him. He hugged me, his embrace reassuring me everything would be fine. The train jerked into motion, and he stood firmly, steadying us.

Luc drew back slightly, looking concerned. "What's wrong?" He removed the puppet from his hand and smoothed his hand over my hair.

"I think I met Dominique's father. Gilles Beaufay. He owns the antique store with the cradle."

"Ah, bon?"

"That wasn't as big of a surprise as finding out my dad lives in Paris. Can you believe that?" I waited for Luc to gasp in surprise and his eyes to widen in stunned amazement. Instead, his gaze darted apprehensively to the puppet in his hand, a guilty expression on his face. "You knew about my dad?" I muttered, taking a step back, slipping from his embrace. "And you didn't tell me?"

"You were so upset about the letters. I was afraid of what you might do if you found out your father lives here. I knew Libby wasn't with him."

"How'd you know that?"

"I phoned him."

My hand snapped to my stomach like I'd been punched in the gut. "You *spoke* with my dad and never told me?"

My God. Was there anybody left in my life who hadn't betrayed me?

"I'm...sorry."

"So he knows Libby's gone?"

"No, I asked only if she was staying there."

"How do you know she wasn't?"

"Because he told me to try her at work. That he hadn't spoken to her in several weeks."

"Maybe he was lying and she's hiding out there."

"I don't think Libby would go to him for help. When she came back, I was going to tell her she must tell you—"

"Well, things kind of changed once Libby left. You should have told me."

"I'm sorry. I expected her to be back sooner. I should not be the one to tell you about your father."

Like I shouldn't be the one to tell Gilles about his daughter?

"Why didn't Libby tell me about him when I got here? Why didn't she tell me about him three years ago when she started writing him?"

"She said you wouldn't understand. You would be upset with her, and you wouldn't care what her reasons were." He looked like he agreed with her.

"When Libby ran off, wouldn't she assume I'd come across him at some point? Or didn't it matter? Because she didn't plan on returning anyway?"

"She's coming back."

"Bullshit. Libby's not coming back. Or maybe you already knew that also. The money's gone, and so is Libby!"

Luckily, the train was pulling into a station, allowing me a quick getaway. The doors slid open, and I bolted out before Luc could break down his theater and follow me.

Luc had lied to my face, same as Evan. Even if he'd done it because he believed it was for the best, he hadn't been honest with me. How was I ever supposed to trust him again?

I tried to forget about Luc for the moment. My gut told me Dad knew where Libby had gone. He was the only person she could confide in who would empathize and not think she was a horrible person for ditching her baby. If I took the *Métro* to Montmartre, I'd have no clue where to go upon exiting the station, so I hiked up to the street and flagged down a taxi. I'd beat down his door and demand to know where Libby was.

En route to Montmartre, Luc called twice. I let the calls go to voice mail. If I talked to him, I'd end up saying things I'd regret. I tended to act impulsively in the heat of the moment lately, like quitting my job. Twice.

Ten minutes later, I stood on the street in front of the address Gilles had given me. Rather than a residence, it was a café. Gilles had written down either the wrong street or wrong address number. Glancing in both directions, trying to decide which way to head, my gaze landed on the café's specials written on a blackboard displayed on the sidewalk. There was no mistaking the sharp, angular print.

Dad was here.

Chest tightening and heart racing, my gaze darted to a waiter in his early twenties then to one in his late fifties and another around the same age. Both older men had gray hair, one a bit taller than the other. I didn't know Dad's height. I could picture him next to Mom, who was really short, so everyone had seemed tall next to her.

I snagged a table and sat down.

One of the older waiters stopped three tables away. I sniffed the air, smelling melted butter, freshly brewed coffee, and puke from my shoulder. No Aqua Velva. They undoubtedly didn't sell it in Paris. I strained to hear the man talking, unsure if I'd recognize Dad's voice even if he was speaking English rather than French.

"Bonjour, Madame. Vous avez choisi?" a man asked.

I glanced up to find the other older waiter standing in front of me. He had a faint tan and a lean build. My gaze locked on a scar slicing his square chin. Dad had a gash on his chin from slipping on the ice while shoveling the sidewalk one winter. The years, and hopefully guilt and regret, had dulled his bright blue eyes. If I removed my sunglasses, would a glint of recognition flicker in his eyes?

I wanted to stand up, and demand face-to-face to know where Libby was. Demand to know why he'd left. Instead, the only word I could force through the emotional lump closing up my throat was, "Orangina." I sounded like some meek little ten-year-old girl.

He turned and left for my soda.

After twenty-four years, all I could say was Orangina? I'd envisioned this day forever. All the things I would say. That I'd pass by him begging on a street corner and dump my Starbucks in his tin cup of change. I'd always imagined it as a triumphant day. I never dreamed that my anger and contempt for this man would be overshadowed by underlying feelings of heartache and pain. Feelings I'd worked years to repress.

Talking with another waiter, Dad let out a hearty laugh. The sound brought back memories of him laughing while tickling me on the living room floor. The time he'd doubled over laughing at our cat, Mitsy, chasing the neighbor's bulldog, Gunther, around the yard until it hopped in our little plastic swimming pool for protection, somehow knowing Mitsy hated water.

My throat closed up even more, and tears threatened the rims of my eyes. No way was I having a meltdown in front of Dad and giving him the upper hand. I surged from my chair and bolted from the café, the sound of his laugh lost in the screams of a red-faced toddler throwing a temper tantrum with his mother. A much more welcoming sound.

I had to get it together and go back for both Libby's sake and mine. After twenty-four years, I needed closure.

But right now, I needed distance.

Chapter Twenty-Two

On the taxi ride back to Libby's, I shoved aside any good memories of Dad, and my tears evaporated before they could hit my cheeks. As upset as I was with Luc, I still had the urge to call him. The first time I'd seen Dad in twenty-four years and I had nobody to confide in. Mom was the last person I'd call. I'd leave that to Libby. Let her be responsible for Mom's meltdown. Yet, as usual, I'd be the one picking up the pieces.

Attempting to get the picture of Dad out of my head, I pulled up my fan page. Ella had replied to my message.

> *I live in Connecticut.* ☹ *But I travel to Europe on business several times a year. Love Fournier. Go have a 2006 Alfa Crux and we'll toast to your future. You'll find an employer that recognizes your worth!*

I replied.

> *I really need a drink. Just saw my dad for the first time in twenty-four years. He abandoned the family when I was ten...*

I couldn't believe the only person I had to confide in, I didn't even know.

The taxi dropped me off at Libby's building, and Gigi trotted over from the flower shop, tail wagging. She plopped down on the sidewalk, and I petted her belly. Would be nice to be greeted so affectionately every time I came home.

"I just saw my dad for the first time in twenty-four years," I told Gigi.

She peered up at me with big, somber, brown eyes, sympathizing with me.

"Yeah, it was hard. You're lucky Cecile would never leave you. You're much too cute." I continued rubbing her belly, and she placed a paw against my hand as if holding it. I smiled. My shoulders relaxed slightly, and my blood pressure dropped below stroke level for the first time since Gilles told me Dad was in Paris. "Thanks for listening."

Upon entering Libby's building, I encountered Gilles Beaufay sitting on the bottom step with the antique cradle. My blood pressure shot back up. A stern expression replaced the charming, dimpled smile and gentle, brown eyes from earlier. "Evette told me you bought the cradle. I found the payment slip with your name and address. You're Libby's sister, aren't you?" he demanded, standing.

I nodded.

"She talked about you often."

"Well, she never talked about *you*," I said coolly.

He looked disappointed but not surprised Libby hadn't mentioned him. His expression relaxed slightly. "So, did Libby ever leave Paris, or did she just leave me?"

"She never left Paris."

He nodded at the cradle. "She's pregnant, isn't she?"

I shook my head. Technically, she was no longer pregnant. "The cradle's for my hotel rep and friend who's pregnant. And I'm..." I almost claimed to be renting an apartment there, but it dawned on me he'd likely seen Hunter listed on the intercom outside.

I couldn't tell if he was relieved or disappointed, or if he even believed me that Libby wasn't pregnant. I wasn't about to hand over my niece to some philanderer who was no better than Dad. Who might not stick around. If, by chance, he took responsibility for his daughter, I didn't want him and his wife raising Dominique. His wife would probably take his infidelity out on my niece and be a wicked stepmother.

"I love Libby," he said. "She's very special. Compassionate, generous, and beautiful. She made me feel more alive than I have in so long."

Kind of how Luc made me feel.

"She gave me the strength I needed to leave my wife."

I raised a skeptical brow. "What about the phone call from your wife?"

"We're separated, getting a divorce."

Maybe a ploy to see Libby. Even if he was being honest, he'd just left his wife and possibly kids. Not a great track record. If Libby didn't return and I told Gilles he had a daughter and he, by chance, wanted to take on a baby by himself, he'd be a single parent. He owned three antique shops and likely traveled all over Europe searching for items to fill them. He'd never be around. Yet didn't Dominique have the right to know her dad?

Yes. Once I knew for sure he *was* her dad.

"I sent letters telling her how I feel, but she didn't respond. Either she didn't care or I hoped maybe she didn't have her mail sent to her new address." He gazed longingly up the open stairway. "She's not home."

"She's out of town."

"Where?"

I shrugged.

"I have to find her. If you won't tell me where she is, your father will."

What if Dad *did* know where Libby was and Gilles got to her first? I couldn't let that happen. Libby would never forgive me. And how dare this guy stick his nose in my family business. If anyone was going to confront Dad and tell him I was in town, it would be me.

"I just asked my dad, and he has no idea where she is. Besides, Libby doesn't want to see you. That's why she left you."

He looked like he'd been sucker-punched, and I almost felt guilty playing him for a sucker. Almost.

—⌒ ⌒—

I'd insisted I didn't need Gilles's help hauling the cradle up the six flights of stairs to Libby's. Furniture was made much better two hundred years ago, and it was like dragging a redwood tree up the side of Mount Everest. I was standing on the stoop of the second floor, glaring up the open staircase, when a young guy stopped and helped me schlep it up to Libby's.

The guy no sooner left when my cell phone rang out. Bruno. The hairs on the back of my neck shot straight up. The call went to voice mail, and I waited a second to check the message. Bruno sounded even more crazed than ever, pissed that I was five minutes late for our meeting at the garden. Thank God. He didn't know where Libby was. He demanded to know where *I* was. I was the hell out of Libby's apartment, that's where. I hadn't thought this plan through or that my no-showing would push Bruno over the edge. I had maybe fifteen minutes before Bruno figured out he'd been scammed and showed up here, taking the door off the hinges.

I stripped off my pukey shirt and quickly changed into a black, sleeveless shirt and black-and-white blazer. I kept on jeans. I slipped on my black designer mules, the blister on my little toe protesting. I told it to suck it up.

This was *the* most important meeting of my life.

I bolted out of the taxi in front of the café where Dad worked. Hovering at the perimeter of the restaurant where the chairs flowed onto the sidewalk, I scanned the inside of the café, spotting Dad waiting on a table. Apparently feeling my stare, he glanced over at me. Our gazes locked. I didn't have my sunglasses on this time, and it only took a moment for recognition to register in his eyes. Libby had likely showed him recent photos of me. He certainly wasn't drawn to me by some innate paternal instinct.

Without excusing himself from the customer, he tentatively walked toward me. Heart thumping madly, I stood my ground, letting him come to me, relishing the apprehensive look on his face. He stopped several feet in front of me.

"Samantha," he said softly.

I steeled my emotions, channeling any hurt I felt into anger. I swallowed the stupid lump in my throat. "Do you know where Libby is?" I said calmly, while my kneecaps jumped up and down like those Mexican jumping beans I used to buy when I was a kid. I tensed my leg muscles, willing them to get a grip.

"No, I haven't seen her for several weeks. Isn't she at her apartment or work?"

I looked for signs that he was lying. Like the twitch in Evan's jaw or how he swept a hand nervously down his tie. I didn't know Dad well enough to recognize his telltale mannerisms, but I knew him well enough not to trust him.

"I wouldn't be here if she were," I said coolly.

He looked taken aback by my bluntness, glancing down at the menu in his hand. "Right, of course. Maybe she's at the hospital. She's due soon." A proud smile spread across his face at the prospect of being a grandpa.

Like hell if I was telling him he'd become one.

I turned and marched down the sidewalk.

"Wait," he called out, following me. "Don't go."

The heels of my mules clicked determinedly against the sidewalk. This time, *I* was the one doing the abandoning.

"Please, Samantha. Stay." His voice filled with desperation.

I spun around. "Funny, I said almost the exact same thing to you twenty-four years ago. 'Please, Daddy, don't go. Stay here with us.' Did you listen to me? No. So why the hell should I listen to you now? Because Libby did? Because she obviously believed all your bullshit excuses for never contacting us."

"I sent you letters and cards." His brow wrinkled in confusion. "I figured Libby was too young to remember but I thought you would."

"What letters and cards?"

"If you never got them, then why'd you send a letter telling me not to contact you? To stay away?"

I rolled my eyes. "So now I'm supposed to believe you stayed away because of some phantom letter I never wrote? How dare you try to blame this on me."

"I'm not, believe me. There's no excuse for what I did. Regardless of your letter."

"Enough with the letter I never wrote."

"I still have it. I couldn't bring myself to throw it away. Wait here. I'll get it." He held my gaze until I reluctantly nodded I'd wait. He turned and entered a door alongside the café, which apparently led up to his home. He likely owned the business and didn't merely work there.

I glanced around, searching for Ms. Duran playing hostess, seating patrons, telling them to sit up straight or they'd get scoliosis. I'd spent fourth grade walking around like I had a board up my butt because I'd respected the wretched woman and believed everything she'd told me. Hopefully osteoporosis had her looking like Quasimodo in *The Hunchback of Notre Dame*.

A taxi approached, and I stepped toward the curb, tempted to flag it down and never see Dad again. I raised a trembling hand then lowered it. I wanted to call Dad's bluff when he was unable to produce the letter.

Moments later, Dad returned and handed me a letter written on a sheet of smiley-face stationary I'd received for my tenth birthday. The letter was brief and to the point, stating I didn't love him, that Libby and I wanted him to stay away. My fingers clenched the edges of the paper, like my hand had gripped the pencil the night I'd written the letter as a form of therapy. The hastily scribbled penmanship pressed firmly into the paper reflected my anger. When the letter was gone from my desktop the next day, I'd assumed I'd inadvertently thrown it away and Mom had emptied the garbage.

Mom must have sent it.

My stomach tossed. How could she have done such an awful thing?

So was this why Libby hadn't told me about finding Dad? Believing I'd sent this letter, she resented me for making him stay away all those years?

I thrust the letter at Dad. "This letter is no excuse. I was ten, for

God's sake. You were the adult. You should have come around regardless."

"I know." He took the letter, shaking his head wearily. "I knew how upset you were, and I hoped if I stayed away and gave you space, you'd change your mind. The longer I stayed away, the more difficult it was to go and see you."

"Putting thousands of miles and an ocean between us didn't make it any easier. You can stop being a husband; you can't just stop being a father."

"I was a shitty father. I worked long hours. I was never around on weekends. I missed half of your birthday parties and Christmas programs. I'm sorry. I just couldn't deal with your mother anymore. She was destroying my life."

He sounded like me, justifying why I'd make a bad mother. Was I so desperate to find Libby because I wanted her to take responsibility for her baby or because *I* refused to take responsibility for my niece? If I dragged Libby's ass back home and forced her to be a mother, how good of a job would she do? How long before she took off again?

"So you decided to destroy everyone's life but your own? I can't believe you left us with her. How did you think she was going to take care of us? Doesn't matter." I turned to leave.

"Don't go, Samantha," a young man called out.

I turned to find Oxford Guy exiting the building Dad had come out of minutes earlier. What the hell? We stood staring into each other's eyes.

"I'm Étienne," the guy said with a faint French accent. "Your brother."

"Omigod," I muttered.

I always figured one of the reasons Dad had left was because he'd no longer wanted kids. But he just hadn't wanted Libby and me. Tears filled my eyes, and I slipped my sunglasses down from the top of my head, refusing to let Dad see me cry.

Étienne stepped toward me, and I held up my hand, shaking my head. "Don't. Just...don't."

I took off, escaping down the narrow, winding streets of

Montmartre. Yet unable to escape my past.

—☙ ❧—

Fifteen minutes later, I was totally lost. My calves throbbed from zipping up and down hills, and I'd almost wiped out twice on the slippery cobblestone sidewalks. I feared if I stopped to figure out where I was, I would have a complete breakdown and collapse on the sidewalk, unable to get up. People would congregate around me as I sobbed uncontrollably, assuming I was some dramatic performance artist. I wiped a tear from my cheek.

Stop crying!

Libby had stayed in Paris to be not only with Dad but with our half brother. They'd been one big, happy family while Mom and I'd been clueless in Milwaukee. So much for Dad being a destitute street bum. He owned a booming café with his loving family. I'd had a brother, or rather, *half* brother, all these years and had never known. Did I have a half sister or another half brother? Had Mom known this and it contributed to her breakdown?

I stalked across a square filled with artists, restaurants, and tourists. I turned a corner and came to an abrupt halt, gazing in reverence up the side of the towering, white basilica, Sacré Coeur, fifty feet away. Several small domes topped towers and turrets, which surrounded a large dome in the center. I felt drawn to go inside and say a prayer, light a candle, or something.

Rather than the ethereal sound of a harp or pipe organ rejoicing from inside the church, the tinny, carefree sound of a steel drum filled the air, along with a man's raspy voice singing Bobby McFerrin's "Don't Worry, Be Happy." Sophie would say this was a sign that everything would be all right. I took it as sign that I should hop the first plane to the Caribbean and get the hell out of Paris.

I walked around to the front of the church to find Bob Marley incarnate, dreadlocks and all. Tourists lounged on the church steps, taking in the panoramic view of Paris, recuperating after hiking up hundreds of stairs from the bottom of the hill.

The Eiffel Tower appeared tiny on the horizon. It seemed so far away. As did my dinner with Evan. Only four nights ago, yet it felt like years with all that had happened. I'd come to Paris expecting a few challenges with the group, never foreseeing both my professional and personal lives going to hell. Never dreaming Evan proposing and not recommending me for the promotion would turn out to be the *least* of my problems.

My gaze swept across the city.

Where the hell are you, Libby?

A car with a faulty muffler chugged up the road alongside the church, drowning out Bob Marley. I peered over at a dented, pea green Citroen with Étienne behind the wheel. Ignoring the no-parking sign, he stopped the car. He cautiously stepped out and walked toward me, our gazes locking. Did he expect me to embrace him like some long-lost brother? The brother Dad had wanted more than he'd wanted Libby and me?

Squaring my shoulders, chin jutted out in defiance, I stood rooted in place. My nose was probably bright red from crying, but at least my sunglasses hid my red-rimmed eyes and emotions. "If you came here on my dad's behalf, you're wasting your time. Nothing you can say will change my mind about him. Not to mention, it's none of your business."

"I would never try to justify what our dad did. It's unforgivable," Étienne said firmly with condemnation. "I was furious when I found out I had two sisters he'd never told me about."

"*Half* sisters," I corrected.

Étienne didn't appear deterred by my comment. "Our father has never been real open. It hurt worse that my mother hadn't told me. And she condoned him not having contact with his own children. If my parents had separated and my father hadn't wanted to see me, would she have thought this was okay?"

I never understood what type of woman would allow the man she loved to ditch his kids and never contact them. She was a teacher, for God's sake; she should have been more compassionate.

"I'll never know. She died ten years ago, when I was fourteen."

That meant he was twenty-four. Ms. Duran had likely been

pregnant when Dad had left. Had Mom known that?

I didn't feel bad for Dad losing his wife, but I grudgingly felt a tinge of sympathy for Étienne losing his mom. I knew how hard it was to lose a parent. I felt like I should say I was sorry about his mom's death, but I couldn't.

"I didn't know about you or Libby until she contacted our father. When he learned she was coming to Paris, he had no choice but to tell me about her. I didn't speak to him for more than a year. Libby came up to London where I live, and I liked her instantly. After my mother died, it would have been nice to have had sisters. Libby sounded like you took good care of her when she was little."

I eyed his Oxford T-shirt. He'd likely gone to an Ivy League school while I'd struggled putting myself through a state university. He wasn't hurting, except for that crummy car. Yet I couldn't imagine what Libby and I would have done without each other growing up.

"How did you find me in Pigalle that day?"

"Libby told me you were coming to Paris and where you were staying. She'd showed me photos of you. She wanted to tell you about me before we met. She said you weren't going to be happy to meet me. I was getting impatient. I hadn't heard from her since you arrived; she wasn't returning my messages." So Étienne was the anonymous caller on Libby's answering machine. "I waited outside Libby's for you and followed you to Pigalle. I wanted to see what you were like. I could tell I scared you when looking at the toys, so I stopped following you. I'm sorry if I frightened you. Dad just told me someone called looking for Libby the other day. Is she gone?"

I nodded.

"I hope she's okay. Last month when I left to go back to London, she seemed sad. I was worried about her. Once she has the baby, I think she'll be better."

Think again. Amazingly, for all the times Étienne had followed me, I'd never led him to the hospital. He seemed genuinely concerned. And it made me feel better Libby hadn't confided in him about where she'd gone, even though I was desperate to find her. But that didn't mean he might not have an idea on where she was.

"Libby had her baby."

His eyes widened in surprise, and an anxious smile lit up his face. "When?"

"Three days ago. She left the hospital Tuesday morning, and nobody has seen her since."

"Why would she have done such a thing?"

I shrugged.

"She wasn't due for six weeks."

"Actually, she was due in two weeks."

He looked confused but shook it off. "How's the baby?"

"Fine. She had a girl."

Étienne didn't seem like an awful guy, but I couldn't bring myself to stand there discussing Libby. Although it wasn't his fault Dad had chosen to be a father to him and not to Libby and me, I couldn't look at him without being reminded of this fact. And having a relationship with him would be a connection to Dad, as if I forgave him.

"I need to go," I said, turning away.

"I may know where Libby went."

I glanced back over at him. "Where? Some castle with dogs peeing in a pond?"

He looked surprised. "It's not really a castle, and dogs pee in a fountain, not a pond. It's two hours away."

A shiver crept up my spine. Sophie's visions had been almost accurate. Or maybe she'd seen a photo of Libby at this place, so subconsciously she knew it existed. Yet how had she known that was where Libby was? Libby had to be there. Libby hiding out only two hours away rather than across Europe with a band of Romanian gypsies meant she hadn't gone far because she planned to return.

I called and told Sophie her visions were accurate. Of course, she wasn't the least bit surprised. Thankfully, she agreed to tag along. No way could I ride alone in the same car with Étienne for two hours. I didn't care to hear about Étienne's life story.

I just wanted to regain some control over *my* life.

Chapter Twenty-Three

From the backseat of Étienne's Citroen, I gazed out at the cattle, as white as milk, grazing on Burgundy's rolling, green hillsides. Charolais cattle, according to Étienne. For all the cows we had in Wisconsin, I'd never seen white ones. The pasture gave way to a sprawling vineyard filled with workers and strange looking tractors riding over the vines, shaking off the grapes. Every so often, a lone bench materialized alongside the road in the middle of nowhere overlooking a vineyard, inviting travelers to stop and enjoy a leisurely bottle of wine and baguette while watching the harvest.

Our drive was anything *but* leisurely.

Étienne's "shortcut" was leading us down narrow roads he cornered like an Andretti wannabe. When he swerved to miss three bicyclists, he assured us the car had an excellent safety rating and put it to the test once again, swerving to miss another group of cyclists then an old man walking a dog.

Very poor, or likely *no*, shocks gave the car the ride of a vintage wooden roller coaster. One more sharp corner and the rattling door—held shut with a bungee cord tied from the door handle to the base of the front seat—would be history.

I really shouldn't rip on the car. The incessant humming and vibrating made carrying on a conversation with Étienne and Sophie in the front impossible. Leaving me alone to ponder things like whether or not my health insurance would cover me in France should I be in an accident. If I even *had* insurance, since I'd quit my job.

Needing a distraction, I checked my Facebook page.

4,822 Likes.

No reply from Ella. I had a few more job offers. One from some obscure brewing company in Australia. I couldn't expect to land my dream job in a matter of hours.

Étienne suddenly grabbed a discarded fast-food bag off the floor by Sophie's feet and placed it on his lap and scribbled madly, peering down instead of at the road. Sophie pointed out a medieval abbey perched on a hill, and his gaze followed hers. Sophie marveled at the sight. I, however, kept my eyes glued to the road, more concerned with what lay ahead than around us. Étienne had been playing tour guide as we zipped past quaint villages, famous vineyards, and medieval abbeys and chateaus. While growing up, he'd spent his summers at their family villa, while I'd spent mine mowing lawns and babysitting. The home had been in his mother's family for five generations. Mom wouldn't be passing down my grandma's wedding ring she'd pawned, let alone a villa.

A half hour later, the sun was low on the horizon, a purplish-pink sunset impressionist artists lived for. We turned onto a gravel drive, and Étienne opened a stone fence's wooden gate. A sign's red script lettering read *Villa de Famille*. How sweet. We drove down the tree-lined drive for a half mile until a quaint, stone house appeared.

Sophie gasped. "The house, it is from my dreams."

Not exactly a castle. Guess her visions embellished things a tad. I wouldn't call it a villa, either, like the sign read, but I grudgingly admitted it was cute. A blanket of wisteria and a perky red door and shutters softened the stone house's rough exterior. A cobblestone patio across from the house held a trellis wrapped in lush foliage and a wooden patio set overlooking a fenced-in garden and a small swimming pool below.

I stepped from the car, breathing in the scent of grass and nature, happy to be alive. Birds chirped merrily, perched on the branches of massive oak trees. Two frolicking bunnies chased each other among the overgrown bushes lining the front of the house. Heart thumping wildly in my chest, my gaze locked on the red door. If Libby was inside, I couldn't lay into her about Dad right off the bat. I had to allow her to explain why in the hell she was hiding out in the boonies and not in the hospital caring for her daughter.

Before we reached the house, Libby stepped out the red door. My shoulders and chest collapsed with relief. Thank God she was okay. Yet she looked far from her usual cheery self. Dressed in the same orange gauze skirt and top she'd worn to the hospital, the skirt's stretched-out elastic waistband hung low on her hips. With her slumped shoulders and glazed-over eyes rimmed with dark circles, she looked like she'd had the life sucked out of her. No trace of the giggling little girl in the mural on her apartment wall. She glanced between the three of us, as if trying to process how we'd all come to be there together. When we picked up Sophie, it had been apparent she knew of Étienne; however, they'd never met.

"Are you okay?" I asked.

Libby nodded wearily.

"You should sit down." Étienne slipped his hand around Libby's, giving it a comforting squeeze.

A twinge of jealousy shot through me at the sight of Étienne holding Libby's hand, caring for her. That was my role. Although I hadn't done a real bang-up job of it over the past few years. And it wasn't merely because Libby had put thousands of miles between us.

The mural on Libby's wall flashed through my mind, of us no longer holding hands thanks to the missing piece. It was true.

Étienne had taken my place.

A lump formed in my throat, and I glanced away from them as we headed over to the patio. Libby wilted into an Adirondack chair, appearing small and fragile cocooned in the large, wooden chair. She peered down at the garden, at a stone fountain with statues of dogs perched along the perimeter, their hind legs raised, peeing water into the fountain. I sat next to Libby.

"Why don't I show you the fountain and the flower garden?" Étienne said to Sophie.

Sophie nodded. "The dogs, I see them peeing every night, but I would love to see the flowers."

Étienne gave her a curious look. As they walked off, I took a deep breath, my heart beating so hard blood pulsated in my ears.

Libby's fragile state made me want to cry. I'd give anything to see her happy, to be crashing funerals with her and Sophie right now.

"Why'd you leave the hospital?" I asked in a concerned, nonjudgmental tone.

Libby's gaze remained glued to the fountain. "I was scared," she finally said in a small voice, like when she was little and wanted to crawl in bed with me after a bad dream.

I perched on the edge of my chair, moving closer to her. "I was scared, too, Libby. My God, I thought something had happened to you. I had no clue what was going on." My voice was starting to rise, so I brought it down a few notches. "I know becoming a mom is a huge responsibility." I'd been thinking a lot about it over the past few days. "But you have a baby. You need to take care of her."

"That's not why I was scared." She gazed down, gathering up the skirt's loose waistband, clutching it tightly. "I was scared because I *wanted* to be a mother. After spending all night with my daughter by my bed, watching her, listening to her breathe, I didn't want to lose her."

Was Libby delirious with fever?

"So you ran away?"

"I never planned on being a mother."

"Well, you are one." I placed a reassuring hand on hers, wanting desperately for us to reconnect.

Pain filled the vacant look in Libby's eyes, and she peered over at me for the first time. "No, I'm not. I never planned on being a mother because I don't plan on keeping my baby. A couple from Nice is adopting her."

I snapped back in the chair, removing my hand from Libby's, staring at her in confused disbelief. "You're putting Dominique up for adoption?"

Libby nodded faintly. It didn't seem to register with her that I'd named her daughter.

"Was the money in the hatbox from this?"

She looked surprised I'd found the money. "I went through a private agency so I could select the best possible parents myself. The Michauds are wonderful people. But I took the money the day

I left the hospital to give it back to them and tell them the adoption was off. Then I went to the garden and saw all these couples playing with their kids. My daughter deserves that sort of family. Like we never had."

"Gilles is getting divorced," I blurted. "Your daughter can have two parents." If I couldn't talk Libby into moving home, I at least had to convince her to keep Dominique regardless of where they lived.

A fleeting sparkle lit her eyes. "You met Gilles?" She spoke his name in the same loving manner he'd spoken hers.

Gilles was definitely the father.

I nodded. "Why didn't you tell me about him?"

"You wouldn't have approved of me having an affair with a married guy with kids. I didn't think it was right, but I can't help who I fall in love with. I can't control my emotions."

I could no longer control mine either. Not that Libby would believe that.

"He still loves you."

She shook her head. "Doesn't matter. We wouldn't work out. The Michauds will be in Paris tomorrow. Their train gets in at five."

My stomach dropped. Some strangers were going to take Dominique away. Once they arrived, could they prevent me from seeing her? Would they let her keep her giraffe blanket or the cradle? I'd never know if the cradle was passed down to Dominique's children. Or if she even had children. My heart raced. Some strangers were going to rock Dominique to sleep at night and tell her stories.

No way was I allowing that to happen.

"I'll give you twenty grand. I'll adopt her." Holy crap. Was I serious? Was I thinking rationally? All I could *think* was that I didn't want to lose Dominique.

Libby looked blown away by my proposal. "This isn't eBay, Sam. She's not going to the highest bidder. It's not about the money. They were willing to pay three times what they did."

"You'd rather give your baby to some couple you don't know than your own sister?" Listen to me. If I'd known Libby was giving her baby up for adoption before she'd had her, I'd probably have encouraged her to do so.

"Your lifestyle isn't conducive to having a baby. You said so yourself when Evan told you he wants kids."

"But I was wrong."

She gave me an incredulous look. "That was just a few days ago."

"Yeah, well, a lot has happened. I quit my job."

Libby's gaze narrowed with suspicion.

"I'm getting one that won't require so much travel. A nine-to-five job." Was I making promises I couldn't keep?

"I want my baby to have caring, compassionate parents who really want her. Who'll always be there for her."

"I'll be there for her." The two-parent part was a bit trickier. I wasn't taking Evan back, and I doubted Luc ever wanted to get married again or that he'd move to the United States.

Since when had I even considered marrying Luc?

"Like you were always there for me?" she challenged, glancing away.

I sat there shell-shocked then finally said, "Like I wasn't more of a mother to you than Dad was ever a father?"

"I'm sure you're pissed about me moving here by him, but I was only five when he left. I just wanted to know him, know why he'd left."

"And you blamed me for his leaving."

"Because Ms. Duran was your teacher? That's insane. You're the only one who blamed you."

"As if you didn't blame me for the letter."

"What letter?"

I was surprised Dad hadn't told her about the letter in an attempt to get himself off the hook and place more blame on me.

I ignored her question. "You still should have told me you found him and that we have a half brother. You've been here three years and never said a word. You know how that makes me feel?"

"If I'd told you, you'd have flown over here and insisted I come home. Dad asked me to stay. He wanted to get to know me. Ever since you got your job, you were never around. I'd rather have had you involved in my life, even though you didn't always approve of it, than giving me money."

"Yet you continued to accept my money?" Libby was being a bit of a hypocrite placing all the blame on me.

"It wasn't for me."

My eyes widened. "Then who was it for?"

"You wouldn't understand."

"I have a right to know."

"Maybe if you knew me, you'd know. You don't even know me anymore, Sam." Libby shook her head in defeat.

When had my maternal instincts been overshadowed by my need for financial stability? I'd once been able to comfort Libby. To heal her pain whether it be sticking up for her when a kid picked on her or putting a Band-Aid on a sore. Not only was I no longer able to make the pain go away, I'd *caused* part of the pain.

"I want to know you, Libby. I'm...sorry."

"I'm so tired." She pushed herself up from the chair with great effort.

"Libby, we need to talk."

"There's nothing to say. I'm giving her up for adoption, Sam." As Libby headed toward the house, the lights on either side of the front door flashed on, casting a yellow glow against the encroaching darkness.

"If you're doing the right thing, then why are you so upset about it? You look like crap, Libby. This isn't what you want." She kept walking. "You're no better than Dad, abandoning your own child." I snapped my mouth shut, feeling like a royal bitch.

Libby paused, her limp body going rigid.

"I'm...sorry."

Without turning around, she walked inside the house.

A tear slipped down my cheek. Now I knew how desperate Scarlett O'Hara had felt at the end of *Gone with the Wind* when Rhett walked out on her. But there wasn't always tomorrow. The couple was arriving from Nice tomorrow. I had to set things right today!

Chapter Twenty-Four

I'd never felt so completely alone in my life. I'd lost Libby, Luc, Dominique, Evan, and my job all in the matter of four days. I had nothing left to lose. I needed to regain control of my life. I needed to get Libby to keep Dominique.

Étienne and Sophie materialized up the stone steps, Sophie carrying her gold sandals, wincing as she walked barefooted across the gravel. The yellow flowers tucked behind Sophie's ears matched her yellow minidress. It reminded me of Luc's cigarettes stuck behind his ears. He hadn't called except for the two times right after I'd bolted from the *Métro*. Although the bars on my phone were vacillating between none and three out here in the boonies. You would think this would be the perfect spot to escape reality, not to find it.

Sophie and Étienne sat, peering anxiously at me.

"Is she okay?" Étienne asked.

I continued staring at the fountain. "She's giving her baby up for adoption."

Sophie gasped, snapping back in her chair. "*Merde*. I cannot believe this. *C'est terrible....*" She went off on a tangent in French.

Étienne surged from his chair, tossing his arms in the air. "She's not thinking clearly. She'd never give her baby up for adoption. She's been taking such good care of herself because she cares about her baby."

"Her mind's made up. We're not going to change it."

"I will." Etienne marched toward the house.

"Étienne," I called out, prompting him to slow his pace. "Let her rest. She's exhausted."

He stopped, his gaze darting between the house and me. His shoulders slumped in defeat, and he paced across the patio. "We need to talk some sense into her. Do something."

"Libby got ten grand from the adopting couple. I offered her twenty."

"Then we'll offer her thirty," he said, rather than acting appalled like Libby had over my attempting to "buy" Dominique.

I shook my head. "It's not about the money."

"There must be some way to change her mind." Étienne glanced desperately around, searching for an answer.

"I don't think so. But...Gilles Beaufay might be able to."

"Who's he?" Étienne asked.

It made me feel good Étienne hadn't known the father's identity either.

"The baby's father." I glanced over at Sophie. "I met him when I went back to the antique shop. Libby still loves him."

"Libby can't put the baby up for adoption without his approval," Étienne said.

"I am sure he loves her." Sophie had one hand to her chest and one held out toward the house, as if she was feeling some cosmic connection between Libby and Gilles. "He would not want her to put the baby up for adoption. They belong together."

"Call him," Étienne said.

"Yes, call him," Sophie agreed. "She is much distressed, like in my visions. A gray aura surrounds her. She does not know what she is doing." Sophie pressed a hand to her forehead, as if she felt one of her psychic migraines coming on. "You must call him *now*."

I slid an apprehensive glance toward the house, shaking my head. "Libby would be ticked. She doesn't want to talk to him." But why? She obviously still loved him, and he loved her. Normally that would be all that mattered to Libby. Now that he was getting divorced, they could be together. Did she not believe he'd actually left his wife? Or maybe she didn't want him to feel like she was trapping him. From the looks of her, it was killing her to give up both Gilles and Dominique.

"I'll call him," Étienne said. "She'll forgive us once she's back with Gilles."

What if she didn't? Hell, she was already upset with me; what did I have to lose?

Dominique, if I didn't do something.

I snatched my purse off the ground and removed Gilles's business card with Dad's address. It listed his store number along with a cell phone. I had only one bar on my phone, so I borrowed Étienne's. I punched in the cell number, my heart thumping wildly, no clue what I was going to say.

Gilles answered.

"This is Samantha, Libby's sister. Libby had a baby, and you're the father." So much for tactfully breaking the news.

Silence filled the line, then he finally said, "You told me she wasn't pregnant." He sounded confused and a bit peeved.

"You need to come see Libby. She still loves you, but she's putting your baby up for adoption. The new parents are coming to Paris tomorrow."

"She can't put our baby up for adoption."

"You have to come and tell her that."

"Where are you? I will come right now."

"Wait until morning. Libby's exhausted. She needs a good night's sleep before seeing you."

Silence. "Okay."

"Before I tell you where she is, you have to promise you'll never leave her and the baby."

"Of course I won't."

"I'll hunt you down and make you regret it for the rest of your life. And same goes if you ever cheat on her."

Gilles remained silent, likely contemplating the downside of having me for a sister-in-law. "Libby is the only one for me."

I gave him directions, and he promised to be there early in the morning. I disconnected and handed Étienne back his phone.

Étienne smiled widely. "This is good. He will come and everything will be better."

Yes. Everything would be better. It had to be.

Luc's optimism was rubbing off on me.

I should call and tell Luc we'd found Libby. However, I was still ticked, even though he'd been trying to protect me by not telling me about Dad and Étienne. It wasn't like he'd done it with malicious intent. Maybe it was best things ended this way. If we made up, leaving would be even more difficult.

My phone beeped, signaling the arrival of a delayed voice mail message. I suddenly had three bars. I dialed voice mail, anticipating hearing Bruno's threats, which were becoming more graphic with each message. Instead, Roger's stern voice brought me straight up in my chair. Rather than making my termination official, he offered me the promotion.

I was the new senior director of corporate events.

After I'd left the hotel last night, Natalie had gone postal over Roger not giving me the promotion. She insisted if I'd been there, Katsumi wouldn't have gone to jail. She'd have gotten her spa appointment and into the fitness center early. Their sheets wouldn't have been lost. Their minibar wouldn't have run out of beer. Roger apologized for not realizing how much I did behind the scenes to ensure a successfully executed program.

My promotion was thanks to Natalie Darwin?

All the outrageous demands I'd fulfilled with a freakin' smile and all the times I'd almost bitten my tongue off rather than bitch-slapping the woman had actually paid off.

Roger said my first duty as director was to research how Natalie could go about adopting Katsumi. I had no clue how to get a dog out of France, let alone into the United States. What if the required paperwork and shots couldn't be expedited, allowing Katsumi to leave with Natalie in two days? Would Natalie demand I smuggle Katsumi out of the country? Would I do it?

A fire ignited in my stomach, and my grip tightened around the phone.

The next message was from Evan, who'd learned about my Facebook page. He told me to post my promotion, that it would be great publicity. With all the female followers I had on Facebook, that'd be a great source for marketing Brecker to women. He was going to talk to the VP of marketing about this.

Rather than realizing my worth, did Roger merely want to capitalize on my Facebook exposure to market Brecker?

"Is something wrong?" Étienne asked.

"Yeah, I just got a promotion."

"This is bad?" he asked, confused.

I nodded, then shook my head, then shrugged. "I don't know."

I'd quit my job, sabotaged this program, and blackmailed Evan to get the promotion. Now, I wasn't sure I wanted it? My qualifications might not have been the only thing that convinced Roger I deserved the promotion, and it ticked me off, big-time! I thought the fan page would make them realize what they were doing was wrong. Not that they would think it was a better marketing plan than the one I'd worked so hard to create.

Sophie uncurled my fingers still wrapped tightly around my cell phone and slipped the phone from my hand. She placed a hand against my burning stomach. "It does not take a psychic to know you should do what is best for you. Physically, emotionally, and spiritually."

What about financially? I needed to regain some semblance of stability in my life, and my job would provide that. I had to suck it up. I had to accept the position until I found another one, since I'd learned today how hard finding a job might be, at least in Milwaukee. I needed control over *one* area of my life. And I couldn't let down the women in my company or the women rallying behind me to get the promotion.

But I refused to share my marketing ideas with Brecker.

I went to punch in Roger's number, but no bars.

"Can I use your phone?" I asked Étienne.

He glanced down at his phone. "I don't have service either."

I peered over at Sophie. She let out a reluctant groan and removed her phone from her purse. A smile spread across her face. "No service. This is a sign."

Yeah, a sign that France could build the most famous tower in the entire world yet couldn't build a cell phone tower in the country!

—◦⟶ ⟵◦—

The house had no air conditioning, and not even the faintest breeze teased the lace curtains on the open windows. I stood in the kitchen fanning myself with the refrigerator door, staring at the contents. Two cans of Coca Light, a carton of eggs, and a hunk of cheese—a pungent odor seeping through its plastic wrap. Half of a baguette sat on the counter. The glass doors on the white cupboards displayed a few cans of fruit and veggies on the shelves. Libby looked like she hadn't eaten in days because she hadn't. By this time of night, the stores were all closed. We'd have to head into town for food in the morning.

I closed the fridge door and peered over at the floor-to-ceiling windows, imagining Dad, Ms. Duran, and Étienne sitting at the wooden table in the alcove, watching birds chirping in the feeders and bunnies frolicking in the backyard. Dinner with the Cleavers. Until Étienne's mother had died.

I went into the living room. The yellow walls and furnishings did nothing to brighten my mood. Nor did the family photos lining the fieldstone fireplace's mantel and the tabletops. I focused instead on the impressionist paintings of peasants working in fields. I was studying one of women harvesting wheat when Sophie's footsteps creaked against the wooden stairs as she came down them.

"She will not open the door," Sophie said. "I think she is sleeping. There are only two bedrooms. We must share a room, and Étienne will sleep down here." Sophie's gaze narrowed on the painting in front of me. A look of fear paralyzed her. "This has much bad energy. The painter was...er...how do you say, much crazy?"

"Insane or psycho. Weren't a lot of them? Van Gogh whacked off his ear." I squinted at the painting's lower right corner, trying to make out the artist's name fading into the green shadows of the field. "It's a Pissaro."

"The painting is good, but the painter is not a good person."

"Pissaro was a bad person?"

She shook her head. "The person who painted this is bad."

Omigod. Pissaro. Were these *Bruno's* forgeries?

"These paintings, we must destroy them. They bring bad luck to those in the house. They are probably the reason Libby cannot think clearly."

Étienne walked inside, his eyes widening. His gaze darted around, landing on a shelf of paperback books. He grabbed a book and pulled his pen from his back pocket. He scribbled frantically on the inside back cover then tore it off and slipped it in his pocket. He really needed to carry around a notepad.

"When did Libby bring these paintings here?" I asked Étienne.

"This summer."

According to Luc, the Pissaros had disappeared from Libby's three months ago. They *were* Bruno's. Thank God Libby hadn't destroyed them or I'd never get that psycho off our backs.

I snatched the paintings off the wall and marched them out to Étienne's car, wanting them far away from Libby. Not like any harm could come to the piece-of-crap car. If it mysteriously blew up, it would be no great loss, except the paintings would be toast and so would I once Bruno got his hands on me.

—◦ ◦—

My eyes shot open, slowly focusing on a silhouetted form standing over me. I let out a surprised gasp.

"It is me," Sophie said quietly. "You were having a nightmare. I woke you up."

It took me a moment to remember I was at Étienne's house in Burgundy and not Libby's apartment. Pascal seemed to hunt me down no matter where I went. There was no hiding from this guy.

Wearing merely my bra and undies, I had sweat gluing the sheet to my bare skin. Sophie perched on the edge of the bed, wearing a Beatles T-shirt Étienne kept there with a stash of extra clothes. She wriggled her butt against my legs, forcing me to move over and make room for her. I scooted up, leaning against the wooden headboard.

"The dream was about Pascal, *non?*"

"Yeah." Here was Sophie's chance to ask him what he wanted and to get him out of my dreams and into the bright light.

"He might still be here." She closed her eyes, attempting to channel him. After a few minutes, she heaved a frustrated sigh. "He is gone. What was your dream about?"

"I was in Pascal's salon with Dominique. It was just the two of us. But she wasn't a baby. She was older and wearing the wedding gown from the antique store. She had long, blonde hair scooped up on top of her head, and I was curling ringlets at the side. She looked beautiful and so happy. We were laughing until...suddenly I turned into Pascal and had a heart attack." I gazed desperately at Sophie. "What does this mean?"

"Well...you work much, same as Pascal did. Maybe the dream says you will not live to see Dominique get married if you continue on the path you have chosen and do not change your lifestyle. But it is a good sign you are seeing Dominique; it means Libby will not put her up for adoption."

As if Libby would listen to my dreams. "She had on my pearl necklace and earrings."

"Hmm... Are you sure this was Dominique and not your own daughter? Perhaps the dream was saying you cannot live without having children of your own." Sophie let out an excited gasp. "This is why Pascal is still here even though his son has forgiven him. To help you and Libby. He needed to help Libby because she helped him."

"By haunting me?"

"By telling you he sees your future and it brings death."

"Everyone's future brings death."

"Not everyone dies so young. He was only fifty-one. You might not be much older when Dominique or your daughter marries. You do not want to die of a heart attack before her wedding, do you?"

"So you're telling me he's going to continue haunting me if I take this promotion?"

"Yes, I am afraid that is very possible."

I had the feeling this was Sophie's career advice, not Pascal's. I didn't need either's advice.

I knew what I had to do.

Chapter Twenty-Five

At seven the following morning, Étienne, Sophie, Libby, and I sat at the kitchen table, drinking coffee and tea. Sophie and Étienne were sharing the stinky cheese and a half baguette while I gnawed on a carrot we'd rescued from the garden. Libby wasn't eating. A mug of tea cradled in her hands, she stared out at the birds in the feeder scarfing up sunflower seeds. She hadn't spoken since saying good morning ten minutes ago.

"I stayed up last night writing the first chapter of my new book," Étienne told Libby proudly, breaking the awkward silence. "My writer's block is gone."

Libby smiled weakly.

"The new moon last night means it is time for new beginnings," Sophie said.

"I was afraid all my research on serial killers was only giving me nightmares. Ideas have been filling my head since yesterday." He pulled the fast-food bag and bookcover from his back pocket and unfolded them, both filled with notes.

"Why don't you carry a notepad?" I asked.

"That wouldn't allow my ideas to flow freely. They need to be spontaneous."

"How many books have you written?" Sophie asked.

"Seventeen."

"Are they all published?" she asked.

"No, none are published. I have received over five hundred rejections. But I know one day I will prevail."

Five hundred rejections and he hadn't given up? Was he a crappy writer, or did he merely have crappy luck and timing?

Regardless, I admired his ability to believe in himself when nobody else seemed to. I had the drive of a pit bull but needed positive reinforcement, such as promotions, to stay motivated. Not initially receiving this promotion was my first major rejection, and look how poorly I'd handled that.

Libby stared into her mug. "I missed Pascal's funeral."

"Samantha and I went," Sophie said.

Libby looked surprised and appreciative.

"He mentioned you in his will," Sophie said.

"I know. Alphonse called me. He was upset. Not because Pascal donated a half million euros to the shelter but because he'd been going with me there every week to give haircuts. Alphonse was proud of Pascal and said if he'd known this when Pascal was alive, things would have been different."

"Why didn't Pascal tell him?" I asked.

"He didn't want anyone to know. He thought everyone would expect free haircuts and it would decrease his salons' prestige."

I thought of Inès's family staying at a shelter. "Where's the shelter located?"

"Near the Venus Café. I do children's art therapy there."

Was that where Gabrielle had gotten her sketchpad from?

A car pulled up out front, crunching gravel, and we glanced in the direction of the front door.

"Who could that be?" Libby said.

Étienne, Sophie, and I exchanged furtive glances. Gilles must have left Paris at five a.m. A car door slammed, and apprehension tightened my stomach. A few moments later, a rap sounded at the front door. Étienne answered the door and returned with Gilles. Seeing Gilles was like a shot of adrenaline, and Libby's sluggish body went ramrod straight. Her shocked gaze darted from Gilles to me. She looked like she wanted to strangle me.

"I told Sam I would call him if she didn't," Étienne said. "You two must talk."

"Libby, he's right. There is so much to say." Gilles walked over and knelt in front of her, as if preparing to propose right on the spot. He placed a loving hand to her cheek, brushing a thumb across it. "It'll be okay. I'll take care of you." He enveloped her hand in his.

I stood, gesturing for Étienne and Sophie to follow me into the living room. "We'll be in the other room."

"We'll go outside," Libby said, dragging herself up from the chair.

Gilles and Libby walked out the back door, onto the patio. Étienne, Sophie, and I moved deeper into the kitchen so we weren't on display in the alcove watching them.

Gilles and Libby hugged.

"That's very good," Étienne said, grinning.

I nodded enthusiastically. "Wish I could hear them." I glanced over at Sophie. "What are they saying?"

"I cannot read minds or lips." Sophie sounded like I was crazy for thinking she could. As if this would be more difficult than communicating with the dead.

Things looked very promising until Libby turned away from Gilles, hugging herself, pacing nervously. Étienne drummed his fingers against the counter. I gnawed at my lower lip. Sophie clutched the locket around her neck. Gilles looked confused then upset, becoming more animated, tossing his arms in the air.

"This isn't good," Étienne said, panicked.

Gilles took off around the side of the house, and moments later, his car spun out on the gravel. We ran outside to Libby. Still hugging herself, she rocked back and forth on the edge of a chair.

"What happened?" I asked.

She shook her head, staring at her bare feet. "You never should have had him come here."

"I'm so sorry," I muttered.

"We thought you wanted to see him," Étienne said. "You still love him, and it is obvious he loves you. Is he upset you want to put his daughter up for adoption?"

"I told him he's not the father," Libby snapped. She stopped rocking, still staring at her feet. "I think Luc is."

My eyes widened in shock, and I placed a hand to my stomach, feeling like I'd had the wind knocked out of me. Thank God Libby was staring at her feet. My mortified expression would give away the fact Luc's and my relationship had evolved beyond friendship. The one time Libby and I shared the same taste in anything, why did it have to be Luc? He'd been helping me search for Dominique's father, and it was *him* we were looking for.

"You told me he wasn't the father," I practically shrieked.

Libby nodded faintly.

"Does Luc know?" I prayed he hadn't known and been lying to me about that also this entire time.

Libby shook her head. "I never told him I think he's the father because I planned to give my baby up anyway."

"And what do you mean you *think* he's the father?" I asked, grasping at a thread of hope.

"Gilles and I stopped seeing each other. A few weeks later, I was so upset, and it was six months since Luc's wife's death. It just happened. Only that one time. Several weeks later, I started seeing Gilles again, but then I found out I was pregnant. I'd had my period after Gilles and I broke up. I read you can still have a period once you're pregnant, but it's not common. I think the baby is Luc's. I can feel it. I had to stop seeing Gilles. I had crazy ideas of telling him the baby was his, even though I didn't know for sure, to force him to leave his wife. Even just now, I wanted to tell him he was the father, but I couldn't. It wouldn't be fair. I told him Luc's possibly the father."

"That's why you said you were due in *six* weeks? So Luc would think the baby was premature and no way was it his?"

Libby nodded faintly.

"I could tell she was Luc's when I looked into her eyes."

That was why she'd cried that night in the hospital, upset over believing her baby wasn't Gilles's.

"But both Gilles and Luc have brown eyes," Sophie noted.

"I don't want to trap Luc or Gilles. I don't know if I believe Gilles will divorce his wife. His family's very religious."

"Don't you think you should tell Luc?" Étienne asked.

"He's not father material. Besides, he'd want me to put her up for adoption if that's what I want."

"No, he wouldn't," I assured her. "You should see him with your daughter. He's wonderful. He loves kids." I pictured Luc with the Mickey and Minnie Mouse puppets in the basket of the Hello Kitty trike as he cruised across the store. The affectionate way he called Dominique *ma petite puce*, even though it was a flea. The concern in his eyes when we'd learned Dominique had a fever.

A tear slipped down Libby's cheek as she stood. "I need sleep before I go back to Paris this afternoon and meet with the Michauds."

"Libby, please think about this," I begged. "You need to tell Luc your baby might be his."

She needed to do a paternity test, but we didn't have time to wait for the results. Luc would want to know he could be the father before it was too late.

Libby's gaze sharpened. "This is my business, Sam. You had no right telling Gilles he was the father. Don't you dare tell Luc he likely is." She glared over at Étienne and Sophie. "Any of you." She shuffled inside.

We all stared at each other.

Which one of us was telling Luc?

"She's miserable," Étienne finally said. "She wants to keep the baby. If you won't give me Luc's number, I'll drive to Paris and find him. He lives in Libby's building, and I know what he looks like. Maybe he can talk her into keeping the baby."

I shook my head. "She might never speak to me again if I call Luc." Then again, she might never anyway. And Libby was all about giving people second chances. If she could forgive Dad for abandoning us, she'd forgive me, right? "I can't believe Gilles doesn't want anything to do with her because the baby might not be his. He was married, for God's sake. Talk about a hypocrite."

"Luc has the right to know he might have a child," Étienne said. "I would want to know. Libby doesn't have the right to make this decision on her own."

Luc possibly being the father put a major wrench in our relationship. Not that we really had one, especially when I'd be leaving now. But none of that mattered as much as the fact that he'd be a good father to Dominique. Yet it wasn't my place to tell him. Look what I'd done by telling Gilles this.

Fifteen minutes later, we sat around the kitchen table, guzzling coffee, still not agreeing on what to do. It blew me away Libby and I were attracted to the same man. Libby didn't love Luc, at least not romantically.

But did Luc love Libby?

I'd only seen them together a few times, but I didn't think he looked at her in that way. How exactly did he look at *me*? In a way that made me feel warm, happy...loved. In a way Evan had never looked at me.

My phone rang in my purse. I pulled it out, finding Luc's number displayed rather than Roger's or Evan's, who were probably wondering why I hadn't contacted them about my promotion. My stomach fluttered. Fate had stepped in.

I answered the phone, walking outside, not wanting Libby to hear our conversation.

"I waited up all night for you to come home," Luc said. "You were so upset when you left, I was worried. You wouldn't return my calls. Now you and Libby are both missing. Where are you? Are you okay?"

His concern and the tenderness in his voice caused my eyes to mist over, but I kept it together.

"What's wrong?"

"I found Libby."

"Is she okay? Is she hurt? Where is she? What happened—"

"She's...okay. She's giving Dominique up for adoption."

"But Libby wanted this baby so much. She would make such a good mother."

"I know. It's obvious she doesn't want to give the baby up. She's not thinking clearly."

"Has she told Gilles Beaufay he's the father?"

"No." She told him you likely were.

"He has the right to know."

So Luc would want to know if he was the father.

Libby told me *I* couldn't tell Luc. Yet she'd just broken down and told Gilles Luc might be the father. Confronted with Luc, maybe she'd tell him this also.

"Maybe you should talk to her," I said.

"If you think that would help."

Palms sweating, I went upstairs to Libby's room and knocked on the door. She didn't answer. The door was unlocked, so I opened it. Libby sat in a rocking chair by the window.

I covered the phone's mouthpiece with my hand. "Luc wants to talk to you."

Libby glared at me. "You called him?"

"No, he called me, worried about you."

She gave me a skeptical look. "What did you tell him?"

"Just that you're giving the baby up for adoption. That's it. I told him I found you, and he wants to talk to you. He's worried about you. He said if you won't talk to him, he's driving here." Minor fib, but she *had* to talk to Luc.

Libby didn't look happy, but she took the phone. I walked out and closed the door, standing next to it. Étienne and Sophie stopped hovering at the end of the hallway and joined me. Étienne and I pressed our ears to the door. Old doors were made so well I couldn't hear a damn thing. Five minutes later, footsteps approached. Étienne and I quickly backed away as Libby opened the door.

"I told him he might be my baby's father," she said, handing me the phone.

Relief swept through me. "It was the right thing to do."

"Yeah, it was. He agrees I should put her up for adoption." She slammed the door with unexpected strength.

Without missing a beat, I called Luc back as I bolted downstairs and flew outside, Sophie and Étienne hot on my heels. He answered.

"How could you tell Libby to put Dominique up for adoption?"

"It's what she wants, and I think she's right."

"When you thought Gilles was the father, you said she should keep the baby! And what happened to you wanting a child? You picked out her name. You've been spending all this time with her.

How can you let Libby put her up for adoption?"

"Dominique deserves parents who can give her everything she needs. Neither Libby or I can provide her with that. I want a child someday when I'm ready. This isn't the time. And I don't love Libby, not like I should love the mother of my child."

"Cutting yourself off from everyone isn't healthy. That's not the way to heal. That's—"

"I have to go." He disconnected.

I stared at the phone in numb disbelief. What had happened to the compassionate man who'd helped me care for Dominique and search for Libby? The passionate man who'd made love to me? I wanted him back!

I peered over at Étienne. "I need a ride to a train station. I'm sure Libby would rather not ride with me in a car for two hours. And I need to take those paintings back. The owner is looking for them." I didn't want to know Libby's involvement with the paintings, I just wanted to keep her safe. I wanted to be packed and gone before Libby got home. To take the promotion and get the hell out of Paris. Libby and I needed some distance before we spoke again.

"I will try to change her mind on the ride back to Paris." Étienne reached out, stopping shy of touching my hand, as if unsure whether or not he should.

I brushed my fingertips over the top of his hand, and my chest tightened. "Thanks."

Chapter Twenty-Six

On the train ride back to Paris, I returned Roger's call, confirming I'd be at the hotel in a few hours to discuss my promotion. Hopefully I came off more psyched about the position than I felt. I should be psyched. It would look great on my résumé and put some stability back in my life. Even if I only took it until I found another job, it would serve its purpose. I was using Brecker, same as they were using me.

I checked my Facebook page.

6,417 Likes.

I felt like a celebrity.

I also felt kind of deceitful not posting my promotion when these women had all been rallying behind me. Not only had *I* won, *we'd* won. If I was receiving the promotion for the right reasons. And Evan would be expecting me to post my promotion. But if I posted it, I wouldn't get any job offers.

I scanned through the posts, coming across one from a woman in human resources at Budweiser. She was quite interested in seeing the company increase sales by 15 percent and wanted to speak with me ASAP. She guaranteed me they had a spot for someone with my ideas, background, and work ethics.

Brecker would die if I went to work for Bud. I private messaged the woman, providing my e-mail addy so we could communicate privately.

Finally. Something was going right.

So why wasn't I doing handsprings right now?

I stopped by Libby's to pack my bags and contact Bruno. Luc's scooter wasn't parked outside. When I reached his apartment, I gripped his key between my fingers, my chest tightening. It wasn't like Luc giving me his key had been the next step in our relationship. Yet returning it symbolized the end of whatever it was we'd shared.

Hoping there wasn't enough of a gap under the door for the key to fit, I bent down and tried sliding it under. The key disappeared inside the apartment. I stared at the bottom of the door, a hollow feeling inside me. I wanted to grab a pen from my purse and fish the key back. Even if I did, having the key wouldn't change things.

Luc and I were over.

I entered Libby's apartment filled with baby stuff and about lost it, my eyes misting over. Maybe seeing all the items would make her change her mind. Having returned Luc's key, I had nowhere to hide everything. Not like I could return the cradle to Gilles's antique store and chance running into him, either. Besides, the Michauds might let Dominique keep it all.

I glanced at the mural on the wall. Libby's and my hands were clasped, joining us together once again. Thanks to Luc, no doubt. He'd filled in the gap around the edges, and the piece of plaster fit snugly in place. The touch-up paint matched nicely, and from a distance, the damage wasn't visible.

But underneath, the damage was still there. Just like between me and Libby.

After packing my suitcases, I exchanged Libby's jeans and my blouse for my black capris and blazer set. I glared at my black mules and the blisters on my toes, unable to believe I'd paid three hundred bucks for a pair of shoes that were likely deforming my feet. The thought of hiking through airports and traveling back home in those shoes about brought me to tears. I tossed the shoes in the garbage and put on Libby's pink flip-flops.

I slipped the little girl puppet Luc had given me on one hand, Minnie on the other, and had them say their tearful goodbyes. Mickey, however, remained stoic. I packed the girl puppet in my carry-on bag.

I eyed the paper roses in the vase on the table. Besides not knowing what became of Dominique, I would never know what became of Gabrielle and Anouk. Whether Inès would get them enrolled in school so they had a fighting chance of obtaining jobs outside the *Métro* station, or if they would find true love. If Inès ever got a job. Hopefully somebody cared what happened to them.

Libby would care. She likely knew them through the shelter. I wrote Libby a note, describing Inès and her daughters and the *Métro* stop they worked at, asking her to do what she could to get Gabrielle in school and Inès a job. I told her they loved fruit tarts and left a hundred euros to offset expenses. I had no clue if I'd continue sending Libby money, not knowing what she was doing with it. Who knew if she'd even accept it.

I opened the balcony doors to check on the flowers and peered across at Monsieur Fleurs sitting on his balcony. I waved goodbye. He picked up a package of plant food from the table and held it up, nodding *merci* with a faint smile.

Cecile's cheerful voice carried up from below. Monsieur Fleurs peered eagerly over the side of his balcony at the florist below. He appeared entranced, hanging on her every word even though it wasn't him she was speaking to. With a look of longing, he watched her until she disappeared inside the shop. He relaxed back in his chair, smiling lovingly at a pot of yellow flowers on the table next to him.

That first day, I'd mistaken him for a pervert rather than a hopeless romantic. He'd never cared about watching anyone but Cecile. Did Cecile realize it wasn't the man's love of *flowers* that brought him into her shop on a regular basis? He appeared to suddenly remember my presence and gazed over at me. I smiled knowingly. Unable to suppress the bright smile on his face, he glanced away, looking embarrassed by his outward display of affection for Cecile.

I had the feeling he'd never told Cecile how he felt. Unless Cecile was married, he should take a chance and confess his feelings for her. Why continue his lonely existence and die with nobody to attend his funeral? It bothered me that Monsieur Fleurs might die without even having *flowers* at his funeral.

I stepped inside, closing the doors behind me.

I erased Bruno's psycho messages, not wanting them to upset Libby when she returned. Mom's message was the only one I left on the machine. I called Bruno, and he answered with a few obscene words. I told him to meet me at the café next to Libby's in a half hour, promising him I had the paintings this time. He was in the middle of threatening to harm not only my family but every person I'd ever met when I hung up. Libby would be pissed at me for handing over the paintings if she knew Bruno was passing them off as the real thing. A part of me didn't want to know if she'd known.

All I cared about was keeping Libby safe.

I sat at the café down from Libby's building with the paintings. Bruno stalked up wearing a Grateful Dead T-shirt and a crazed look. He snatched the garbage bag from the chair next to me and peeked inside at the paintings, a proud look consuming his face.

"I'm giving you these on one condition. That you never contact Libby ever again or the cops will catch wind of your paintings."

His smile vanished, and I feared he was going to suffocate me with the garbage bag. A sly grin slowly spread across his face, and he arched an approving brow, as if to say he liked my style. "I have what I need. I will leave Libby alone. These are very good. I will be famous one day. Everyone will want my paintings as much as they want Pissaro's."

Bruno stalked off, bursting with pride.

Bruno was seriously delusional yet passionate about art. Too passionate. In a weird way, I was jealous of his passion. Everyone I'd met in Paris had a passion for what they did and for life. Luc's puppet performances brought joy into people's lives and enabled him to carry on his wife's memory. And he'd rediscovered his passion for cooking. Sophie helped both the deceased and the living find peace so they could move on. Étienne's passion for writing enabled him to persevere despite a depressingly high number of rejections. Gilles had a passion for Libby. Monsieur

Fleurs's passion for Cecile had grown into a passion for flowers. However, I wasn't envious of Pascal Rochant's passion for money, his job, and success, which had led to his self-destruction and, ultimately, his death.

Although Sophie claimed Pascal was haunting me because he wanted to prevent me from turning out like him, she was wrong. Unlike Pascal, I didn't have a passion for my job. I felt like I was the only person in Paris without a passion.

Now that I was leaving Paris, I feared I'd never find one.

I walked next door to the flower shop, discreetly glancing toward Monsieur Fleurs's empty balcony. Gigi popped up from her cushion by the door and greeted me with a wag of her tail. Alternating bright purple and yellow flowers adorned her collar. I scratched behind her floppy ears. Unable to say *au revoir*, I stepped inside the store, armed with my French lexicon. From the little bit of interaction I'd had with Cecile, I knew her English wasn't even as good as my French.

"Bonjour," I called out to Cecile, who was busy with a customer but returned my hello with a cheerful smile.

I perused the flowers. Red roses symbolized passion and love. Too sappy and prosaic. I was studying a pot of daisies when Cecile walked up. I glanced at her dainty hands. No wedding ring. I didn't want to be responsible for arranging a forbidden liaison.

I asked what her favorite flower was that symbolized love.

She smiled and, without hesitation, walked over to a pot of yellow daffodils like she'd given Luc to give me. She placed a hand to her heart. "Your love...is, er, all to me." She continued in French, losing me after *le soleil*, the sun. She smiled, realizing this. "The sun...it shines...when we..." She motioned between the two of us.

"Are together?" I offered.

"Oui, c'est ça."

"How sweet." And she'd chosen these flowers for Luc to give me. Guess I wasn't the only one playing matchmaker.

I bought the flowers and asked if she could personally deliver them to the gentleman across the street with the balcony full of flowers.

Her cheeks flushed, and she wore a demure smile. "Monsieur Levasseur." She glanced in the direction of his apartment even though it wasn't visible from inside the store.

"He is *très gentil*," I said.

She smiled. *"Oui."*

I left the shop hopeful, praying one of my matchmaking attempts that day would be successful.

I went up to Libby's to grab my luggage and refused to get teary-eyed. I zipped in and out of the apartment without looking around. I walked past Luc's staring straight ahead. I schlepped my suitcases down the stairs then hauled all three out onto the sidewalk to wait for the taxi I'd managed to call and reserve by myself. As I petted a curious Gigi sniffing my luggage, the familiar hum of Luc's scooter approached. Nervousness vibrated through my entire body. Our gazes locked, and apprehension filled his eyes as he drove up the sidewalk and parked by the metal pole in front of the building. He removed his helmet and raked a hand through his hair. We stared at each other. Gigi broke the awkward moment, trotting over to Luc, tail wagging.

Luc smiled at the beagle. *"Salut,* Gigi." He crouched down and petted her. Hearing the soft lilt of Luc's voice speaking French to Gigi caused me to melt, same as it had the first time he'd spoken to me. The day I'd discovered Libby was pregnant and feared Luc was the father of her baby. I still didn't want him to be the father, but not because I felt he'd make a bad one but because it could be difficult being in love with the father of my niece.

Luc stood, and Gigi trotted back toward the flower shop, pausing momentarily at my side for one last pet.

Luc glanced cautiously over at me. *"Salut."*

I smiled faintly. *"Salut."*

I wanted to make one last-ditch effort to change Luc's mind about Dominique. However, I doubted anything I could say would make a difference. I couldn't change how Luc felt. It would only cause us to part on bad terms. Leaving was hard enough without having Luc upset with me.

He gestured to my luggage. "It was much easier to carry down the stairs than up, I hope."

Far from it. Carrying it out of Libby's apartment, past Luc's, and down the stairs was one of the most difficult things I'd ever had to do in my life. Right now, I would carry it back up the stairs a thousand times to hear Luc ask me to stay.

"Are you going to the hotel?"

I nodded. "Back to work."

"That's good. What you wanted."

Right. Precisely what I'd wanted...four days ago.

"When do you go home?"

"Sunday." In two more days. That was two more days we could spend together. I willed Luc to ask me to dinner tonight. Except I had a farewell reception to work.

A black Mercedes taxi pulled up to the curb. I ignored the car's trunk popping open and the driver stepping out. Luc addressed the driver in French, and the man got back in his car, leaving the trunk open. Luc carried my garment bag and large suitcase over to the car and stuck them in the trunk. He closed the trunk, staring at the car a moment before peering over at me. His brown eyes softened, gazing deep into mine.

"Do you think one day you might come back to visit Libby?"

I shrugged, unsure if Libby would ever talk to me again. It'd be awhile before I spoke to her. I was hurt. "I hope so."

He nodded. "Me, too."

I swallowed the lump in my throat. *"Au revoir."*

Luc shook his head. *"À bientôt,* not goodbye. I'll see you again soon." He placed a kiss on my cheek, his breath warm against my skin. I fought back the tears flirting with the rims of my eyes. He kissed my other cheek, and his lips lingered. *"À bientôt,"* he whispered against my skin, and I instinctively pressed my cheek to his lips.

He drew back, and a chill consumed me. I turned without meeting his gaze and got in the taxi. If I looked at him, I'd lose it.

As the taxi pulled away, I prayed for Luc to come running after me, yelling for me to wait, asking me to stay. But the only sounds I heard were Gigi's barks and the sobs catching in my throat as tears flowed down my cheeks.

_⌒ ⌒_

I had the taxi driver wait outside the hospital with my luggage, promising him an extra fifty euros. The couple from Nice was due there in four hours. I walked slowly toward the nursery, feeling like every one of my internal organs was shutting down.

I passed the empty receptionist desk, spying Nurse Perky at the end of the hallway, the only nurse in sight.

I could kidnap Dominique.

I could waltz right into the nursery, snatch Dominique, and waltz out. But smuggling her out of the hospital would be easier than smuggling her out of the country. I assumed even a baby needed a passport or some sort of paperwork. Five minutes on the streets of Pigalle and I could easily find someone willing to whip me up a baby passport overnight for fifty euros.

Kidnapping wasn't an option unless I planned to live my life on the run. Hiding out away from everyone I knew held a certain appeal, but that was no life for my niece.

On to Plan B for Bribe.

Libby couldn't be bought, but maybe the Michauds could. Maybe they were more desperate for money than a baby.

I could offer them fifty grand to forget about the adoption. What if they became greedy and threatened to tell Libby unless I gave them more money? I didn't care about the money, but I wouldn't want Libby to find out what I'd done. The plan could definitely backfire. Besides, Libby would just find another couple to adopt Dominique, and I'd be out all that money. I wasn't thinking rationally.

I walked into the nursery, a tear slipping down my cheek. Needing to get it together so Dominique didn't sense my sadness, I paused before walking over to her incubator, wiping away my tears, taking a calming breath. The giraffe blanket covered her small form. She gazed up at me, and I was certain recognition registered in her eyes. Was she too young to recognize me? She was definitely too young to ever remember me and the time we'd spent together. Time I would never forget.

I bolted from the nursery without saying *au revoir*. I didn't want this to be goodbye.

Chapter Twenty-Seven

As I walked across the hotel lobby, I tried desperately to shove the vision of Dominique cooing softly in her crib from my mind. I had to focus on something positive, like taking this promotion knowing I could quit in the very near future to go to work for Brecker's biggest competitor. I wanted the position just long enough to help office morale by promoting Rachel to my position and Hannah to meeting planner—if she still wanted to be one after this week. I'd implement all the changes I'd tried to get Lori to do. I could do some serious good for my co-workers. Paving the way for future women executives in the company.

Twenty-two grand more a year meant nothing without anyone to share it with. The promotion and financial stability had never been all about me. I liked being able to help out Libby, although I now realized she'd also needed me, not just the money. I'd wanted a house for Dominique, Libby, and me. If I hadn't been able to help Mom out of her financial jams when she went on spending sprees, who knew what would have happened to her.

The fact that a burning sensation hadn't ignited in my stomach the second I'd entered the hotel was a positive. However, I didn't feel elated, ecstatic, or...much of anything.

I was numb.

As I neared the hospitality desk, Natalie Darwin was screaming at Hannah, Katsumi yipping at her feet. My stomach burst into flames.

Natalie's glare locked on me, and I reluctantly continued toward her. "Well, there you are." She eyed my pink flip-flops with disapproval. She shook off my attire and continued, "Just look at this."

She held up a colored chalk sketch of herself. Her chin and nose came to severe points, and the small birthmark next to her nose resembled a large wart. The slanted, green eyes captured her devious nature. Rather than a portrait, the artist had captured her true essence in a caricature.

"I look like the Wicked Witch of the West."

The resemblance was uncanny.

I clamped down on my lower lip, afraid I was about to start laughing uncontrollably like that day at the puppet show.

"You don't look like the Wicked Bitch of the West."

Shit. My Freudian slip of *bitch* rather than *witch* didn't go unnoticed. Hannah let out a surprised gasp, and Natalie eyed me, undoubtedly trying to determine if she'd heard me correctly. And here I'd always been worried about slipping up and calling her *Bat*alie to her face.

Natalie glared at Hannah. "What'd you do, drag some bum off the street to draw this? I mean, really, you are completely incompetent. You haven't managed to do one thing right this week...." Natalie was off on a tangent, and Hannah's eyes were misting over, her lower lip quivering.

My urge to laugh hysterically vanished. "Hannah didn't hire a bad artist on purpose. The hotel recommended him."

Natalie let out a disgruntled huff. "She should know by now that concierge is worse at his job than she is."

A sob escaped Hannah, and she turned away. If I were a crier— the past few days being the exception—this bitch would have had me in tears on a daily basis over the past thirteen years. Instead, I'd kept my feelings hidden inside. Thanks to Natalie, half my stomach lining had likely been burned away. And now that she thought I owed her one, she would make my life even more of a living hell. The concierge was the only person who had dared to set boundaries with this woman.

Fighting for my job had given me self-respect. I wasn't about to lose that along with everything else I'd lost that week.

"Maybe if you hadn't pissed off the concierge from day one, he wouldn't be so vindictive," I said.

Natalie snapped her head back in surprise. She quickly recovered, raising her nose in the air. "I never said anything to him that wasn't true."

I glanced down at the sketch. "Yeah, well, maybe that artist didn't *draw* anything that wasn't true."

Natalie let out a horrified gasp. "You ungrateful little snot. After everything I've done for you over the years—"

"What *you've* done for *me*? Like the time Bahamian customs arrested me for trying to sneak your delayed luggage out of baggage claim because you insisted they were too lazy to have it cleared by the end of the trip? Or the time you lost your wedding ring on the beach in Hawaii and left me to look for it while you got a massage, and I was stung by a jellyfish and spent the night in the emergency room?" My hands balled into fists at my side. I wanted to knock this bitch flat.

Natalie's red lips pursed into a thin, straight line. "You were merely doing your job. Which I cannot *believe* I got back for you."

"You didn't get me my job back, I did. Besides, I don't want my job. Screw my job!"

Katsumi let out a yip.

I glanced down at the poor dog squirming to free herself from the pink, faux-fur-trimmed sweater. I glared at Natalie. "By the way, Katsumi isn't a French Asian designer. She's a porn star."

Natalie rolled her eyes as if to say *Really, Samantha, you'll stop at nothing.*

"Go check out a porn mag. Or pick up a newspaper. She's dating the president's son. She's all over the media. If you could read *French*, you'd know that." Slam.

Natalie let out an appalled huff, and I couldn't decide if it was directed at me or Katsumi. She turned to leave, and I snagged the leash from her hand.

"The concierge said the owner wants his dog back."

She grabbed for the leash, and I snapped my hand back, glaring at her. Bring it on. She backed down. Without saying a word, she marched down the hallway.

"Holy shit," Hannah muttered. "That was awesome. You are so totally my mentor." She hugged my trembling body. Katsumi let out a victorious bark.

"Yeah, but she's going to take this out on you and make your life a living hell." What happened to my determination to help my co-workers? Now they had not only Lori's programs but also mine to deal with. Hopefully I'd still paved the way for women at Brecker and Roger would realize they'd no longer put up with discrimination.

"She can't," Hannah said. "I'm quitting. I'll have to wait until I get another job. I don't know how the hell you've done this job for thirteen years. You always kept it together and made it look so easy. I mean, sure, I knew you got stressed sometimes, but you rarely showed it."

I liked this Mini-Me better than the one I'd witnessed yesterday.

"Rachel's gonna shit when she finds out she and Allison are the only ones left in the department, along with this clueless guy from Dallas," I said. "At least she's got a lot of bargaining power when it comes to asking for a raise and my old position, along with demanding some changes in the department. They can't afford to have everyone quit. As your mentor, I should advise you to never burn bridges, especially if you're going to need a reference. At least I won't need a reference for the position with Budweiser."

A panicked look seized Hannah. "Didn't Rachel e-mail you?"

My gaze narrowed. "I didn't get an e-mail from her. Why?"

I whipped out my phone and checked e-mail. Nothing. I checked my spam folder to find Rachel's message. My anti-virus program must have filtered the subject header as spam: BUDWEISER BEER A FAKE. Rachel said she'd made a bogus post by Budweiser, offering me a job so I'd have bargaining power. Omigod, Rachel. I just committed career suicide without having another job. Roger was never going to give me a decent reference after I bitched out his wife. Shit! I went on Facebook and deleted Rachel's post from Budweiser before someone from their company saw it.

Knowing it would do me little good to call Roger and explain what had happened, I called Evan. He was in his room working.

When he started congratulating me on my promotion, I immediately cut him off and told him Roger wouldn't be giving me a reference, let alone a promotion. He agreed to meet me in the lounge.

I headed toward the lounge, passing by a hotel sign advertising a cooking class with the hotel chef. It was open to the public at 150 euros per person. The chef should make recipes for food and beverage groups in-house, like what Luc did for Brecker, and the groups could do a cooking class with him. Companies would pay big for that.

Ten minutes later, I sat in the lounge drinking a Malbec, dreading my confrontation with Evan, who was undoubtedly going to insist on checking me into the nearest psychiatric facility for evaluation.

Evan entered the lounge dressed in a crisp, white oxford and black slacks. He zoned in on me, looking concerned about my panicked call. I remembered why I'd fallen for him three years ago upon meeting him at the company Christmas party right after he'd started with Brecker. He had this presence, exuding a sense of confidence that drew me to him. He was driven, and we understood the demands of our jobs and placed few personal demands on each other. Things between us hadn't been personal for some time.

He sat down, and before he could say anything, I recounted my blowout with Natalie. Rather than telling me I'd majorly screwed up both my career and life, he laughed. "You know how many times I've wanted to tell that bitch off? God, I wish I could have seen that. Bet it was priceless."

"You're missing the point here. I've held my tongue for thirteen years. I could have held it at least until I had another job."

"You're not taking the position with *Budweiser*?" His upper lip curled back when he said Budweiser. He was obviously still ticked about my blackmailing him.

I shrugged. No way was I confessing that the offer had been bogus.

It seemed like an appropriate time to apologize for blackmailing him but I wasn't sorry. He'd put me in the position to use whatever weapons I'd had to. Still, I said, "Sorry." I just wanted to move on.

Evan's shoulders relaxed slightly. "I'll give you a recommendation if you really think the job will make you happy."

I was unsure how to respond. A smart-ass retort like *As if you care if I'm happy* seemed inappropriate since he looked like he did care.

"I couldn't tell you I hadn't recommended you for the promotion. I was your boss. I thought you of all people would respect that."

That was kind of a slam.

"You can't stand schmoozing, and that's a big part of the position. I honestly didn't think it was a good fit for you. I thought this promotion would make you even more miserable." He peered at my wineglass, a pensive look on his face, then met my gaze. "Believe it or not, Sam, I want you to be happy. You haven't been happy in a long time. And I guess maybe we made a better couple professionally than we did personally."

Evan's jaw didn't twitch, and he didn't smooth a nervous hand down the front of his pressed shirt. He was being sincere. He'd been more in tune with my feelings than I had been with his, or my own, for that matter. I wondered if Rachel had exaggerated about him saying I wasn't a people person and my department would lose employees if I became manager. Wouldn't have been the first time she'd embellished a story for her cause. However, Evan had lied, telling me the position hadn't been filled and then warning me I was jeopardizing my promotion by leaving the group to be by Libby's side in the hospital. He could have said nothing.

"How's Libby doing?"

I nodded, pressing my lips firmly together, unable to talk about it without crying.

"That's good." His smile faded. "So what are we going to do about the condo?"

"You keep it."

He looked surprised. "You're the one who found it and fell in love with it. You should keep it."

"I'm thinking about buying a house." The thought of no longer needing a house for Dominique caused my stomach to lurch. "Would be nice to have a yard with a flower garden." Besides a flower garden, I envisioned myself sitting on a wraparound porch overflowing with potted flowers, like Monsieur Fleurs's balcony. Maybe some wicker furniture to relax on at night and watch people pass by walking their dogs. "And maybe I'll get a dog." I smiled at the thought of Gigi greeting me with a wagging tail every night when I arrived home from work. I needed some unconditional love.

Evan stared at me in disbelief. "A house with a garden? You always said yard work was for people with no life. And a dog? You've never shown interest in caring for a living plant, let alone an animal. What next? You gonna organize neighborhood block parties and invite people over for coffee and home-baked cookies?" Evan shook his head in disbelief. "You've changed more than your hair color this week, which looks good, by the way."

I nodded, smiling down at my pink flip-flops. "Yeah. Guess I have." More than he'd ever know.

_꧁ ꧂_

Unable to stay at the hotel and risk running into Natalie or Roger, I booked a room at a boutique hotel—i.e., rooms the size of Luc's puppet shed. I checked into my room and sat at the desk, preparing to go online and change my flight so I wasn't flying back with the group, when I realized I'd left my laptop at Libby's. I couldn't believe I'd done that. The thing was like an appendage. It was a company computer, so I needed to return it.

I checked out my Facebook page on my phone.

8,015 Likes.

My Likes were exploding. I felt like I'd let all these women down by not taking the promotion after they'd all rallied behind me. I'd probably have to take the page down or Brecker would sue me for defamation.

I opened a message from Ella. She was very sympathetic about my whole Dad situation. Her husband had remarried and moved to

California and didn't stay in touch with their daughters. This brought tears to my eyes. I told her I'd write more later, that I was a bit too emotional right now. I could see us doing more than drinking Malbec together. I could see us being friends, and not just on Facebook.

I still couldn't believe Rachel had posted that Budweiser comment. But the more I thought about it, the more I realized I'd been more psyched about telling Brecker to take the promotion and shove it than I had been about going to work for Budweiser. They would expect me to work sixty-hour weeks with no vacations, like Rachel had boasted on my fan page. I no longer wanted to give that to a company. I no longer wanted to be a puppet. I wanted to be a puppeteer, run my own business. I'd never seriously considered starting a business because of the financial investment, instability, and uncertainty.

Why not freelance with my marketing ideas? If some microbrewery in Colorado and an obscure brewery in Australia were interested in hearing my ideas, others would be also. I needed to think globally. I could freelance my marketing ideas to a brewing company anywhere in the world.

My Facebook fans would admire me for turning down a promotion and not selling myself short to a company that didn't respect my abilities. After all, I'd achieved the promotion yet made the risky decision to start my own business, be my own boss. I now had 8,000 fans and growing to help me spread the word about my new business. I had a following.

I no longer felt so alone.

Chapter Twenty-Eight

I gazed apprehensively up the open staircase, wondering if Libby was home. Taking a deep breath, I walked up the stairs with greater trepidation than the day I'd arrived. Emotionally spent, no energy to argue, I would merely get my computer and leave. I walked past Luc's, relieved his scooter wasn't parked outside. Heart thumping, I knocked on Libby's door. She called out for me to enter. I walked in to find Libby seated on the futon with Dad. Dad's and my gazes locked. He gave me a cautious look, and I glanced away, taking a calming breath, willing my heart rate to slow, and attempting to keep my face void of emotions.

I walked over to my laptop on the table. "I just came to get my computer."

"Please, stay," Libby said.

The tension in the air slowly lifted.

"I just got here, but I'll only be a moment." Dad peered at Libby. "Are you sure you want to give your daughter up for adoption?"

Libby nodded, staring at Sylvie La Souris—the stuffed animal mouse—lying on the cocktail table. She picked up the mouse and rested it on her lap, fidgeting with its whiskers. "She'll be better off having two loving parents who'll make sure she has everything she wants and needs."

"Two parents are never a guarantee, Libby," Dad said. "Look what I did. I've had to live with it my entire life. Look at Étienne's mother dying. Your daughter's adopted parents could be in a car accident tomorrow, she could go into foster care, live with people you didn't choose for her."

Libby started rocking, staring at the cradle, hugging the mouse.

A tear trailed down her cheek. "I know that."

"So you're giving her up because you honestly don't want her?"

A meek sob caught in Libby's throat, and she swallowed it. Dad placed a loving hand on Libby's knee. I was suddenly seven years old, and Dad was rubbing my knee while driving me to the hospital, reassuring me everything would be all right after I'd been stung by a bee and my eyelid was partially swelled shut. I shoved the memory aside before my eyes watered with tears.

I took a cautious step toward Libby, wanting to wrap my arms around her, comfort her, but unsure how she'd react. Just because she'd asked me to stay didn't mean everything was better between us.

"I wouldn't make a good mother," she said.

"You'd make a wonderful mother." I went over and knelt down next to Libby.

"I'm scared. I don't want to give her up, but I don't know if I can do it alone. And I don't want Luc to feel responsible."

"You wouldn't be alone," Dad assured her. "Étienne and I are here to help you, and I swear to God, I'll never leave you again." He sounded sincere, yet I had a hard time believing him. I couldn't imagine ever trusting him again. A tear slid down his cheek. Unnerved by his display of emotion, I glanced away. "I think, if you give her up, you'll regret it. And regret can eat away at your soul. Don't do it, Libby, unless you're sure you can live with your decision."

"I'm here, too, Libby." I placed a hand on her shoulder. "I can stay awhile if you want me to."

Libby nodded, placing a hand on mine, squeezing it. A warm feeling washed over me, and I glanced at the mural, at Libby's and my hands intertwined. I smiled, promising myself I'd never allow us to grow apart again.

Dad followed my gaze to the mural. "I remember taking that photo out by the garden. It was Easter. You two looked so nice in your dresses."

Dad recognized the photo when I hadn't. Not exactly what I needed to hear. And I didn't need to stroll down memory lane with him either.

"This isn't fair to the Michauds," Libby said. "They've been expecting a baby. I'm sure they have the nursery all decorated. This is going to break their hearts." A tear slipped down her cheek. "I'm an awful person for doing this to them."

"No, you're not," I said, fighting back the tears now threatening my eyes. I could steel my emotions toward Dad but not Libby. I wiped away a rogue tear. "They might be hurt at first, but they'll understand one day. They'll adopt another child."

Dad offered to contact the agency and ask them to notify the Michauds of Libby's decision to keep Dominique, and to hire a lawyer if needed. Libby gave him the ten grand to be returned to the couple.

Dad had helped convince Libby to keep Dominique. Yet that didn't even begin to make up for the past.

Dad opened the door to leave, peering over at me. "I hope one day you can forgive me." He walked out, not waiting for a response.

I'd be civil to him for Libby's sake, but I couldn't see myself ever forgiving him. Really, it wasn't about forgiveness. It was about being worthy of a relationship and my love. He had a long way to go to deserve either. At least now I had closure, which gave me a sense of peace.

I took Dad's place on the futon next to Libby.

Libby laid the mouse inside the cradle then brushed her fingertips over the painted bunnies on the headboard. "This is perfect." She glanced around at the baby stuff scattered throughout the room. "Everything is. I can't believe you bought all this stuff. How'd you even know what to buy?"

I smiled. "I had some help." Now wasn't the time to get into Luc's and my relationship, or whatever it was we'd shared.

"And I like the name Dominique. How about Claire Dominique? I've always loved the name Claire."

"Sounds perfect." Luc had named my niece Dominique. I just prayed he hadn't indeed been naming *his* daughter.

I peered over at the mural. "We'd gotten those dresses for Easter. I'd been upset Mom had dressed us alike. But I wasn't smiling in the picture."

Libby tilted her head to the side, studying the mural as memories appeared to fill her head. "I hadn't wanted my picture taken. I'd wanted to hunt for eggs. I'd gotten up during the night to hide the eggs but couldn't reach the dyed ones on the top shelf, so I'd hidden the ones in the carton, which hadn't been boiled. You started laughing, and Mom yelled at you."

I'd forgotten all about that. Mom had gone ballistic, afraid we wouldn't find all the eggs and the house would stink when they rotted.

"I felt so bad when Mom called you a rotten egg when it was all my fault. I ruined your Easter. So when I painted the picture, I put a smile on your face. Made me feel better. After Dad left, you always made sure I smiled, which couldn't have been easy for you."

Here *I'd* felt bad about that day.

A tear trailed down my cheek, and I wiped it away.

Libby placed her hand on mine. "I'm sorry I didn't tell you about finding Dad."

"I'm sorry you didn't feel you could."

"I know things were much harder for you. I never should have said those things at the villa yesterday. I appreciate everything you did for me when we were growing up. I don't know what I'd have done without you. Just wished you could have been more of a sister rather than a mother. I don't blame you for not being able to forgive Dad. There's still a part of me that'll never forgive him. It's hard. I've stayed here more for Étienne than Dad."

"I was really hurt you didn't tell me about him. I felt betrayed. Yet seeing Dad was a good thing. I feel like I've gotten closure."

"And I'm sorry I never told you I've been using a lot of the money you send me to buy supplies for my art therapy classes at the shelter."

"Do you know two little girls, Gabrielle and Anouk, and their mom, Inès?"

Libby nodded. "They stay at the shelter. How do you know them?"

I told Libby about my encounters with the family.

"I'm glad my money was able to help them. I'd like to help them more."

Libby smiled. "They could use the help." Her smile faded. "I saw you took the paintings from the villa. I'm guessing you met Bruno. I have to tell you...your money also bought his art supplies."

My stomach dropped. "You were using my money to make forgeries?"

"He was supposed to be doing the paintings for a charity art auction. He owed someone money and had to leave town for a while, and I learned that he had buyers for the Pissaros who thought the paintings were authentic. So I hid them at the villa."

"Well, he's gone and will never bother you again."

The phone rang. At least I knew it wasn't Bruno.

"I don't feel like talking to anyone." Libby dropped back against the futon, heaving an exhausted sigh.

The machine picked up, and Gilles's concerned voice filled the room. Libby straightened, her gaze darting to the phone, a hopeful expression on her face.

"Libby, I know you don't want to speak to me, but please call me. I need to know you're okay. I love you no matter who is your baby's father. I'm sorry...." He hung up.

Libby smiled. "Guess I better get a DNA test done." She nibbled nervously at her lower lip. "I pray Gilles is the father. I love him so much."

I planned on lighting every candle in Notre Dame, Sacré Coeur, and every other church in Paris, praying Luc wasn't the father.

Chapter Twenty-Nine

An exhilarating rush zipped through me as I tried to catch my breath, peering down at the iron gridwork maze of the Eiffel Tower and at the 674 steps I'd just conquered. A crisp breeze cooled my cheeks. I loosened the pink scarf around my neck and pushed up the sleeves of my new fuchsia sweater even though I'd barely broken a sweat thanks to the heatwave ending.

I strategically weaved my way through the throng of tourists on the second platform of the Tower, squeezing into a spot along the guardrail. As lights flickered on across the city, I located Libby's building where she and Gilles were giving Dominique her evening feeding.

Gilles was as ecstatic as I was about him being Dominique's father. Libby planned to move in with Gilles, and I was taking over her lease. Granted, it was a tad small, but I didn't need air conditioning in the winter, and I'd bought a gas-operated blow-dryer. It had flowers, a dog, and friendly neighbors. Precisely what I wanted in a home. Monsieur Fleurs gave me a bright smile now whenever I encountered him and Cecile out walking Gigi. And an apartment truly was all about location. I had the best view in Paris. A view of Luc.

I glanced at my watch. Luc was ten minutes late.

What if he no-showed?

I peered over the guardrail at the specks of people below as if I might spot Luc. I'd asked him to join me for dinner at a small café in the Tower to celebrate Dominique being home. I hadn't mentioned my idea for a new career that involved him. My life had never been so unsure since the day Dad had walked out.

And I'd never been happier.

Assuming Luc showed up.

I hadn't seen him since vacating Libby's apartment with my luggage three days ago. Libby had met him at the hospital for the paternity test. He'd supported Libby in her decision to keep Dominique, but she'd sensed his relief when he'd learned Gilles was the father. She'd been unable to deliver the news in person, since he hadn't been home for two days. Hopefully he hadn't been avoiding me. We'd left so much unsaid I wasn't sure exactly how he felt.

A guide herded off a tourist group, and Luc walked toward me dressed in jeans, a white poet's shirt, brown vest, and a brown fedora that matched his eyes and held no cigarettes. Our gazes locked, and my entire body went warm, despite the cool breeze.

Luc held up two hot dogs. A chef after my own heart.

I smiled. "Just what I was craving."

He handed me a hot dog and placed a kiss to my cheeks, his breath warm against my skin. His lips gently touched mine, lingering before he drew back. I slid my tongue along my lips, savoring the refreshing taste of cinnamon and Luc.

He quirked a curious brow. "You're still here."

"I leave Monday."

He frowned, glancing down at his hot dog.

"But I'll be back after you return from your puppet tour. I'm going to be your new neighbor."

The corners of his mouth curled into an intrigued smile. "You're moving in with Libby?"

"She's going to live with Gilles."

"Ah, well, you'll probably need help carrying all of your baggage up the stairs."

I nodded, a giddy smile spreading across my face. Bless those steps. If it hadn't been for those steps, Luc and I never would have met that first day, and I'd never have gone back to his apartment that night.

"What will you do for a job?"

Perfect segue into my business proposition. Besides marketing my ideas to brewing companies worldwide, I wanted to pursue my cooking class idea. I told Luc about the hotel's program and my idea for classes geared toward companies visiting Paris. I'd run it by Isabelle, my sales rep at the hotel, and she was onboard, willing to offer it to corporate clients. Their chef, like most hotel chefs, didn't have time to conduct such a class. Hopefully Luc wanted the position.

"I think that might be a good idea. I miss cooking. You were right. As long as I'm my own boss, I'm the puppeteer, not the puppet." He tapped his hatband. "I quit smoking."

"Congratulations." He also wasn't wearing the Celtic cross necklace. Time to move forward.

I took a bite of hot dog, glancing up, noticing the panoramic windows of Jules Verne restaurant were directly above us. An elegantly dressed couple sat by the window, peering in awe at the city. Reminded me of myself a week ago. I smiled, a warm feeling washing over me. I'd take a hot dog over escargots any day.

I took a bite of hot dog, and mustard dripped onto my hand and my sweater sleeve. I licked it off my hand then riffled through my purse for a wipe, realizing I was out. I'd never been out of wipes.

"I don't have any wipes."

A sly grin curled Luc's lips. "You're living dangerously now."

"Guess I am."

Luc pointed out the Marais area, his office—the Luxembourg Gardens—and then east of the city where his parents lived. "I went to see my parents for a few days."

"How'd it go?"

He nodded, still staring out at the city. "Good. They now understand why I'm happier being a puppeteer. My dad apologized for saying I was throwing my life away and that being a puppeteer wouldn't bring Fiona back." He turned toward me and brushed baguette crumbs from the fringe of my scarf, his hands grazing my breasts. My breath hitched in my throat. He continued brushing a gentle finger over the fringe, gazing deep into my eyes. "I was so surprised when Libby told me I might be the father I didn't know what to do. I didn't want to love someone again only to lose her.

Then I realized I didn't want to lose Dominique or...you."

Hope fluttered in my stomach. "I didn't want to lose you either."

Luc wanting children no longer scared me. I believed not only that he'd make a good father but that I might not make such a bad mom. It wasn't like I had to make a decision right now.

Luc tossed our hot dog papers in a trash can. He grasped hold of my scarf and drew me toward him. I curled my fingers around his hands, never wanting to let go. "Why don't you come with me on my tour? You could help."

Hmm... I could be a full-fledged puppeteer. But no strings attached wasn't all it was cracked up to be. At least not with Luc. I wanted there to be strings.

"I need to go to Milwaukee to put my stuff in storage and straighten things out, but I'll be back."

Mom had Ken and her travels to look forward to, so hopefully she'd take the news well that I was staying in Paris for a while. Libby and I agreed not to tell her about Dad. We didn't want her thinking we'd both abandoned her for him.

Luc slipped his arms around my waist, and I slid mine around his neck. He brushed a gentle kiss against my lips. "I don't know what would have happened to me if I hadn't met you. I'm falling in love with you," he whispered, his mouth almost touching mine. "I never thought I would love a woman again."

The word *love* seemed to float into my mouth and warm my entire body. I swallowed the lump of emotion in my throat. "I'm falling in love with you." Saying those words had never felt so right or made me feel so completely happy.

Our lips touched, and we deepened the kiss as the lights of the Eiffel Tower twinkled on, dancing around us, immersing us in a soft, yellow glow. Right then, I knew Paris wasn't about haute cuisine or couture, it was about passion. A passion for life. Luc had brought me back to life, making me more passionate about *myself*, opening up my mind and heart to discovering the other passions that lay ahead of me in life.

My passion for Luc was just the beginning.

About Eliza Watson

When Eliza isn't traveling for her job as an event planner, or tracing her ancestry roots through Ireland, she is at home in Wisconsin working on her next novel. She enjoys bouncing ideas off her husband, Mark, and her cats Quigley, Frankie, and Sammy.

Connect with Eliza Online

www.elizawatson.com

www.facebook.com/ElizaWatsonAuthor